# A TRUE AMERICAN PATRIOT

## A NOVEL

## DANIEL J. O'CONNOR

PERMUTED
PRESS

A PERMUTED PRESS BOOK
ISBN: 978-1-63758-833-8
ISBN (eBook): 978-1-63758-834-5

A True American Patriot:
A Novel

Cover art by Cody Corcoran

**PERMUTED**
PRESS

Permuted Press, LLC
New York • Nashville
permutedpress.com

Published in the United States of America
1  2  3  4  5  6  7  8  9  10

# Advance Praise for
## *A True American Patriot*

"Dan O'Connor has written a fast-paced novel focused on a multitude of national security threats drawn from today's headlines. For readers who like constant action and out-sized heroes, A True American Patriot is for you."

— **Robert M. Gates,** Secretary of Defense 2006–2011

"Dan has taken a life filled with serving and protecting our nation and with his unique ability, captured past, current, and future national security and geo-political events to create a fast-paced, entertaining book everyone will enjoy reading. Whether you were on the front line, behind the scenes, or never served, this book has something to offer for everyone. Looking forward to Dan's second book."

— **Scott Whipp,** Executive, Phigenics LLC, West Point Graduate, and Gulf War Veteran

"A fast-paced action thriller.... Only a master of his craft like Doc O'Connor could write such a masterpiece."

— **J. Soltys,** former CIA Officer, retired Navy Special Operations SEAL/Senior Explosive Ordnance Disposal Technician, former U.S. Customs Special Agent, and former Deputy U.S. Marshal

"Authenticity, not just action, is what sets A True American Patriot apart from other thrillers. The author displays a real world knowledge of foreign and domestic settings and of the characters that populate this fast-paced tale. I lived and worked in high-threat environments in Africa and South

America and Dan O'Connor knows whereof he speaks. His book is a riveting read—a fiction but based on the real stuff. Readers will have a hard time putting this book down."

**—Carmen Martinez,** Ambassador of the United States (ret), Minister-Counselor, Senior Foreign Service, Chief of Mission in Zambia and Myanmar (Burma), and thirty-three years of service in Brazil, Venezuela, Thailand, Ecuador, Colombia, Mozambique, Myanmar (Burma), and Zambia

"*A True American Patriot* is an amazing debut spy thriller written by a real spy! Dan O'Connor has woven his twenty-six years of successful experience protecting our nation's most precious intelligence assets into a breath-taking espionage adventure. With our country's most prolific intelligence asset in the cross-hairs of both relentless and brutal adversaries, Dan shines the light on the cunning strategies and ruthless counter-measures necessary to overcome barbaric efforts to cripple our intelligence capabilities. Absolutely, a must-read!"

**—Phil Houston,** twenty-five-year CIA Officer and *New York Times* Bestselling Author

*To Carmela, my wife and my one love, who kept hearth and home together during our many years of travel in services to the missions which support this great nation. I so look forward to our future years together.*

# CHAPTER ONE

# ON YOUR SIX O'CLOCK

THEY WERE IN THE AIR approaching Dubai International Airport in the United Arab Emirates. The Professor, a little-known but very powerful world figure in certain foreign capitals, stared out the airplane window at the unfolding cityscape like a child, checking boxes in his mind. He always liked to mentally catalog interesting buildings by name, height, and style. The plane was now in descent. The Professor had been here many times but not recently. Now, the array of skyscrapers that stretched out before him was even more incredible than he remembered. The tallest building in the world (since 2010) was in Dubai. It was 2,716 feet tall and was called the Burj Khalifa.

After passing through customs and immigration, the Professor and his colleague moved into a waiting limousine. The ride to Abu Dhabi would take about one and a half hours. Traveling bumpily through the desert, they passed elderly vendors selling bottled water strung on the backs of camels. In the desert, water is the key to survival. Fortunately, their driver had ensured the car was already well stocked. Once they arrived in Abu Dhabi, they once again passed buildings that were shining and new. The place didn't match the sheer density of Dubai, but Abu Dhabi was quickly growing into a remarkable modern metropolis. The Professor knew that the rest of the Arab world would one day look like this.

The Professor covertly held the level of a U.S. cabinet official with special status. He had near-instant access to the president of the United States, and a select number of kings, prime ministers, queens, and heads of terrorist networks also knew him well. He was considered a brilliant mathematician who understood not only numbers but also the hidden algorithms of human motivation.

This U.S. president regarded the Professor as a kind of national treasure. Therefore, POTUS ensured that the Professor's personal background was kept secure. It was shared only with those who really had a "need to know."

The Professor provided intelligence to the president. He was a "force multiplier" and had prevented nuclear, chemical, and biological attacks on the U.S. on more than one occasion. None of these threats had ever been made public, of course. The Professor was also a patriot. He had no desire for praise or recognition. He had only an unwavering desire to see the enemies of his country fail.

It was a mild evening, and the Professor was scheduled to meet with a longtime friend and high-level government official in the lobby of the Emirates Palace Hotel, followed by a relaxed dinner. As usual, Devlin "Doc" O'Connell was at the Professor's side. Doc always wore a subtle half-smile, a mini smile that adversaries invariably found impossible to interpret. He was the Professor's security adviser, protector, and close friend.

Doc had learned a long time ago to never ignore his innate judgment, a combination of instinct and practice honed over long years, from the hard streets of the Bronx to the mud huts of Afghanistan. Doc often felt threats prior to actually seeing them. In this instance, while getting off the elevator in the lobby with the Professor, Doc instantly knew they were in danger. The hotel lobby was loaded with guests and friends, and the noise level was barely manageable. Staff personnel were practically sprinting back and forth to fulfill requests. Doc surveyed the area and knew in a matter of seconds that there were two, maybe three, assassins present; the variable was a woman dressed in a full burka. The men were clearly professionals: trained and hard, and trying their best to look bored. Doc could not immediately determine whether the woman was in or out, making her, potentially, the most lethal threat of all. As Doc and the Professor moved through the lobby, all three were standing in fixed positions. They stayed in place as the Professor walked eagerly toward the main entrance to greet his old friend, who was just pulling up in a brand-new level-five armored Mercedes Benz.

The advance was the car in front, and security personnel were jumping out as it coasted in. More security officers were on foot and had been waiting at the entrance; with a subtle nod, they gave the green light: safe.

The next vehicle then rolled in, carrying the principal, who was waving on the inside of the bullet-resistant glass and smiling at the Professor. An armored SUV that carried five armed, highly trained security officers, with locked and loaded automatic weapons at the ready, also rolled in watching everything and everyone.

A minute before, the first assassin had walked behind Doc and the Professor in the lobby at a reasonable distance as they went out the large glass doors of the main entrance. Doc noted the large bumps under his clothing and identified two automatic weapons; an MP5 submachine gun was hidden under his right side for spraying, and another was wrapped around his left side. The assassin was also cupping a stun grenade.

The second assassin had somehow quietly gotten ahead of them and was waiting outside the Palace Hotel; Doc spotted him by the long gun peeking out of a car window. He was the sniper; he had the right angle and was vectored generally on the entrance. Doc moved around the side of the Professor so that the sniper would have less of a target and be forced to reevaluate his shot.

Doc's biggest concern was still the female assassin who was floating around somewhere and was now out of sight. Suddenly, from the corner of his eye, he caught a glimpse. She was walking purposely out of the rear right side entrance, not yet near the motorcade but heading in that direction. The choreography was now in full motion.

The first assassin threw his grenade at the SUV and then engaged the security officers with his two hidden MP5s. The team leader was opening the motorcade door, and the principal was turning his body to exit. Doc's instinct took over. He grabbed the Professor and hurled him into the limousine just as a large-caliber bullet whizzed by his head. The sniper's bullet proceeded to blow the team leader's head off. Doc launched himself over the Professor's body, and once inside the car, he threw the Abu Dhabi government official down on top of the Professor while pulling the door shut. With everyone pressed into the floor wells of the vehicle, he yelled at the driver to gun it; the car's tires squealed like a free stallion suddenly spooked.

A few seconds later, they made it to the fastest lane of the highway at top speed. The female assassin had by now made it to the center of the Palace Hotel entrance and detonated the strapped-on bomb that had been concealed by her robes. The blast, it would later be determined, killed at least one hundred people, including the entire security detail. The front of the Hotel collapsed, floors pancaking one on top of another; it was a scene from hell.

From the speeding car, Doc called the American embassy using a secure radio code and advised the Marine guards there that they were running hot, had two government principals, one U.S. official and one other high-level U.A.E. government official, along with one local security driver en route. Doc requested an expedited entry through the rear gate. He provided a quick situation report and ordered the embassy to immediately raise the threat level to maximum. The Marines sprang into action and were waiting for Doc's armored Mercedes when it pulled up a few minutes later. At the rear embassy gate, they saw Doc's face and waved the Mercedes in while covering the surrounding area.

Once secured within the embassy compound, the first task at hand was to figure out whom the hit team was after—the Professor, the foreign government official, or both. Doc made some phone calls and set up an emergency exfiltration plan for the Professor and himself. The U.A.E. government official was transported to his own compound by another armored motorcade accompanied by military assault teams and a couple of tanks on both ends. In three hours, the Professor and Doc were wheels up on a foreign private government jet back to the U.S.—all markings had been removed. The flight home would take sixteen hours. A carefully prepared security venue in the U.S. would serve to protect the Professor and Doc for a short while until they had an exact grasp of the enemy they were up against.

# CHAPTER TWO

# THE CAT OF NINE LIVES

IN FLIGHT AND AFTER SOME heavy sleeping, the Professor thanked Doc profusely for saving his life and that of his close friend. Doc nodded nonchalantly as if accepting a cup of coffee. The Professor asked Doc if he thought he, the Professor, was the primary target of the attack. Doc responded that it would all take some time to analyze. He noted that the team was well trained and fully committed. He told the Professor that the three-person assassination team had picked them up in the lobby and trailed them outside. They clearly had foreknowledge of the Professor's and Doc's presence and time in town, plus the exact timing of the arrival of the senior foreign government official's motorcade. If the assassination team were only after the foreign government official, it would have made more tactical sense to set up outside the main entrance and simply hit the official when he exited the vehicle.

Doc went on to explain to the Professor some of what surfaced once things were in motion. The first assassin who threw the stun grenade at the SUV and then engaged the local security detail was a diversion; otherwise, that shooter could and would have tried to kill the official himself—as well as Doc and the Professor. But he did no such thing.

Assassin Number One was successful in his objective. The sniper, Assassin Number Two, fired at the moment when the official started to lift off his seat in the car.

"At that point," said Doc, "we were all in his line of sight. When I lifted you into the armored car and threw you beneath the foreign official, it served two purposes: to reverse the official's momentum, and to get the vehicle off the 'X' as soon as possible."

While the Professor pondered all of these factors, Doc said that, again, it would take some time to determine the hit team's actual target. He said that it was unlikely that both the Professor and the foreign dignitary were targets, as the chances of success would have been diminished.

Meanwhile, despite the failure of the assassination attempt, the assassin team was still successful in literally taking down the Palace Hotel and ending many lives in the process. The propaganda and media outlets would no doubt give this incident both domestic and global coverage for some time. This was generally what the terrorists wanted.

The Professor asked Doc what his personal instinct said as to who the primary intended target was.

Doc paused for a minute, looked directly at the Professor, and asked if he was really sure that he wanted an answer to his question.

Yes, he was sure.

Doc nodded slowly but first asked the Professor if he had ever heard the joke about two guys in the woods and an angry bear.

The Professor shook his head.

Doc told the story: Two guys were walking in the woods, and suddenly, a very large bear appeared out of nowhere and was five yards from them. The bear diligently smelled the air twice and suddenly began chasing them. Of course, both men immediately started running as fast as possible. While doing so, the one guy asked the other guy what they did to arouse the beast. The other guy never answered his question, but he picked up their pace of running as the bear was getting closer. Finally, while huffing and puffing, the first guy asked the second if he thought they could out-run the bear. Guy number two answered that he did not need to outrun the bear; he just needed to outrun him. The first guy then did his best to keep up, but found himself dropping back. The bear was now right behind him. He mentally prepared himself for his own death as he slowed even more. To his surprise, the bear ran directly by him and continued his chase after the second guy.

The point of the story was that many threats are general in nature. Focused threats are very different. They are often initially taken as general, but this is a disguise: they are actually pointed and personal. The attacker(s) is going after the scent and will not stop until he is either successful or is put down.

Doc said that his feeling thus far was that the Professor was the primary target. The fact that the assassin team waited until the motorcade arrived was camouflage. "Instead, they vectored onto you personally," he said, "but looked to the motorcade as a disguise that would not let their true objective be obvious.

"All three were professionals, and the operation was carefully executed. The fatal explosion was also meant as backup—it was another means to hide the fact that you, the Professor, were the target, in case the sniper missed."

The Professor sat back and pondered it all and then asked Doc, "What about right now?"

"They will still come for you, as it is likely 'personal.' Whoever this group is, you are being hunted, and they will not stop."

Pressed by the Professor, Doc conceded that in his judgment the unseen enemy was likely al-Qaeda. The operation matched their tactics and typical objectives. Moreover, the risk had not abated, as their sense of time was flexible—they study, learn, wait, and act again. The operational commander, not just the assassins, would surface with time. But this was no time to rest.

On that note, the Professor told Doc to get some rest himself—he needed it and certainly deserved it.

Doc closed his eyes, but they both knew he would not sleep until they were in a designated safe house surrounded by trusted associates.

The Professor had started to take it all in ethologically (French and Latin for the character of human and animal beings). He had known Doc for many years and knew it could be a fatal mistake to take his thinking lightly.

The Professor thought for a moment. We all die one day, but this situation was practically unbearable. On the other hand, he had Doc for protection. But would it be enough?

# CHAPTER THREE

# HOME OF COMFORT AND SAFE HAVEN

THE PLANE LANDED AT STEWART International Airport in upstate New York, a generally serene environment where landowners and farmers had lived for generations. Many people, tired of the Manhattan rat race a mere few hours south by car, would drive up on occasion to take advantage of the beautiful mountains and the land to recharge their batteries.

The Professor and Doc were met at a standing helicopter by two fully armed pilots. They were soon in the air en route to their safe house. The property was developed exactly for this situation. It consisted of twenty-five acres of land with breathtaking views of both the surrounding fields and the Shawangunk Mountains. It was a perfect place to regroup and recover from the past disconcerting few days in the Middle East.

The compound was self-sufficient in all respects including utilities (solar panels), housing (large and small residential structures), a two-acre pond, and an extensive cutting-edge camera system. It also contained discreetly heavy

and light weapons of all kinds, as well as hidden underground tunnels exiting in several directions for fast departures. Food rations, water, horses, mobile transportation,
helicopter pads, and sophisticated communications systems were all in place with redundancy. An invisible electric
perimeter fence (wattage dependent on circumstances),
unrecognizable to even the professional eye, provided an
added measure of security.

During the next couple of days, the Professor reviewed his
schedule and also reviewed Doc's personnel file mentally
yet again. The Professor had the capacity to absorb and
retain information flows almost effortlessly. However, in
some respects, the Doc's personality was a Rubik's cube.

The Professor first met Doc when Doc was only sixteen
years old. At the time, the Professor was a visiting professor
at Columbia University, a strolling, virtual, small metropolis
of its own in the heart of New York City. While walking on
a side street in Harlem, the Professor had been suddenly
surrounded by three rough men demanding his money
and his clothes. One punched the Professor in the stomach
and tore off his coat. Another of the men put a switchblade
to the Professor's throat. Doc was walking across the street
with one of his older sisters on their way to the University.
He saw what was happening, flagged a nearby taxi, and
told the driver to take his sister to the Columbia University
entrance. Then he crossed the street.

Doc—full-grown and about 190 pounds of solid muscle,
stepped into the circle and told the men that they'd had

their fun and they should move along; the Professor was his uncle. The leader of the three looked at Doc then laughed. He said that they'd just been released from prison and he had better disappear or they'd put him the hospital, or kill them both. Doc nodded and stared at the man holding the knife to the Professor's neck, where a slow but steady stream of blood was running. He slowly lifted his hands, saying he wanted no trouble. He then stepped back and slammed the ball of his foot into the knee of the man with the knife; he crumbled with his leg inverted. Doc threw an uppercut to his chin and snatched the stiletto now in the air. Doc moved in on the leader before the first man even hit the ground and butted the center of his face hard. Lights out. Doc then spun and swung his right elbow into the temple of the third assailant. Within three or four seconds, all three men were on the ground totally unconscious.

Doc grabbed the Professor, his coat, and his wallet and moved him quickly away. He took out several Band-Aids from his coat pocket and placed them with pressure on the Professor's throat. The bleeding stopped, and Doc told him to get the cut cleaned when he could. The Professor, dazed by the speed and viciousness of the counterattack, kept looking back at the three fallen men. When they arrived at the University gate, Doc told the Professor to take taxis from now on and walked away. The Professor was still in shock, and all he could mumble was a broken, high-pitched "thank you."

Spotting him again from afar, the Professor saw Doc wearing a subtle smile.

The Professor vowed to never forget that young man. He remembered vaguely seeing Doc's sister in the taxi as she got out and it drove away. The Professor found her walking with a friend on the University grounds a few days later. He introduced himself and said her younger brother had gotten him out of a jam, and he just wanted to thank him properly. The sister, whose name was Beth, told him that her brother was generally very hard to locate, but she promised to pass on the Professor's gratitude. The Professor realized she was protecting her brother. Calculating the odds, the Professor figured he would be unlikely ever to see Doc again. But in his mind, he somehow felt there was still a small probability.

# CHAPTER FOUR

# FATE COMES TOGETHER

A FEW YEARS LATER, ON one of his earliest overseas missions, the Professor was told by his superiors that he would have several U.S. Secret Service personnel accompany him to ensure his safety. The Professor said that he did not want such support. It would inhibit discussions with his contacts abroad and also make him uncomfortable and therefore less effective. After considerable debate, it was decided that the Professor would have just one security expert with him at all times who would appear to be simply an executive assistant. When the introductions occurred, the Professor and Doc were equally dumbfounded, as each remembered the other.

Their superiors had mentioned to the Professor that Doc was one of their most unusual and effective operatives. He had a remarkable record for someone his age, with an impressive number of difficult kills in action (KIAs). If the Professor followed his guidance to the letter, they were quite confident that he would be safe. Following that mission, the Professor requested that Doc always accompany

him on sensitive trips both domestically and internation-
ally. He had also been given Doc's full U.S. government
physical and psychological jacket.

The read in the file was extensive. It described Doc as
an imposing young man at 6'4" and 225 pounds in top
physical condition. He was not just in good shape but also
in fighting shape. The difference it cited between these two
conditions—good shape and fighting shape—was critical
when threats occurred. Professional athletes can be in top
physical condition, but that does not mean that they are
fighters. Even a talented boxer, for example, is a fighter
of sorts in the ring and able to go fifteen rounds in a bout
when needed. But once in the ring, only certain punches
or strikes are allowed. Doc understood that no such restric-
tions existed in his training or in his business in the U.S.
military. Being in fighting shape was always a constant for
Doc, as was keeping his street smarts honed at all times.

His expertise in firearms of all kinds, knives, blades,
scalpels, and poisons was also fully developed. More importantly, Doc had been trained to see attacks coming prior
to an adversary's first move, and he learned to excel at it
effortlessly.

As the Professor read on, it was clear that Doc also ema-
nated a very dangerous presence. In public, civilians tended
to unconsciously look away rather than make eye contact.
And yet, at the same time, many again unconsciously were
pulled toward him, as if he provided some sort of aura of
safety and protection.

Real professionals in public would make him out initially
as military—likely Special Forces (SOF) or an intelligence
officer, or perhaps even a federal law enforcement type.
Upon further review, they might discount initial impressions

and surmise he did some serious prison time. This was due to various but somewhat faded, slight scars on his face and arms, as well as his general overall comportment. Whatever the case, he was always seen as someone nobody wanted to ever confront or challenge. Even mental psychopaths, sociopaths, and professionals that were quite comfortable with extreme violence tended to avoid him.

The psych review concluded that he has an active with a "quiet interior," which permitted only a limited number of close friends (and respected authoritative figures/superiors). However, it was also emphasized that he had an explosive side to his nature—a boundless, external, lethal capacity—that was, best kept, for the most part, under wraps. There was, in the psych professionals' estimation, about a 1 percent chance that if provoked due to a continuous, massive amount of stress and extreme danger, he would become unhinged for a short while. Such an explosion would most likely destroy any bad actors or adversaries within his radius. At the same time, he would still continue to protect anyone he perceived as truly honorable.

Doc's makeup included extremely fast mental calculations that were simply extraordinary. He liked to focus his approach as follows:

Rule Number One: Weapons are either at the ready or are improvised instantly in service to the following tactics: surprise, speed, and violence of action (and then a fast retreat) with his principal—in that order.

Rule Number Two: Time is the overall vital ingredient to survival.

Rule Number Three: Never, ever give up—no matter the odds.

Psychological youth background and development: Doc was born one of nine children (six sisters and three brothers—he was the first male). His father was a highly decorated U.S. Army foot solider with multiple medals awarded (two Purple Hearts and one Bronze Star) for combat in World War II. His mother was a homemaker. Shortly after the war, his father was honorably discharged, and he very happily came home to his wife and children. They all lived in a very small apartment in Bronx, New York.

Their three-bedroom apartment had two sets of bunk beds—these were for the girls, with three girls in each bedroom, and Doc slept on the living room sofa along with the two smaller children. Their parents had a very small bed in what was considered a one ultra-small storage room that was half the size of either of the two full bedrooms. Despite their cramped environs, Doc's family was a happy one.

All the children especially enjoyed their father coming home at the end of his second week of work (when he got his paycheck). He would bring home bags of food and a few goodies like ice cream and chocolate. Their mother doled out the treats in proportion to how well each of them were doing in school; the one who was doing best was given a very slight portion above the rest and had "talking rights." Then, the father was diagnosed with pancreatic cancer and was dead in five days.

At age five, Doc was told that he was now the man in the family. His mother said he was responsible for all, in accordance with the Irish tradition at the time. Doc had taken this to heart and it had a profound effect on his psychological makeup. He now saw his mother and sisters and baby brothers in a new light. He registered everything he could about each of them. He watched how they were, both when alone and with each of them separately. How they were with outside friends and nonfriends. The nonfriends were his keenest concern so he studied them carefully without his siblings knowing it.

Psychiatrist comment: This has, as a result, placed Doc into a special and lifelong conundrum. Doc, as an extremely young child, was forced to understand serious and heavy questions about life very early on. Most of all, he felt the weight of ensuring that his mother, his sisters, and the two infant boys were always protected.

Doc has since applied it to himself as an adult by way of answering a couple of self-devised theoretical questions: When one is born into this life, are they here to do many (good or bad) acts to themselves or to other people? Or are they specifically here for one act and one act alone? If so, when this one act has been completed, is their time on this planet done?

Many Asian cultures believe and perceive that this life is simply a matter of "fate." That is to say the existence on this earth is not only preordained, but for a select few individuals, it is designed for exactly one specific act in time.

In the world of executive protection, the answers to these questions were absolutely pivotal for Doc. But in sum, Doc became deeply disciplined and motivated from his early years forward. The streets of the Bronx were the proving grounds for his development both physically and psychologically.

He learned to take on all comers in very tough street fights, regardless of size or age, to make sure that his sisters and brothers were always protected. He taught himself to be fearless and one step ahead of any situation. The street battles were constant, and he learned to not only use and take his punches wisely, but to use his brains to outfox his competitors. In time, when he walked his sisters to school, no one dared to test him.

As Doc grew into a very formidable man, he sought out the highest level of training and the most sophisticated challenges—mental and physical. His battlefields became more comfortable despite circumstances of any kind. His early promise to protect his family evolved into a commitment to his military colleagues in combat, and ultimately into his bond with the Professor, who was now most in need of safety and protection from unknown actors, who most assuredly wanted the Professor dead—and very soon.

CHAPTER FIVE

# LET THE GAMES BEGIN

BACK AT THE PROPERTY, THE Professor called Doc in
and asked him what he thought about traveling to Russia
and China. The Professor had contacts and friends in both
countries and said he had received numerous invitations—
lectures, and sensitive meetings with various upper echelons including the presidents there. More saliently, POTUS
wanted him to go—and as soon as possible, for very serious reasons of national security. Doc replied that regular
but generally unseen movements were, in a high-threat situation, somewhat welcomed—and they had already spent
more time on the property then he liked. As long as the
specifics of the schedule were kept on an absolute need-
to-know basis and the timing could be lightly manipulated
to throw off the formal schedule, then Doc felt it was fine,
and even smart, to go. Moving targets are much more difficult to kill.

Doc understood, of course, that when POTUS requested
something of the Professor, it was never something to be
turned down lightly. Doc also knew that the property could
be easily made to look as if the Professor was still on the
grounds. Doubles, selected by Doc for their innate abilities, would mimic each of the Professor's movements and

routines every day and evening. Hence, it was decided that the Professor and Doc would commence their journey the following evening under heavy darkness.

The next day, Doc received a secure phone call from the national security advisor. He stressed the absolute need to protect the Professor at all costs.

"Consider it vital to U.S. security interests," Doc was told. The secretary of defense (SecDef) also wanted to talk with Doc. Doc called into the Pentagon immediately and was told to stand by for a secure line. Within one minute, the SecDef reasserted to Doc that this was a critical mission and that failure was not an option. The Chairman of the Joint Chiefs of Staff (JCS) was handling this directly from the Pentagon.

The SecDef also said that only six individuals were aware of the operation—POTUS, NSA, the Chairman/JCS, Doc, the Professor, and the SecDef. The Chairman/JCS, who was on the secure line as well, indicated that he had SOF personnel already on the ground: two red teams—one in each country. The numbers of each team, about ten each, worked in shifts so coverage would be around the clock. The two teams were under strict orders: the Professor and Doc would be brought home safely at all costs. They were to be an invisible outer ring of security and would operate via nonverbal signals and gestures—direct physical contact was to be kept to an absolute minimum.

Doc was well acquainted with such protocols from several missions he had run himself. He also understood the need to keep him, as well as the Professor, alive: Doc would likely take in large portions of data with or without meaning to. If the Professor was killed, Doc would be the best secondary source of any new intelligence. Finally, Doc was told that he was the inner-ring protector of the Professor and would ensure that the Professor was brought home regardless of his own personal, or his SOF colleagues', safety. Doc acknowledged the orders, confirmed his role, and thanked the chairman very much for his support.

Doc and the Professor departed the safe haven quietly and on sharp alert. They used one of the underground passages, then multiple vehicles, and finally arrived at a small military air base, where an unmarked plane waited and was ready for their takeoff immediately.

After flying to the West Coast, they were met in a discreet hotel room previously swept, along with its surrounding rooms, for surveillance devices. Three different analysts came at prearranged times for the briefing. Experts in the countries of concern provided updates that were both historical and timed. The fact was, Russia and China were enjoying their closest relationship and it was historically unprecedented. The Professor's mission was to determine the odds of three distinct geopolitical possibilities—and whether they were either likely or inevitable in the very short-term future via the impact on U.S. national security.

First, given the ongoing and intense trade war with China and its slowing economy due to the coronavirus ravaging the planet, was China really going to make an overwhelming military push to acquire Taiwan? The small island, with its remarkable production and distribution capacity, would seriously boost China's economy. A successful takeover would also increase the power and prestige of the Chinese leadership. But China knew that its operational success in having recovered Hong Kong, and the relatively low or hidden violence that followed, was unlikely to be similar in Taiwan.

They seemed to be considering it more. Some recent events even made it to the media. One could reasonably believe that they were planning to make a move—and soon. Furthermore, the South China Sea artificial islands that had been built up by China as a new coastal barrier were also serving as a warning to the U.S. that the "Panda had indeed grown up" and might indeed be willing to take on the U.S. military.

Second, Russia was hungry to display its renewed military strength and was greatly interested in swallowing the whole of the Baltic states for the oil, gas, and other natural resources they possessed. Their newest scientific short-range and long-range nuclear supersonic missiles hinted at new strategic thinking. And Russia, like China, was deeply concerned and frightened of its population turning on their leadership thanks to poor quality of life and possible economic collapse.

Third, were both parties tied as close together as U.S. intelligence had been led to believe? They'd clearly grown closer as far as appearances were concerned. But were they equally motivated to act—now—on their ambitions? To what extent did they fear the U.S. war chest? Did they truly believe that together they could destroy the United States and that its overwhelming power had diminished to the point that, while they might not want to take the U.S. on directly, they could push the edge to the point of war's inevitability? Had they jointly concluded and believed that if geopolitical major events were compiled fast and close enough together, the U.S. military, along with America's allies, no longer had the capacity to handle multiple crises erupting in tandem on the world stage?

The Professor thanked each of the analysts—who, he noted, left no hard or digital copies of anything behind—for their time. The Professor had already done psychological profiles of all of the respective senior officials within each country. The sensitive ones were reserved for individual heads of state. And with the data dump the Professor now had, Doc could see that it was likely that the Professor would be able to put the necessary analytical pieces together.

The two left the hotel, accompanied by U.S. airmen dressed as civilians to another unmarked U.S. airplane that looked like a simple military cargo transport. But inside, the aircraft was clearly outfitted for a black mission. The U.S. Colonel in charge had two full crews for rotating shifts, allowing the trip to refuel in the air; the flight would be nonstop. And the plane was loaded with relatively sophisticated communications and jamming equipment, plus hidden weapons systems, including bright green, covered, self-destruct buttons on every console—buttons that no one on board was thoughtless enough to call attention to on the trip.

Once in the air, the Colonel came to the cabin Doc and the Professor were sharing. Once they were wheels down, he said his orders were to immediately go wheels up en route back to CONUS. Additionally, the Colonel was apprised that their return transportation modes were to be determined by Doc exclusively. It was a security and safety measure for all of them. The Colonel stated plainly that he was not aware of the mission's details outside of his transportation requirements, and his crew knew even less. They would remain in a nearby U.S. military base on a constant ready/alert status. And the Colonel would follow Doc's every command to the letter at all times.

The Colonel added that he would be standing by for Doc's word as to where and when they would like to be picked up. Doc would tell them whether their next flight was declared and authorized by the host country—like this ride—or if they would be flying below the radar via stealth aircraft.

"I prefer the latter," the Colonel said, "as it tends to get one's blood moving from time to time."

# CHAPTER SIX

# A CELEBRITY IN HIS ELEMENT

ARRIVING AT THE SMALL AIR base, a high-level Chinese official greeted them. Two stretch limousines were waiting planeside. The ride from the air base to the hotel brought to the Professor's mind the sheer vastness of the population of just Beijing alone. And the incredible industriousness of the Chinese people: riding, walking, running, working, and constantly thinking at a pace and depth that is almost impossible for so many Westerners to imagine. The Professor was jerked out of his reverie as his limousine stopped hard at the hotel's main entrance.

The official escorted them into the Imperial Palace Hotel, wished them a productive visit, and left. The lobby was a hive of activity and languages. A bellboy and a hotel manager came over and asked if they could accompany them to their room that turned out to be a large suite on the fifteenth floor. Before departing, the manager gave the Professor a list of all of the official meetings on his schedule. Doc tipped the bellboy.

Both knew that they would be closely watched at all times—sound and video feed collecting via recording devices were standard practice in China. Neither had brought any papers, computers, documents, or books. The Professor would rely on his memory palace—a difficult but time-tested memory technique that allowed him to consign everything seen or heard into a sort of file cabinet in his mind, to be recalled whenever needed.

Doc knew better then to spend his own time trying to mimic any of the Professor's abilities. However, he did have a narrower but similar capacity to examine instantly a friend or foe and judge or react accordingly. In other words, he could always recall a face.

Tired from the long ride, Doc and the Professor decided to skip dinner and sleep. Doc took the suite that was assigned to the Professor and the Professor took the other bedroom: a basic security measure. Doc also placed some simple "tell tales" (relatively invisible markers and minia-ture traps) throughout the suite.

Doc was well aware that his "friends" had at least one or two players in the hotel on their side, but nothing could be taken for granted.

That night, during what was often referred to in Doc's business as the "witching hour" of 3:30 a.m., when one's sleeping cycle was usually deepest, a fire alarm went off. Then, there was a blaring announcement that guests were to go to the nearest staircase and proceed out the front lobby of the hotel. Doc checked on the Professor, who was getting his pants on and told him to stay close. Then came a serious pounding on the door—a female voice was urg-ing them to get down the stairs right away as the smoke was increasing rapidly. Doc looked through the 180-degree peephole and saw no smoke in the corridor. He jumped out onto the balcony terrace and looked in every direction: still nothing.

Doc's sense of nearby danger kicked in. He instructed the Professor to stay in the bathroom with the door locked until he called that the coast was clear. Looking again through the peephole, he could see a woman, definitely Asian and probably Chinese, her face pretty and her long hair wrapped tight around the back of her head. She seemed calm, as if she were checking to see if they needed any more chocolate squares for their pillows. The telephone in the room rang. A person at the desk shouting that all guests needed to go to the nearest staircase right away—in Chinese. Doc asked if staff on the fifteenth floor were warning guests.

"No," said the caller. "That's why we're calling all the rooms."

The banging on the door continued.

Doc hollered that he was getting dressed and that the woman should go warn the other guests.

"No, it's urgent that you both come out."

The door lock twisted, key card inserted from outside, to no avail; Doc had engaged the lock chain and deadbolt when they first entered. But now, a man entered the picture and began kicking the door, trying to dislodge it from its hinges.

The door was solid so Doc stacked some heavy furniture against it to buy time. He quickly grabbed his "mountain climbing equipment," as he described it when they disembarked, had the Professor come out, and placed him into a harness, then quickly did the same. He cracked one of the side windows with a glass breaker, tied the line of the device to three different anchors in the suite, and attached the two harnesses to the line.

He yelled a brief thank-you to the two outside the suite door. Doc then heard gunshots—some aimed at the front door lock no doubt, but also bangs from down the hall in the corridor to the left, and then to the right. Doc calculated an exchange of fire from three different angles. Their friends were moving in.

Doc secured the line to the harnesses, told the Professor to close his eyes, helped him climb over the balcony railing, then clambered over it himself. They spun down via a special mechanical device Doc had packed and landed on an outside balcony two floors below.

Doc unleashed the harnesses and collected the line. The suite was empty and silent, and there were no signs of smoke. Now another announcement was blaring, saying that the fire alarm was in fact a false alarm. Surprise, surprise, Doc thought to himself.

Doc told the Professor that the threat was probably gone for now. He knew that their attackers had not seen outside the building—and no enemy would believe that they would be crazy enough to stay in the same hotel they'd been ambushed in. For now, their assailants outplayed, Doc and the Professor could concentrate on recalibrating in the morning.

At breakfast, Doc told the Professor he'd decided that they would stay in their new suite. Doc figured that their friends were their best defense; if another attack occurred, he was sure they'd have their backs.

He had the front desk move their suitcases and toiletries to a new suite on a different floor. Doc knew that his close friends would for sure increase the number of security personnel covering their new room given the recent attack that had just occurred.

Doc knew that these relatively simple security measures would cause the attackers to stand down—media coverage on the Professor, who was such a popular figure in all of the universities and scientific corporations, would result in heavy press for sure. Additionally, no one was aware of the inner ring of special operations support and probably figured the two shooters were in the local gangs. The Professor, trusting, as always, Doc's judgment, tried his best to focus on his meetings that day.

The Professor had a full schedule. Most of the day was spent giving mathematical lectures to crowded rooms at universities around town followed by Q&As of the sort that the Professor always enjoyed. Corporate and government scientists attended as well and always seemed highly impressed with his often theatrical and futuristic answers to complex questions.

The Professor was in real demand, which allowed him to set up one-on-one lunches, dinners, and visits to various restaurants or very small teahouses, often impromptu. This, too, the Professor enjoyed—it allowed him to renew relationships with various Chinese friends, discuss their next career moves, and so on. Occasionally, a high-level official would be included. And for security, Doc was always present.

Almost all those whom the Professor and Doc met reflected their professional specialties and professed their love of the mainland. Throughout the day, Doc was able to pick out a few of his friends, discreet in the audiences or restaurants, sometimes near, sometimes far, always blending into the scene to ensure their invisibility. Thus assured—those guys would move like Olympic athletes should any threat arise—Doc could keep close watch on the inner circle.

As the Professor made his rounds over the next few days, he and Doc settled into an end-of-night routine of taking an hour-long stroll. They both knew the importance of routine in these sorts of circumstances, and they planned their routes every morning. China is not for the lighthearted, the Professor found himself musing on the third day. Its leadership works from the top down, in ways few Westerners can grasp. The aim is to keep the populace under control at all times. Visitors to China generally aren't aware—but should be—that they are not protected, or in good hands, in this land. Hopefully, thanks to Doc and the forces deployed to protect me, I am, the Professor thought. But we'll see, I suppose.

CHAPTER SEVEN

# A REAL PEARL
# FROM AN OYSTER

ON HIS FOURTH DAY IN China, the Professor was thinking about an attractive female Chinese colleague whom he'd not spoken to in more than two decades. She had attended one of the previous evening's dinners and stayed in the background, but the two had nonetheless locked eyes. Never one to miss a meaningful moment, Doc had clocked their nonverbal exchange but put it aside, as the Professor evidently had. Maybe the Professor wanted to ask her out. Who could say?

The event was sponsored by a big-time Chinese company that was in high demand globally, thanks to its production and technological prowess. Attendees were young and old, male and female, and included a wide array of significant people who actually ran the companies. As the Professor was being introduced around, the lady in question acted as if she were meeting the Professor for the first time. The Professor didn't react, controlled his suddenly racing pulse, and went on his way.

The exchange lasted only a second, but Doc could see she was a friend of some sort—definitely not a foe. By and by, the Professor casually introduced her to Doc just as the Professor was walking to greet another guest. Doc grabbed a drink from a fast-moving waiter and put it in her hand. She handed the cocktail back to Doc, raising her right hand to object, and pressed a small hard drive into his left hand. Doc, unfazed, scanned the crowd, and within a second, wedged the hard drive back behind his oversized belt buckle.

Doc had been wearing that belt buckle since arriving in country. The inside portion of the buckle was coated with a chemical that prevented penetration by x-rays. Doc closed in on the Professor's position and threw up a subtle hand signal/code (a rubbing of his chin consistently) that indicated that it was time to depart—but casually. The Professor, who had been sitting with a few friends, apologized—he had another engagement—and thanked them for their wonderful hospitality. Doc and the Professor then walked right by the hard-to-miss Chinese surveillance team and made their way out.

As they left the building, Doc saw one of his friends lurking nearby. Doc carefully signaled: no physical threat expected but time of the essence with a sensitive package in tow but not yet validated. Doc and the SOF team, over the previous years, had developed an ability to signal to each other as deaf mutes did without missing a beat. The more subtle and low-key the better when sending and receiving messages that were quite understandable to those that had the training. Individuals who knew each other well, due to a military or intelligence environment, where lives were lost or saved, were often able to operate covertly when necessary. Doc then indicated that they were in need of an encrypted throwaway computer. They also needed a temporary safe haven outdoors for the Professor and Doc, with any of the routine surveillance personnel at ease for a couple of hours.

The friend nodded, relayed the message to control, and awaited response. Within two minutes, the friend had moved well ahead of Doc and the Professor; a loose cufflink signaled that the Professor and Doc should follow him from a mild distance. The SOF operative was moving at a slightly rapid pace and directed them along a medium-size moonlit riverbank that included a significant flow of constant water that was pleasing to the eye. Walking in silence, they made a sharp turn, and Doc saw instantly a small laptop computer in a doorway. Doc kneeled down to tie his shoe, and when he rose, the computer had been safely stowed in his jacket, all in one unseen movement.

The two continued their now more casual walk. They passed by two pretty Chinese ladies of the night—their faces made up just so and their attire, by China standards, but not overwhelmingly, provocative. The women were carrying a few bottles of liquor and appeared slightly drunk. Doc looked at them carefully and realized that they were two operators he had known several years ago. They had even worked together on a couple of missions. The pair continued to walk straight to the Chinese surveillance team, and Doc now understood the unfolding plan.

Doc and the Professor kept walking, and then Doc doubled over as if he had sprained or broken his ankle. The Professor helped Doc to a nearby bench. It was quiet and dark, and only a sputtering park light above them provided any illumination. Doc pulled the flash drive from his belt and told the Professor to load it up on their new laptop. The Professor, too, now understood what was happening.

The drive loaded almost instantly. The Professor saw that the information was encrypted and password protected. No way in. The Professor accessed his internal memory palace and was motionless for a few seconds. Then he softly tapped in a few keystrokes, and the computer was open.

Doc asked, "How did you do that?"

The Professor said he simply reviewed his former relationship with his friend of twenty years ago and remembered what passwords and encryption—allowing for updates—she would have used.

Doc looked down the road, amazed but still watchful. The Chinese surveillance guys were deep in conversation about how much the two ladies of the street would cost— the same two ladies Doc had recognized a few minutes ago. They were willing to oblige them in reaching paradise this evening—because everyone had consumed, by now, multiple gulps of the ladies' very strong whiskey.

The Chinese surveillance team leader was the first to mouth off, telling his men that the old Professor and his big assistant were nothing but a pain in his ass. "With the big idiot crying like a baby, they are clearly not going to be running away from us any time soon."

Doc stood up, limped around the park bench, and howled about his ankle. He howled some more and leaned against the bench in agony—providing good cover for the Professor and his newfound laptop. Doc heard laughter as he gripped the bench tighter.

The Professor had begun muttering every letter and word. The drive also included numerous diagrams and real time tables—along with weapon types, plans, and a clear leadership roster—downloaded onto the laptop. Mathematical formulae came fast and furious—weapons systems, WMD—but the Professor absorbed them effortlessly.

Doc would occasionally try to stand up on one foot and scream and then sit down hunched over to continue covering the computer and the treasures it contained.

The Professor now looked like he was melded to the computer. He was a robot, converting the data streams pouring down on him at an extraordinary clip. Looking over his shoulder, Doc could sense only this: it was a military plan that was already well on down the road and possibly even finished. Hunched over the Professor, Doc was trying to take in everything he could see. Whether he could understand it or not was immaterial; he might be able to recall it.

After about two hours on the bench, Doc wailing aloud all the while about his predicament and moaning about the perils of Chinese hospitals, and with the Professor locked onto his screen like a chess master, they were ready to wrap it up.

Doc had suspected early on that evening, after passing the ladies of the night, that the wooded park around them was part of the staging area for this operation. Doc figured that their entire team was surrounding the area to create a no-go zone for anyone curious about a lonely professor at a park bench. Their team knew as soon as Doc relayed his nonverbal signals that this was top priority. They knew Doc well, and knew he would take this kind of operational chance only if absolutely necessary. If any other Chinese surveillance members had strolled by—or even an innocent individual—they would have been taken out. Any midnight stroller would have met their maker that night.

On the move again, Doc breathed a sigh of relief that that didn't happen.

While they walked, Doc asked the Professor whether he thought they could keep the data in some way, but the Professor said it wasn't possible. This was super sensitive intelligence so both the computer and the flash drive would have to be destroyed immediately.

Doc looked down the road, saw the fun was still alive, and made like he was going to soak his ankle as he sat on the riverbank. He tucked the computer inside his jacket and removed the flash drive. He then casually lit a cigarette and, using the lighter, melted the inner and outer sides of the computer together, smashed it hard onto a block of the black tar that paved the walkway, and dropped it all into the fast-flowing river.

He then smashed the flash drive in half, twisted more of it into smaller pieces, melted it with his lighter as well, and then threw that into the river too. To an onlooker, it appeared that he was simply throwing pebbles into the water.

The Professor stood up and put his arm under Doc as they limped along out of the park. They spotted a couple of taxis but waited a few minutes for their crack surveillance team to follow them to the hotel. Right before Doc and the Professor walked into the hotel, the Professor leaned forward and whispered into Doc's ear that timing, from this point forward, was critical. Doc nodded; that phrase, coming from someone as understated as the Professor, meant that they were now at maximum risk. Doc glanced around and saw one of his friends huddling with a small group outside the hotel entrance. Doc knew that the man, who was ethnically Chinese, was feigning laugher while scanning Doc for cues or instructions.

Doc clenched his right fist tightly and then expanded his fingers a couple of times as if he was shaking out his grip. The friend looked at him for less than a second, subtly nodded his chin downward, and looked away. Doc and the Professor went into the hotel lobby and then up to their suite. With his nonverbal signal, Doc had just warned his friends to stay even closer, if feasible, without revealing themselves to the Chinese surveillance team. That signal also relayed to his friends that physical danger was now extreme, not only for Doc and the Professor, but also for each of them.

# CHAPTER EIGHT

# TRUST
# BUT VERIFY

THE PROFESSOR SLEPT SOUNDLY FOR a couple of hours but then was fully awake. Doc could see that the Professor was deep in thought.

The Professor knew that in the spy world, misinformation and misdirection were common. However, the depth, scale, and diagrams of nuclear, biological, and chemical weapons, along with the most senior leadership structure with names and future replacements—all the information he had just consumed—were impossible to fake. No country in the world would ever use such vital intelligence as a "dangle"—a term of art that meant false but appealing. The global threat was real, and it was all tied to Russia as well.

Doc did not get much rest either. He spent most of the night thinking forward about how best to protect the Professor. Doc knew that he could build in more substantial countermeasures. Nevertheless, at the end of the day, all attacks would have to be handled as they arose in real time, as they showed themselves.

Doc also now understood why the Professor was selected for this mission. There was no chance that the Professor, or anyone else for that matter, would be able to get a hard copy of the intelligence. Nor could the data be brought back to the U.S. in any kind of a timely manner. The information had to be read and retained on the spot, in real time.

As for the Professor's former friend, Doc could only surmise that she had been successfully recruited a long time ago to spy for the United States. She had likely never set foot outside of China due to its very tight and rigid security measures. In the Chinese totalitarian system, people with access to sensitive information were, by definition, deemed threats and were watched carefully at all times by the internal Chinese intelligence services.

Doc was sure of one thing: this woman was tough and adroit. Somewhere down the line, she had probably been hurt or scared by her superiors. Doc was curious about her current position in the Chinese government and what she wanted in return for her service to Uncle Sam. Doc also did not rule out, but thought it was a long shot, that she had heard that the Professor was coming to China and that was when she had decided to make sure of her move. If that were the case, it was a bridge that both she and the Professor had to cross without delay.

Past professional experience had taught them both that it was imperative that they stick to their routine. Any attempts to shorten their schedule would raise suspicions. That in turn would mean arrest. They had two days left in country. That time would be taken up with presentations at two other Chinese universities and large functions at night. The first day went well.

Today's evening reception was the most densely crowded thus far. The university president insisted on moving the Professor around from one small group to another throughout the evening. Toward the end of the reception, the president introduced the Professor to a group of four renowned science professors and two female mathematicians who were also linguists for the Chinese president himself. The Professor again spotted his female former colleague but shifted his attention to the four researchers. The two female linguists turned their welcoming smiles to Doc, who politely shook their hands. They spoke for a few minutes to him in English, and Doc used a few of the lines he knew in Mandarin.

The Professor's former colleague asked Doc if his time in Beijing had been productive. He responded softly in English that it has been exceptionally so. Doc also noted that although they had learned so much from the online journals and articles right here, they ultimately had to "let them go" and fluttered his hands. She responded in English with a smile and asked if he had a wife or children. He said he sadly did not—did she? She smiled and said that yes, she did have one young daughter, who was her sunshine ever since her husband died many years ago.

She added that it was her great dream one day to send her to the U.S. as the Chinese value U.S. education greatly. Doc said that he could not agree more, as he himself always learned a lot by coming to China.

She said that she was most pleased to hear such a positive opinion. Doc then said he understood her dream and that the timing was actually perfect—Doc and the Professor had two very close friends here in Beijing now.

Doc said, "I'm sure they would be most honored to meet your daughter and escort her to the U.S."

The woman's face beamed for a spilt second. Doc then saw a flash in her eyes and a barely noticeable nod.

In those few seconds, Doc initially drew a dark conclusion from the girl's strange look. But his instinct told him that it wasn't directed at him. It seemed more likely that she was thinking about her husband. Was he murdered? If so, the killer would remain a target for her; his days might well be limited.

Just then, the university president came over to Doc and the two women and said that they had not had the chance to speak enough with the Professor. The Professor agreed, shook their hands, and they smiled in return. The university president then whispered to the Professor that he had personally invited one of the women, who was actually the first linguist to the president of China. She was with him often, but almost always when he met with visiting heads of state. The Professor bowed lightly in her direction.

The university president bowed as well, then smiled and said it was urgent that they move on to meet other guests. As they started to walk away, the woman said softly to Doc that the president of China was looking forward to seeing the Professor tomorrow afternoon. She bowed and on her way up from the bow, glided a small note into the Professor's palm and then moved on to other attendees.

A few minutes later, in the men's bathroom, the Professor passed the note to Doc while whispering in his ear to do everything possible to fulfill the "special request"—and sooner rather than later.

In all the years that Doc had been with the Professor, this was the first time he had ever expressed a requirement so emotionally. Mathematicians were not known for exposing their feelings.

With the bathroom faucet running, Doc looked directly at the Professor and said, "Roger that; it will be done."

The Professor then whispered to Doc that the woman's name was Zhaohui Xiaoqing, but she should be referred to simply as "the woman."

# CHAPTER NINE

# THE PANDA

WALKING BACK TO THE HOTEL as usual, Doc and the Professor sat at a new bench for a minute so Doc could rub his "sore" ankle. While bending over to massage his leg, he made sure that the Chinese surveillance team was a reasonable distance down and up the path. Doc then signaled that he was doing a dead drop at the bench. The Professor and Doc resumed their walk, and Doc saw an operative, one of the "ladies of the night," walk by with a small dog. This time, her apparel indicated that she was an exceedingly wealthy woman.

The woman stopped by the bench and sat down to give her dog a treat. Members of the Chinese surveillance team quickly swung by to stay on top of the situation. They had just gotten word on their radios that the Professor and Doc were going to meet with a high official the next afternoon.

The surveillance team captain relayed to his team the following message: stay alert. Their targets were apparently more important than they had thought. Meanwhile, the SOF operative stealthily retrieved the bench dead drop, looked around, started walking, and then read the notes that had been left, committing their contents to memory before destroying them.

The first note was in Mandarin and the second was in English; both included the correct authentication words. The first provided a very specific pickup location with exact coordinates that included air photographs/diagrams, bio-data, and a photo of a young, pretty Chinese female. The message added that her name was Mei Baozhai and that she was fluent in both English and Mandarin. Doc had added a communication order for the U.S. Colonel that had transported Doc and the Professor to China to put his coffee down.

In the second note, Doc instructed the Colonel directly to remember that he was under Doc's command. Doc then suggested that the Colonel stretch his limbs to get his blood flowing: he was to arrange for an F-22 stealth aircraft to arrive at precise coordinates no later than tomorrow evening. The Colonel was further advised that there would be friendlies on the ground at the site and they would transfer the young lady immediately upon his aircraft touching down.

When the plane reached friendly airspace, the Colonel was to contact the Chairman/JCS and advise of the package en route per Doc's orders. Once on the selected U.S. Air Force base, the Colonel was to take a clear photograph of himself and the young lady with the stealth aircraft in the general background. The Colonel was to forward this to Doc when requested, via Doc's encrypted cell number.

The note also included an order to his friends. The team leader was to split his team in three. Two elements would separately support the Professor and Doc. The third would recon the provided coordinates, ensuring a secure and protected area for the incoming bird. They were to use the Professor's or Doc's name with her to establish bona fides. The young lady would also be expecting two of the team's females to approach her and tell her how much she would enjoy attending a U.S. university. Should any conflict occur, the third team was to protect the young lady at all costs and get her airborne.

The note also requested that the team leader advise Doc once the bird was back into safe airspace. Additionally, as an aside, the note stated that the Professor and Doc were now on call to be visiting with the president of China sometime tomorrow afternoon.

That evening in the hotel suite, the Professor and Doc had their first true rest since arriving in Beijing and both slept for around five uninterrupted hours. When they woke up, they received their first real bad news. It was a coded message from the safe haven in upstate New York. Doc's grandfather had just passed away. It was a brain aneurism and he passed quickly.

However, they were able to provide him with outstanding support in his final hours while he regaled them with World War II stories.

Doc understood that this meant that the figure who was standing in for the Professor at the property had been assassinated. The "stories" meant that they had successfully apprehended the sniper and were able to access quite a bit of information. The sniper was from the Middle East and belonged to an affiliate of al-Qaeda. The sniper had revealed that the "Professor" was to be assassinated to fulfill a contract between his organization and the Russian government. Doc had decided not to pass this information on to the Professor until he could digest this new information and calibrate their next steps.

Shortly after, Doc asked the Professor if the next leg of the trip—to Russia—was a definite necessity. The Professor nodded: yes, it was. Given the likely audio surveillance in the suite, they both knew there could be no further discussion.

At about noon, while Doc and the Professor took a walk, their friends had been able to signal to Doc a thumbs-up on the transport. The bird had passed into safe airspace about an hour ago, and they would be advised again once the package had been delivered.

In return, Doc signaled to his friends that an attempt to take out the Professor had occurred in the past twenty hours in another country where he was running a "double." The double was dead, and the operation was run by an al-Qaeda affiliate but was actually covertly contracted by Russian officials. Doc motioned for the team leader to communicate all this to Chairman/JCS. Doc then issued another order/signal that this all be relayed quickly to the second operational team on the ground in Moscow.

Everyone on Doc's team needed to know that the Russians were very interested in removing the Professor from the chessboard. As they continued their walk, Doc finally briefed the Professor.

A stretch limousine arrived at their hotel at 2 p.m. The driver did an expert job navigating the heavy traffic, and they arrived at the Great Hall on time. A senior staff servant met them, bowed deeply, and in Mandarin told them it was a great honor to have them visit the palace.

After being shown the grounds, they were escorted into a side room adjacent to the president's main office. Tea was served, and they were told they would be summoned as soon as the president was available. Two security guards in formal garb stayed with them.

About a half hour later, the Professor and Doc were greeted again. One of the president's personal staffers told them that the wait would not be much longer. He asked if they would like more tea. The Professor said that he hoped they were not causing difficulties in view of the president's schedule.

The staffer said, "Not at all."

A few minutes later, several military and various security officials marched past at a fast clip.

The Professor recognized every one of them, but he didn't show it. The staffer then invited them into the president's office. Upon entering, the president walked across the room and shook the Professor's hand with a broad smile and made a small nod to acknowledge Doc. Standing off to his right was the Linguist that Doc and the Professor had seen the night before. The president spoke, and the Linguist relayed that the president asked them to please have a seat and pointed to a sofa. The staffer left the room. The Linguist motioned for Doc to sit in the rear next to her.

The president of China, sitting behind his wide mahogany desk, expressed satisfaction that the Professor was visiting China once again. He had heard great things about his mathematical genius. The Professor looked at the president, smiled, and said he was just becoming a feeble old man that liked to babble every chance he could get about his silly ideas with a truly educated audience. The president smiled more and even chuckled a bit.

The president said that he needed more such scholars, especially ones like the Professor, men who were both humble and visionary.

The Professor bowed his head slightly and remarked how smart and effective the president had been in moving his country so far and fast economically. And what he had been able to achieve, the Professor went on, was nothing compared to a president that not only loved his country deeply but also permitted his citizens to thrive and excel in all areas. The Linguist finished translating the Professor's comment, and the president waved his arms in the air to express his great fortune.

# Chapter Ten

# THE PANDA GETS POKED BY AN EXPERT

THE PRESIDENT LEANED FORWARD AND said that he would like to ask for guidance. The Professor said he would be most happy to be of some small value given how gracious the president and his universities' professors had been. The president nodded and then asked what the Professor thought of the current U.S. president.

The Professor responded that the president was, at bottom, a tough and shrewd man. In public, the American president's image had many faces, not unlike being at a fair and watching each of the tricks and amusements at each stall. The president, in this regard, could be considered the circus manager, often purposefully playing the role of a clown himself. The Chinese president was listening carefully.

"However," the Professor continued, "the man is actually quite brilliant, and the essence of his genius is his ability to measure and see deeply into the hearts of friends and adversaries alike while remaining, himself, something of an enigma. To underestimate such a man would be a major mistake," he concluded.

The president shook his head slowly and asked the Professor if he really thought this was the case. The Professor said he most certainly did. He added that he was not a man to take such questions lightly. The Professor said that when he measured, via his most intricate mathematical calculations, various likely scenarios around the world, the U.S. president and America always came out on top.

Doc was totally absorbed in the conversation and watching for the telltale signs that body language always gave away. The Chinese president's posture flared for a moment. His eyes flashed. There was discontent, disbelief, and anger there. For a millisecond—no more—he looked unhinged. Doc had seen that look before—on the faces of psychopaths.

Doc knew that the Professor had gone too far. He had purposely antagonized the president, trying to access his inner core. It was a highly dangerous maneuver.

The Professor went back to humility mode and told the president that he was getting quite old and therefore was not really able to evaluate a sitting U.S. president. He apologized for his shortcomings in not being of some major value to him. The Professor then congratulated the Chinese president again for all of his successes—creating a modern country, eliminating poverty. The Chinese president's smile opened a bit more widely, and he bowed ever so slightly. The president began winding up his remarks by saying how rapidly the world was changing, and how inevitable China's rise had become.

"No one," he concluded, looking the Professor directly in the eyes, "can stop China's inevitable ascension."

The Linguist escorted them out after they bowed to the president. Along the way, she pointed to the ancient artwork on the walls and seemed to be conversing with those artistic wonders. She whispered that she has been ordered by the president to go to Russia in the next few days as a linguist to the Chinese foreign minister due to the extraordinary sensitivity of the meetings scheduled there. She noted that it would be her very first time out of China.

The Professor nodded and pointed at one of the larger paintings, saying loudly that it was a favorite of his; he proceeded to stare at it for a couple of minutes. Doc practically whispered to the woman that, coincidentally, they, too, were traveling to Russia shortly. Doc recommended a hotel (theirs) and a small local restaurant. The Linguist nodded appreciatively. Doc then mentioned that they had successfully transported her daughter to the U.S. She glanced to one of the other paintings and told Doc that she would do all possible to assist them in the future. Their special relationship was sealed.

Approaching their waiting limousine, Doc leaned forward and said to the driver that the Professor wanted to walk back to the hotel. The driver started to politely protest. It was too late; they were gone. As they proceeded down the nearest side walk, Doc saw a couple of Ministry of State Security (MSS) officials get out of a vehicle parked a short distance behind their limousine. The officials walked across the street parallel to them. Soon, they were able to blend into the massive crowd. The extraordinary buzz of activity was almost disorienting.

Once absorbed in the heavy crowd, Doc noticed that a few of their friends were coasting along with them. Doc and the Professor then saw several police officers in the near and far corners ahead listening intently to their radios. Doc understood what was happening. They were being given physical descriptions of the Professor and Doc, with instructions to identify and hold. Their MSS followers had lost them.

Doc did not like what he was seeing. He and the Professor ducked into a store and purchased a random array of clothing, much like other tourists. In a restroom, they switched clothes and put on sunglasses and hats. Doc motioned to one of their friends that they needed even more cover, and the operative pointed ahead of them. On the next block, they saw a lady walking into an underground store. She then turned into what appeared to be an old and unused train car. Once they were inside, the SOF operative changed the Professor's clothes again.

Due to the Professor's slender size, the operative dressed the Professor as a woman—complete with wig, boots, eyeliner, dress, bra, beret, pocketbook, and lipstick. She told him to lighten his voice if anyone questioned him and to let her do the talking once they were above ground. The Chinese had a very strong facial recognition system, and it was probably used more in China to control its citizens then anyplace else in the world. The Professor wasn't happy, but went along.

Doc then heard two police clambering into the train car. They walked directly up to him, and one asked him in broken English why he was there. Doc replied swiftly that he was a little tired from all of the walking around and just wanted to lie down for a while.

One of the officers picked his radio off his belt and began calling for a supervisor. Doc could not chance it. He threw a roundhouse punch to the side of the officer's skull;

he dropped like an old sack. Before the other officer could even react, Doc put him in a chokehold and held firm until he blacked out.

Doc took their handcuffs off their belts, locked each of them around one of the two poles in the train, and took their radios. He tied their legs together and put tape on their mouths. He knocked on the conductor's door and shouted that they all had to move now. The operative took one of the radios, raised the intended supervisor, and told him that the two subjects had been positively spotted about five miles back. The operative then said they were getting only static and threw the radio down, smashing it.

Doc and the Professor followed the operative upstairs onto the street; they saw one of her colleagues in a car and got in quickly. In the car, they were safe for now. Police and surveillance teams were headed to the false location. Doc barked out orders. One: they needed to get to a secure house as soon as is possible; two: they needed to send an urgent encrypted communication to the Colonel that a bird was needed ASAP for exfiltration to Japan or Guam.

Provide timing ASAP—critical intelligence to deliver for Chairman/JCS, SecDef, and POTUS. Vital information cannot, repeat cannot, be sent electronically or hard copy. Preferred pickup venue would be at same location as was used successfully with the last package if feasible.

Within an hour of driving, the safe house was identified and utilized, communications were sent as ordered by Doc, and the Colonel had responded.

Bird One will arrive at venue in exactly three hours. Your operatives will be on site and advise Bird One via digital signal of friendly welcome and will visually waive off bird by hot signal (fire or lighting flare) should hostiles be present, then Bird One will retreat. Seats available only for Professor, Doc, and Pilot. Time of Bird One on the ground limited to less than one minute; engines will remain ready for returning hot take off and remain under Panda radar once packages are secure and doors locked. Have been advised by Chairman/JCS it is now approved that internal team on the ground also follow established protocol exfiltration immediately.

Doc and the Professor prepared for their departure with yet another set of heavy disguises. They did not like having to lay low in the safe house with time standing still. However, the alternative out on the street was probably worse, so they just reviewed, over and over, the vehicle routes designed to get them to safety. By now, the false lead on the street would have been revealed as a red herring. Two operatives went by the Professor's former hotel and saw police and Ministry of State Security (MSS) officials standing watch. Thanks to the facial recognition software installed around the country, the Professor would remain a "woman," but both he and the Doc would don hats and sunglasses to shield their identities. The team commander was notified that the hotel was compromised and ordered two other operators to follow through on Operation Phoenix Rises.

This was a backup: multiple prearranged explosions designed to eat up MSS personnel and slow down Chinese cyber and face-recognition experts. Once the operatives carried it out, the city was in chaos. Soon carefully orchestrated paper threats were found claiming that more attacks were to come. The pressure on local law enforcement was extreme.

The operational team had Doc and the Professor exiting the safe house via a hidden underground basement door that allowed them to move, unseen, into a large truck. The truck contained numerous vegetables and hay along with a smelly donkey. Doc and the operational team leader agreed that it was better for the Professor and Doc to travel alone. The team members—all ethnic Chinese—would lead and follow in a caravan style.

Doc and the Professor had no trouble with the first and second legs of the trip. They blended in with farmers and at the second venue changed apparel and vehicles without any attention.

At the beginning of the third and final leg, Doc was starting to relax. But soon they were pulled over—amazingly—by two of the same MSS officials they had encountered in the city. When the first, who spoke a little English, approached the car window on the driver's side, he did a not-so-subtle double take. He asked the Professor some questions, and Doc responded in broken Chinese. When he continued to question the Professor, he was answered in even better Chinese, jarring him. Doc could see that the official was straining hard to put the pieces together; these guys probably had digital photographs on their cell phones and car computer. Doc's instinct whispered to him, and he silently cursed what he was going to have to do (and do fast).

He was not concerned about the armed officials but rather the SOF operations team. Doc knew that once he and the Professor were airborne, the internal operational team could have much more difficulty with their own exfiltration via a deep U.S. submarine waiting for a signal off the coast. For them, time would be of the essence, and an incident here and now would only make things worse.

The officer went back to his vehicle and spoke with his partner. Doc could not permit these officers to contact Beijing or give away their location. He had only one option, so he told the Professor to get low on the floor of the car. The Professor did as he was directed.

Doc got out of his vehicle and walked to the MSS car, keeping his arms up and spread wide while asking something in garbled Chinese. The MSS driver got out of the squad car to evaluate the situation for himself. Doc timed his strides very carefully so that they were both opposite side doors at exactly the same time. The MSS official started to ask what Doc had been saying.

This gave Doc license to move in closer. Doc noted that the other MSS official was still sitting on his seat and was unable to see them—Doc or the first officer—from the chest up on his side of the car. Doc, with his hands still held high, struck the standing officer's windpipe hard, crushing it. Doc then caught his falling body and shouted at the other MSS officer, "Something is wrong!"

By the time the officer understood the situation and raised his gun, Doc had already taken his fallen comrade's gun from his belt and proceeded to shoot him between the eyes.

The Professor and Doc continued on to the arranged site. Protocols relayed via code words indicated that all was secure and the package was waiting. Stealth Bird One landed, and Doc and the Professor were airborne within five seconds, carefully under radar screens of the Chinese. All members of the internal operational team commenced heading to the coast from slightly different routes for their submarine exfiltration. One hour later, Bird One reported departing hostile airspace and entering friendly space. An additional confirmation came from the operational team leader reporting on an encrypted communications channel that all of his personnel were accounted for and enjoying the underwater cruise home.

# CHAPTER ELEVEN

# INTELLIGENCE BRIEF

BIRD ONE WAS ABOUT TO land in Guam at Doc's last-minute order. This decision was kept secret until the last minute as a security measure. Doc had sent earlier an encrypted message that instructed that no mention of their arrival be made. He also requested that the U.S. base commander ensure their access to a secure video/audio conference within for the Professor to communicate with Chairman/JCS, SecDef, and POTUS upon arrival, regardless of the time window in D.C. They would not be staying in Guam more than three hours, and they would then need another military aircraft to take them to Moscow. The Professor had told Doc that they needed to stick to their itinerary so as to not raise further suspicions. The Professor had sent a letter to the Chinese president saying that they regretfully had to depart his wonderful country that evening quite unexpectedly—a treasured colleague in Russia was ill.

The stealth F-22 landed smoothly, and two military Humvees were waiting in the hangar. The base commander greeted the Professor and Doc as they all got into the Humvees and drove to the far side of the base. No pleasantries were exchanged. This other side of the compound was heavily fortified, and armed military police officers waved them through. They went directly to a concrete bunker, out of sight until they were deep inside the covered building. They were escorted to a large conference room and advised by the commander that the secure video/audio was ready and the White House was standing by.

The Professor motioned to Doc to stay in the secure room and have a seat. When they were alone, Doc tapped the button on the console. The images of POTUS, SecDef, and the Chairman/JCS immediately came on live, as did their voices. POTUS kicked off the meeting with some pleasantries but knew that whatever the Professor had was going to be serious. Therefore, POTUS requested they get right to the heart of the matter.

The Professor first nodded to Doc and then looked directly into the POTUS's eyes. He said that while in China, they had come upon some extremely dangerous intelligence. China, jointly with Russia, was about to stage a full-on attack of the United States homeland, and its allies, within the next two to three weeks. At first there were smiles, but within seconds, all realized the Professor, a low-key man, was dead serious. The SecDef, who had been drinking a glass of water, spontaneously spit it out. All three officials then leaned forward.

The Professor went on to say that to protect a source, he would refer to this person as "the Colleague." The Professor continued: while traveling to various universities, they were able to make contact with someone the Professor had known decades before. For some reason, the Colleague had disappeared but had now resurfaced. The Colleague was now a close adviser and highly regarded confidante to the Chinese president.

During a large gathering, the Colleague appeared and did an excellent brush pass to Doc, slipping him a drive. The data it contained was incredible.

It listed all personnel at the top of the Chinese political structure, including meticulous profiles of the Chinese president on down. Weapons systems including China's nuclear weapons and other WMD capabilities were described in great detail, along with chemical, biological, and radiological weapons. Air, sea, and land weapon systems (aircraft, ships, and so forth) and satellites were all listed with inordinate detail. The sheer volume and sensitivity of the content on the flash drive, of troop sizes, Special Forces compositions, and tanks was remarkable. Additionally, memoranda of agreement with Russia and North Korea, including military operations and standards, were also present. Extensive plans for wide attacks against the United States homeland and allies in Europe and then around the world were drawn up with dates and times for military operations by China, Russia, and North Korea—all within the next three weeks.

The Professor took a long breath and stared directly at POTUS, the SecDef, and Chairman/JCS, who all had their mouths wide open but were silent. The Professor closed his brief by stating that due to the extreme sensitivity of the contents on the flash drive and small chance they could successfully get it out of the country without compromising the data or themselves, he had decided that the only way he could successfully transmit the sensitive material was by word of mouth. He had memorized the data and destroyed the files. Moreover, the Professor said that given his decades of viewing such documents, he had no doubt this informa-tion was real—not part of a disinformation campaign.

The Professor reminded POTUS that he possessed a vir-tually limitless capacity to remember and recall data. His eidetic memory was that strong.

POTUS continued to stare at the Professor. He looked at the SecDef and the Chairman/JCS in the room and asked for their thoughts. Both men seemed dazed for a few seconds, and then they awoke. SecDef said that what the Professor had relayed was terrifying if accurate. Chairman/JCS chimed in that there had been a dramatic increase in military operations of each of the three countries mentioned—China, Russia, and North Korea. Up to this point, the JCS had believed such activities to be "showing off" as a means to impress the individual homelands. The Professor's brief, if accurate, would mandate that the JCS radically increase their own exercises.

The Chairman/JCS continued, "Our public relations people could portray it as a showmanship exercise to match the three countries while actually sending the message that we are challenging them. It could also be made to look like we have had 'terrorist' intelligence. Our submarines and surface ships could both deploy covertly off our coasts, and surface carriers could be more visible in the Atlantic and the Pacific. This could provide some immediate top cover across the board for the coming week. The media would no doubt see through these collective activities eventually, but there would be no headlines for another two to four days. Finally, we would need to quietly brush off and shine up our nuclear capabilities/missiles and ensure that every-thing is as needed."

POTUS's face grew red but he nodded. He told the SecDef that he was authorized to follow through on these new exercises across the board. POTUS called in the national security advisor and said that they would meet within the next two hours to review and bring in the National Security (NSA) director, Secretary of State, SecDef, Director of Intelligence and Director of Central Intelligence, Director of the FBI, and Director of Homeland Security. POTUS ordered the national security advisor to get briefed on the meeting in detail (minus the Professor's stated special ability) and then bring each of the other directors up to speed right away. This should be done with low-key visible arrivals and departures so all were prepared for a "routine" meeting. POTUS ordered that all were to understand that this was being handled at the maximum level of security.

POTUS told everyone to leave except for the Professor and Doc. POTUS looked at Doc and asked if he concurred with the Professor's brief. Doc nodded. POTUS asked the Professor what he thought their next move should be. The Professor said that a Chinese delegation was heading to Moscow in the next couple of days for an "extremely important" meeting—the inference being that it would be a timed decision for the Chinese president and the Russian president.

The Professor recommended that he and Doc continue on their previously scheduled visit to Russia using the same cover that they used in China. They would do their best to obtain additional information for POTUS and report back whatever further military and diplomatic actions they advised.

POTUS asked why he believed that he could acquire more intelligence in Russia, and the Professor stated that his Colleague from China was in the Chinese delegation. POTUS smiled and then nodded and ordered them to proceed. The Professor said that they would be departing Guam within the next three hours. Furthermore, if it was at all feasible, they were going to quietly meet physically with their Colleague to obtain more real-time intelligence for POTUS.

He stressed that this Colleague had such overwhelming knowledge of the Chinese president and his inner circle that he was going to try and get the Colleague to stay in place and keep the U.S. apprised. However, his intuition was that the Colleague might actually be of more value to POTUS and the U.S. if she came to the U.S. permanently. She possessed knowledge that could help dissolve the Chinese relationship with Russia. Moreover, North Korea was a wild card in this mix—as usual. If the now-close relationship with China and Russia were to be dissolved, he would expect the North Koreans to lash themselves even closer to the Chinese leadership.

POTUS made it clear that the Professor had full authority to do what was needed. Finally, the Professor advised POTUS that if either or both of them were to be killed during this mission, a new flash drive with all of the data that was originally seen on the Chinese flash drive had been duplicated by them to the best of their abilities while they were traveling back to Guam, and the information was en route to Washington.

Just then, a stealth F-22 fighter jet, with escorts, landed at Andrews Air Force Base. The recovered intelligence they carried was now available for full examination and exploitation.

Before departing for Russia, Doc contacted the pilot who had flown the young Chinese woman to Washington, D.C., and requested that he forward the digital photo of her as soon as possible to Doc via their encrypted communication. The photograph soon appeared on Doc's encrypted cell phone. The young woman was beaming with a wide smile and bright eyes, with the pilot standing next to her, as she held up a new U.S. passport (with the stealth airplane in the far background). Doc then carefully placed the photo deeper into his encrypted digital device, ensuring that no one could access it except him.

They were now airborne en route to a designated and approved Russian military air base.

Doc thanked the Colonel (the same one aboard during their previous flight) for another ride, and the Colonel advised that as was done with the former China arrival, he would be on a close U.S. military base in a nearby country friendly to the U.S. He told Doc that he would again be on call at all times, with another backup, in the operations center. Pilots, too, would be on a constant ready status around the clock for another quick evacuation if needed. The Colonel passed Doc a set of coordinates—a semirural venue outside Moscow that the operational advance team had already checked out and believed to be viable.

Doc thanked the Colonel again and said he owed him a beer at the minimum. The Colonel smiled and said he would enjoy that, along with his entire air wing. Doc said he'd remember that.

The Colonel told Doc, "Be careful. If you can't be careful, be good. If you can't be good, then by all means, don't name the baby after me."

Both men laughed at the old military joke. The Colonel nodded and said, "Be safe and bring that Professor home."

Doc then shook his head, saluted the Colonel, and gave him a thumbs-up.

# CHAPTER TWELVE

# THE BEAR

THE U.S. MILITARY AIRPLANE LANDED on schedule. Doc and the Professor were greeted on the ground by a two-star Russian general and his aide. The aide translated the general's welcome and guided them to a limousine while they were awaiting their luggage and visa stamps. The general waved away customs. Doc sat in the front seat, measured the driver quickly, and then watched as the aide hustled their four suitcases into the trunk. While the vehicle got moving with the general and the Professor sipping some vodka, Doc smiled inwardly at their two extra but smaller bags.

He had wagered in his own mind that they would not be checked by customs, so he added them to this trip prior to leaving Guam. Various weapons, sophisticated lethal devices, as well as some professional makeup, hairpieces, mustaches, and glasses were carefully hidden inside these extra suitcases. Doc had not forgotten for one second that the Russian government had contracted with Middle Eastern terrorists to take out the Professor and Doc—once likely in Abu Dhabi and then again at the safe haven in upstate New York when the terrorist sniper had been apprehended and then persuaded to cooperate.

Doc knew from experience that the Russians did not routinely have the eye for detail that the Chinese had when it came to the small things. However, the Russians were more vicious, relentless, and ruthless while often sucking down booze without effect all day and all night. Doc believed that what made their vaunted Spetsnaz forces so fearsome was not having any of their booze during their overseas missions or during their training domestically. Also, the Russians had truly brilliant nuclear scientists, while the Chinese relied more on simply stealing as much and as quickly as possible.

On the other hand, Doc knew that it was quite possible that the two-star general who was now cordially transporting them could have authorized the false-flag attacks. His motivation was still unknown, and his riding along might simply be to determine if either Doc or the Professor suspected him. Doc spotted the trailing vehicle tailing them from a long distance behind—a security detail. Doc made a mental note to ask the Professor to give him a briefing later on this particular general.

As they pulled up to the beautiful Hotel Baltschug Kempinski Moscow, the general said to the Professor that perhaps after a couple of his university presentations were done, they could have dinner together at one of his favorite restaurants. The Professor agreed, and Doc opened the car door for the Professor to get out, then lightly assisted the doorman with getting their luggage out of the trunk. Doc grabbed the two special but significantly smaller cases; they were very light and no burden. He took one and handed the other to the Professor. Doc and the Professor then headed up the steps. As they did so, Doc noted the follow-up security vehicle arriving. Four athletic-looking men now stood near the general's limousine. The hotel staff automatically looked away from them.

The desk was accommodating and sent Doc and the Professor up to the seventh floor right away. The room was a large suite. A basket of fruit was on the front table for the Professor, as was a large bottle of vodka with plenty of ice nearby. No doubt, the rooms were all set for maximum surveillance. The Professor and Doc looked at the room and then at each other for a couple of seconds. Doc suggested to the Professor that perhaps they could go for a nice walk, and the Professor said that it would be a great idea to shake off some of their jet lag.

As they strolled along outside, Doc and the Professor discussed pleasantries of their surroundings. Doc was able to catch each member of their surveillance team and noted the street video surveillance cameras inside and outside on each of the buildings in each direction.

By the second hour, Doc was even able to recognize some markings that the internal operational team clearly left for them. Doc was also sure that as they returned to the hotel, he observed about three of their "friends" well outside the Russian surveillance circle but watching him and the Professor carefully and taking note of the direction that Doc and the Professor were walking.

They knew Doc was purposely making the route easy for the Russian surveillance team so that they could become comfortable and relaxed when trailing Doc and the Professor.

Once back in the lobby of the very busy hotel, Doc looked around and took note of two women, both beautiful. One looked hard at the Professor for a second and appeared to register his physical traits closely. The other was sitting a far distance across the lobby, and she glanced Doc's direction and then away. Doc immediately catalogued both women and pretended to not see either of them. While the Professor continued his banter, Doc guessed that the first was a Russian operative while the second was one of the "friendly" team members who departed as soon they made eye contact.

Doc was instinctively sure that the operative who had zoned in on the Professor was not part of the Russian surveillance crew but rather had a mission of her own. As the Professor and Doc walked by her to the elevator, Doc glanced down at her hands to signal that they hardly noticed her presence. Doc noted a callus on the woman's right hand between her thumb and her forefinger. Doc knew that this was for sure the result of handling a grip on a firearm frequently. The woman was a professional.

Doc was not concerned of any immediate threat—she was probably assessing her target for either kidnapping or execution at a later date. For a second or two, he joked to himself that perhaps she was a honey trap, famous in Russian intelligence. The FSB trained particularly attractive women to lure a target into incriminating circumstances and then proceed to blackmail them forever. However, Doc's own estimate was that she was not a "sparrow," but rather a hardened operative and assassin.

Doc knew that the next time he laid eyes on her, he would have to kill her without hesitation. Doc was pleased that he had the foresight to bring the appropriate gear to this stop.

Doc and the Professor were ready for some sound sleep. Knowing that their "friends" were in shadows, spoke native-level Russian, and were likely in either one of the adjacent rooms or below or above their own suite room was a relief. They awoke after six hours and prepared for the day. The Professor's first presentation was at one of the largest research and development institutes, full of scientists, mathematicians, and professors of physics—all eager to listen to the Professor's views and projections. The Professor had visited the same institution about seven years ago, and his talk at that time was greeted with warm enthusiasm.

Prior to leaving the suite, Doc deliberately left a complete schedule for the next couple of days to make it easy for surveillance personnel that covered their room. A separate copy had been sent to the internal operations team by encrypted communication and contained much more depth—walks, coffee breaks, and such. Doc and the Professor would not go anywhere that was not known to their friends.

The limousine and ready driver were provided and covered by the institute. The Professor and Doc got in the back seat en route to the headquarters building. Upon arrival, security was at the main entrance, and the Professor and Doc were welcomed and escorted into the auditorium. Both were rather surprised by the standing room–only audience, and the Professor smiled and walked on stage and was met by the director of the institute.

Doc went up to the stage too but remained off to the side of one of the curtains. By his estimation, he could physically get to the Professor in fewer than three long strides if something untoward happened. Moreover, he was able to see the entire audience and saw some of the faces that he had seen in yesterday's walk—friends. He also saw in the group a few familiar faces that he had done operations with in years gone by.

The Professor thanked his audience for coming and told them that he remembered half as many on his last visit. He gave them a broad smile. The Professor opened with a couple more jokes and then moved directly into his scholarly mode, sharing his past, present, and future views of the scientific world.

The show went on for two hours, and then an endless number of the audience members raised their hands. The institute director closed the meeting with a promise that the Professor was staying for some refreshments and snacks at which time he would be open to more discussion. The audience broke up, and the Russian surveillance team, along with the institute's security officers, came in closer to the Professor.

After another hour, the crowd started to depart. Doc spotted the same FSB woman he had seen in the hotel lobby. Doc quietly caught one of his female friends' eyes and remembered that she was the friend that had exchanged eye contact with Doc yesterday. He gave her a signal regarding the FSB agent they had both seen. As the Professor and Doc moved swiftly out of the main entrance with the crowd finally moving as well, one of his other friends, who had also gotten the message on a hidden radio system, had already proceeded toward the threat.

The first friend operative (known from the lobby) reached over to the FSB female, asking her if she knew how to get up to the second floor. When the FSB operative paused for a slight moment, another operative slid a needle directly into her heart from behind in less than a second and then removed it just as quickly. The woman collapsed to the floor, but the crowd figured that she just fainted and ignored her. Both friendlies disappeared into the crowd while Doc and the Professor were getting into their limousine. All signs would point to a heart attack.

In the evening, there was a gala event for the Professor. After getting a light rest in their hotel suite, they decided to take another walk to clear their heads.

Doc and the Professor talked about various routine issues until the Russian surveillance team was more distant. Doc told the Professor that once the gala had finished, when they returned to their hotel suite, Doc was going to excuse himself and say that he was going to go to bed. Doc would beef up his bed to make it look like he was sleeping deeply. With the lights out and cameras not being able to see much, he would slip out the rear door in disguise and use the stairs and lower elevator to get out of the building. Doc said he would be back within a few hours, and the Professor understood that Doc would not be taking such a risk unless it was very important.

Prior to leaving Guam, Doc had ordered the special operations commander and the team leader to have a few operatives find the Chinese delegation. In particular Doc wanted to know all movements by the senior Chinese Linguist. They had successfully provided him an encrypted communication with the Linguist's hotel room number and also her specific walks and routes that she did at the end of each day after meetings with Russian senior officials. The team noted that she, too, was under heavy surveillance, but the surveillance crew was less than diligent. As a result, she was able to lose them occasionally—and in these instances there was a specific restaurant she frequented.

Doc quietly slipped away to the streets. He was in disguise, and he did not see anyone taking an interest in him, with the exception of his friends who were there but constantly shifting their own operatives so that they would not be of interest. Doc saw the Chinese Linguist on one of her routine routes and heading to the restaurant. Doc walked on her street side, looked at several restaurants and as she closed the distance, turned to look at her, and asked in English if she would recommend one. The Linguist glanced closely at him and suddenly realized who he was. She smiled and pointed to one that she said was her favorite. He thanked her and proceeded to the entrance, watching all around the both of them for the next block. The U.S. friendly team was also looking carefully for any local surveillance around Doc or the Linguist.

They entered the restaurant together and sat at the very back in a relatively dark booth. After the waitress took their drink and food orders, the Linguist asked Doc if the Professor was well. Doc said the Professor was very well, sent his regards to her, and she asked if the U.S. surveillance team outside did too. Doc laughed softly and nodded. He took out his telephone, tapped a button, and placed it on the table for her to see. It was the photograph of her daughter, and she seemed to freeze for a full minute. Doc turned off the phone, and the photograph was automatically sent back into his archive. Two tears rolled down her cheeks, which she removed with the back of her hand. Doc told her that her daughter would be afforded the best opportunities in the U.S.

Doc told her that the Professor had already ensured that from the President of the United States. Her face beamed again and she bowed slightly, asking that he tell the Professor that she would never ever forget this kindness. She then reached subtly across the table and softly grabbed both of his hands. With the one on top, she pressed his hand softly; with the one on bottom, she lightly pressed a flash drive into his palm. Doc looked directly into her eyes, bowed his head slightly, and said that it was truly his honor. The waitress came over to the table with their drinks and dinners. Doc used the time to gently slide the drive into the compartment of his belt buckle.

She talked to him about what had happened many years ago. She had been in the Chinese Royal Court and met a man she fell in love with but who was not Chinese. They had a secret affair, and a daughter was born. Unfortunately, the Chinese president also loved her. When he found out that she was bedded with someone else, he had a Chinese man executed in front of her, erroneously believing that he had been her lover. When her secret daughter was born, he originally believed that it was his daughter. However, after killing the innocent Chinese man, he found out that she was not. He waited until her daughter was twelve, and then the Chinese president raped her and planned on killing her for her indiscretion.

She set up and executed a plan that would appear as if he had succeeded. He did not know, and never learned, that she moved her daughter around continuously to protect her and prevent her death if she was ever discovered. She then thanked the Professor. This presidential demon could never hurt her daughter again. This was all she wanted in her remaining years of life. The Chinese president had no morals or convictions. He saw himself as the next king of the world. He planned on destroying not only the U.S., but also the Russians, and all other governments daring to challenge him and his country's glorious future

Doc recalled seeing the Chinese president in his office. That look of sheer mania on his face was slightly askew before his quick adjustment for cover. Doc asked the Linguist whether she thought the president would deploy nuclear weapons (or other WMD) to achieve his ultimate goal. The Linguist answered yes without any hesitation. Moreover, she said to read carefully the nuclear sections on the new flash drive, and that it contained deep evaluation of Russian documents.

"The Russians have given much to the Chinese as a show of good faith," she said. "However, the Chinese also claim to have a senior Russian asset under control. His name and the majority of the documents that he has passed to the Chinese are also on the drive. They are fairly low level, and it seems the asset is playing with the MSS to some degree."

The Linguist continued that this Russian asset was somehow being blackmailed by the MSS, and the safety of his family had been threatened. It was not clear yet whether the Russian military officer was going to cave or not.

Doc thanked the Linguist for her thoroughness, hiding his own surprise at the depth and breadth of their impromptu meeting.

Doc asked if they could have one more meeting in two days at another designated restaurant. She paused and said that would be acceptable if she could lose the Russian surveillance again. Doc asked what airline her flight to Beijing was on, and she said her entire itinerary was on the flash drive.

Doc had one more question: Would she be more valuable as an intelligence asset in Beijing or now? The latter would mean her going directly and permanently to the United States.

She said that when they met in two days, she would give him an answer. She thanked him again for his candor, support, and said to please forward that to the Professor too.

Doc said he would and that the Professor also wanted to pass on that his vote would be that she come to the U.S. right away. She looked at Doc closely and smiled.

Doc placed the money on the table to cover their tab. He set the time and place for their next meeting. Then he departed first to ensure that she was not walking into a trap.

# CHAPTER THIRTEEN

# THE GIFT THAT KEEPS GIVING

UPON EXITING THE RESTAURANT DOOR, he started back on his path to the hotel. He knew that if he had been followed, his friends would signal him along the way. He also knew that the special disguise he was using was invaluable in protecting him from the growing facial recognition technology in Russia. The new flash drive he carried unquestionably contained data vital to the U.S. once again. Doc had to find a way to both view and memorize the new data with the Professor immediately. They then had to get this second flash drive out of the country and into the hands of POTUS.

Doc decided that he would take the chance of going back into the hotel room. He would get out of disguise, appear to wake up, and come out of his bedroom to ask the Professor if he felt like a late-night dinner and perhaps a drink or two. The Professor said he was up for it, and a nice walk as well.

Outside, they followed their usual walking routine and played at small talk. Doc asked if he thought his old friend, the U.S. ambassador to Russia, would be interested in joining them for dinner. The Professor said there was only one way to know, and he promptly used his cell to give him a call. After an exchange of pleasantries, the Ambassador said that he could not as he was unfortunately in the middle of a silly skirmish with two of his staffers in the embassy.

However, he insisted that they come anyway to the embassy; he would send his car and driver, and they could then have a drink or two with sandwiches and catch up on old times. Within a few minutes, the Ambassador's car pulled up. When they arrived at the embassy, the Ambassador greeted them at the main entrance and embraced the Professor warmly. He shook hands with Doc and motioned both to follow him.

They were escorted to a secure conference room the Ambassador figured could give them some privacy. The skirmish the Ambassador claimed to have had actually been a sham—the Ambassador knew that Doc and the Professor were in town and had been generally briefed on the purpose of their visit.

Doc indicated that he and the Professor needed this secure room to review, organize, and absorb data that they just acquired. They were left alone, and the Professor and Doc proceeded to memorize the data.

Upon his completion of the flash drive review, the Professor requested that the embassy place a secure audio and video call to the White House to speak with POTUS immediately, with only Doc and the Professor attending. When POTUS got on the line, the Professor explained that they very recently acquired another flash drive from the asset named Colleague at their current venue.

POTUS's first question was whether this Colleague was the same individual that he had been briefed on. Yes, and

Doc and the Professor continued to believe the source to be valid and reliable. The Professor further noted that the sheer quality of the information and his running numerous mathematical equations on the numerous weapons systems including nuclear, chemical, radiological, and biological, as well as military planning and operations were truly astounding. POTUS said that it was his understanding that the first flash drive that they had gotten in China had proven itself to be completely accurate and fully substantiated by senior analysts from the Pentagon and other approved agencies.

The Professor advised that the second flash drive portrayed Russian operational plans, capabilities, and intentions plus more updates from China and its intentions too. POTUS said that the Pentagon has seen and confirmed massive movements by their respective militaries—both Chinese and Russian. All of this while both countries continued to cling to it all being "just conducting joint exercises." The first flash drive, now thoroughly validated, was used continuously to watch these moves. The second flash drive would remove the shroud totally as very real threats were definitely on the table.

POTUS could now be heard yelling at his staff to call in the entire national security team to the situation room now, or, if out of town, to get on secure video links, within thirty minutes. POTUS then asked the Professor what his take was on this breaking situation. The Professor said that from his instincts, his own analysis, and his observations to date of both countries' leaderships, plus the flash drives' internal documents, he felt that an attack was indeed very possible—if not imminent.

The Professor said what concerned him the most was American leadership practicing group denial. "In other words," he said, "we could have another Pearl Harbor attack on our hands, but with a much heavier punch.

"China and Russia are combining their capabilities and zeroing in on the U.S. for a great surprise. This latter or second flash drive indicates that both countries' leaders are looking at an attack time of a few weeks."

POTUS's face drained of color. After a full minute, he looked into the Doc's eyes and asked the Professor again what he would advise.

The Professor lowered his voice and expressed to POTUS the need for immediate action. First, he would have the U.S. Secret Service called in to significantly increase POTUS's personal security and that of his family. All plans for the bunker and other safe haven means should be enhanced, upgraded, and evaluated now. The Professor noted that although publicly unknown to the populace, in all previous wars, America's attackers had always tried to assassinate the existing president.

The Professor added that he would put an initial heavy emphasis on North Korea. From the Professor's perspective, after taking in the fact that North Korea was completely controlled by both China and Russia, it could be used as an initial punching bag to show their seriousness. The Professor said he believed that neither China nor Russia would allow North Korea to use its nuclear weapons, the readiness and/ or actual full development of which remained in question. Both flash drives indicated that North Korea was really a tool for China and Russia, and its leader nothing more than he appeared—a young, fat boy out of his depth.

The Professor went on:

"Bring our allies into the threat nexus now and send SecDef and the Secretary of State to visit and seek their alliance with us in a public manner. The advisers and counselors in the situation room need to draw up more immediate options and actions by our military. Our Homeland Security has to dramatically increase its readiness for the population. The CIA and NSA intelligence should be driven to put all their networks and assets at the highest levels with gloves taken off now. POTUS should make a State of the Union emergency address informing the populace what is happening and what is at stake." This was the sort of thing many seniors still remembered about the Cuban Missile Crisis in the 1960s.

In this presentation, the Professor suggested that POTUS imply that the U.S. government and national security components had been watching this situation from the very beginning, thus warning the U.S.'s adversaries to bring it on if they dared.

The Professor recommended to POTUS an upgrade to the U.S. Defense Condition (DEFCON) from its current setting of DEFCON 4: above normal readiness/increased intelligence watch and strengthened security measures, to DEFCON 3: increase in force readiness above that required for normal readiness—Air Force ready to mobilize in fifteen minutes. (Below is a chart showing the remaining DEFCON 2 and 1 Standards.) If the aggressors physically moved with any substantial attacks on the U.S., or even looked like they might by way of nuclear, biological, chemical, or radiological attacks, then POTUS should reset to DEFCON 2. There was no way around this dilemma, and POTUS had no other recourse than to stand up and caution these adversaries that hostile actions would not be tolerated or permitted.

"Moreover, they will regret their actions immediately and our response will be swift, expansive, and unrelenting. POTUS should end the speech by relaying that citizens from all around the world built this country from the ground up. They are proud and fearless warriors at heart, and they will prove it to all who want to tread on them and their loved ones. It is a mistake to underestimate them in any way or at any time."

| Readiness Condition | Exercise Term | Description | Readiness |
|---|---|---|---|
| DEFCON 1 | Cocked pistol | Nuclear war is imminent | Maximum readiness |
| DEFCON 2 | Fast pace | Next step to nuclear war | Armed forces ready to deploy and engage in less than 6 hours |
| DEFCON 3 | Round house | Increase in force readiness above that required for normal readiness | Air Force ready to mobilize in 15 minutes |
| DEFCON 4 | Double take | Increased intelligence watch and strengthened security measures | Above normal readiness |
| DEFCON 5 | Fade out | Lowest state of readiness | Normal readiness |

POTUS seemed to have recovered from his initial shock, and understood why his job was called the hardest in the world. He thanked the Professor and Doc. In turn, they asked POTUS if they should send the flash drive content for eyes-only distribution via an encrypted communications system and he concurred. The faster the analysts could harvest the data, the faster they could determine its overall value and validity. It was imperative that "the Colleague" was protected in all respects, so the analysts should act as if all of their findings had been produced by America's incredible technical advances, and not human per say. POTUS indicated that the Professor and Doc were to call him on an encrypted line whenever they obtained more information.

POTUS also instructed them to tell both the Russian and Chinese presidents or their deputies that they, the Professor and Doc, were the U.S. president's "back channel" for means of communication directly to POTUS but off any records. Furthermore, if either of them got killed or hurt in any way, the price their killers would pay would be higher than anything they could imagine, and that was a 100 percent promise directly from POTUS.

The embassy secure communications office, on maximum readiness, proceeded and distributed the flash drive documents on need-to-know and eyes-only bases as ordered by POTUS.

Doc was very impressed with one of the embassy staffers in particular. He was called the Chief. In the secure conference room, the Professor and Doc explained to him alone that there was a particular piece of information that was purposely remitted from the batch on this second flash drive. Doc ordered that the Chief, and the Chief only, was to immediately depart back to Washington ASAP. He was to create an explanation or a personal story for his unanticipated travel if any of the Russian officials made inquiries about his return to the U.S.

Doc then provided the Chief with a specific telephone number to memorize; he should use only that number.

Once he made contact with the Professor's longtime friend, he was to request an in-person meeting with him. Doc provided a name. Doc noted that if the Chief provided this name to anyone at all now or in the future, with the sole exception of their chosen contact, he would be imprisoned for espionage and spend the rest of his life behind bars.

Doc asked if he understood the order and mission completely. The Chief answered that it was crystal clear. Doc then put a sensitive nondisclosure document on the table that expressed the same warning, and the Chief signed it without even reading it carefully. The Chief clearly understood the seriousness of his mission.

Doc provided the name to the Chief and asked him if he knew or had had any contact with a particular Russian general identified in the second flash drive. The Chief said that he did know the general somewhat, but they had only chatted together at diplomatic receptions in town. The Chief then relayed to Doc, without being asked, the general's personal habits, disposition, family, and real rank within the Russian military structure. The general was regarded as a true up-and-coming favorite of the current Russian president—a close counsel and even a confident. Doc and the Professor thanked the Chief for his service and the mission given to him today.

He was told to go downstairs, get in the waiting vehicle, and obtain his first-class digital ticket waiting for him at the airport. Their contact would be expecting him. Hence, he was to first brief him with all he knew about the Russian general. As the Chief nodded and got up to leave, Doc looked at him and said,

"Pass on the Professor's highest regards to the contact—and one other thing."

The Chief asked what that was.

Doc said, "If the Professor and I are able to turn the general to our cause, we're going to strongly advocate on his behalf to the contact. We're going to also request and insist that he become the general's best friend, so he needs to get back to Moscow as soon as possible."

The Professor and Doc had both concluded by his demeanor during this impromptu interview, and his orientation from their perspective, he would be the right choice for the job.

The Professor and Doc looked at their watches and realized that they had been in the embassy compound for two hours. They called in the Ambassador and asked him whether there was a way of getting into his residence without being seen. The Ambassador nodded. The Chief told them to follow him and grabbed a full bottle of whiskey on the way out. The residence was reached through a short connecting tunnel, and they ended up in the Ambassador's basement.

The Chief walked them upstairs to the main level and then poured some whiskey on their clothes. Doc and the Professor then each took a long swallow and even placed a little on their hair. They looked at the Chief, who nodded and then put his finger to his lips. Doc smiled and the Professor gave the Chief a quick handshake.

Then the Chief went back the way he came, and Doc and the Professor stumbled out the front door, laughing and giggling along the way. The driver opened the door for them and rolled his eyes at the drunken men. They made it to the hotel, keeping the act on going up on the elevator and into their room. Then they both went to bed and fell asleep. In the morning, they each had long showers for final effect and left their laundry out to be serviced. Their tight schedule was reviewed, and they left to begin the new day.

The first meeting was a breakfast with a CEO of another major Russian institute. The Professor and the CEO were having their technical conversation that quickly went above Doc's knowledge base. Doc looked interested just enough. In between the various technical terms, he subtly looked around the room and counted the Russian surveillance team members. He counted two inside the room, two in the lobby, and a remaining two sitting in their vehicles outside, eating their breakfast. Doc figured that the two in the lobby lost the coin toss. Doc welcomed the bored and tired looks on their faces. He immediately took a mental photograph of each of them and catalogued it for retention.

The Professor and Doc then went to a different location within a drab and colorless corporate building to meet with a few young scientists. It turned out that they were competing with each other to hear the Professor's views and thoughts of the future of spaceships and satellites. The Professor fielded their requests and asked them which universities they each represented, and they all enjoyed telling him. Then they confidently claimed theirs was much better than any of the others. Doc smiled at this and figured that the one who did not engage was likely the FSB intelligence officer who was just checking to see if all was well.

After the meeting, two scientists lingered. One started walking toward the Professor and then looked over at the other one. They exchanged a rapid glance, and the scientist quickly decided to forget his question and left for an appointment he had forgotten. The FSB officer smiled and calmly approached the Professor and said that he very much enjoyed the discussion.

He then moved in closer, as did Doc, and lowered his voice, saying that his FSB director was wondering if they would enjoy a luncheon together. When the Professor said of course, but that he would have to cancel his next engagement, the FSB agent said that was no problem as it had already been cancelled. The agent gave the Professor a card with the address and name of the restaurant, thanked them, and put on a plastic smile directed at Doc. Any sensible individual offered a luncheon by the head of the FSB would know that it was not a matter to trifle with.

They walked briskly to the restaurant and arrived on time. At the main entrance were two very large individuals with long suits standing adjacent to the door. Doc observed that they were not only carrying Glock 45s as side arms, but also had under the right side in their jackets compact U.S. Army submachine guns, specifically a 350 Brugger and a B&T APC9K—the newest and hottest weapons used to defend VIPs. Additionally, looking at the inside bottom of their suit pants wrapped just above their ankles, he saw they wore long knives. These boys certainly came prepared.

However, Doc also knew that their hardware was probably to defend against gangs and various Russian mob organizations. Doc found that interesting. He logged it into his mind because he would have thought that the D/FSB was more powerful (not just equal) to such entities, but perhaps not.

The two rather quiet U.S. tourists, the Professor and Doc, were true lightweights in their minds. Within the next minute, a level-five armored Mercedes vehicle with a lead and a follow, and fully equipped take-down teams, arrived at the restaurant and pulled up in the front and back, challenging anyone to breach the hard security circle.

The Professor and Doc stood aside while the FSB director got out of the back seat. Doc saw that he was closely escorted with two surrounding levels of security bodies that could not be broken. Doc thought from his own experience, however, that a powerful explosive being preset and detonated at the venue would have ruined their showing-off message to any takers. Doc also wondered if they'd had a few bomb-sniffing dogs sweep the area, but with all their bravado of an on-stage arrival, he suspected not. Doc absorbed this too.

He knew that the best protective security teams were those that traveled silently, as this required adversaries to spend a lot more time making sure they had the right target. The one thing that all players in the business understood was that to mistakenly take out the wrong target meant that they themselves would generally be the next target themselves. Doc again weighed it all in his mind.

There were only a couple of tables with customers, and all of them were well spaced. The director motioned for the Professor and Doc to join him—right after his security team leader patted both of them down thoroughly. The director was silent for a moment, and then asked them if they were enjoying their visit to the motherland. The Professor, who also paused for a half moment, said that other than a small hangover, the visit has been quite nice. The director laughed loudly and said that the best remedy was a shot of vodka.

The restaurant owner rushed over to pour three glasses and then dismissed himself. The director saluted the Professor and Doc, and all three then drank to both good health and their deep love of their respective countries. The waiters then rushed to place different plates of appetizers and then a main course on the table. The director began waxing aloud about all of the beautiful sights in his country and swallowed several more shots of vodka.

After the dessert and clearing the table, the director motioned for coffee—cappuccinos—and for the waiters to depart along with all of his security officers—except for the director's team leader. He was told to leave the room but stay within view.

The director then said to the Professor and Doc that they needed to talk privately. The Professor agreed, waved toward Doc, and said that he could be included and trusted completely without reservation. Doc, he said, was a man that could not betray even if tortured. The director looked at Doc and said that the FSB file they had on him concluded the same. However, the director smiled and said that it would still be fun to watch him fight a few of his own hand-picked bodyguards, as their profiles are quite similar. Doc's countenance didn't change.

The Professor looked directly into the director's eyes and said that the U.S. president had decided to use the Professor and Doc as a back channel means of communication in a serious effort to dissuade those that are posing and maybe planning a major threat to the safety of the United States. Therefore, they were in a position to speak to him candidly.

"It is and will be very soon apparent to all that our two countries are in a terrible situation and a third country, China, is the primary cause. My algorithms make it clear that Russia will not surface the winner.

"This war of China and Russia going against and trying to destroy the United States will be a failure. And even if it were to succeed, the Chinese president will turn on you immediately. Your only valid response at that time will be to use your nuclear firepower to obliterate China, but in such a scenario, Russia will most definitely lose the majority of the motherland with the only real portion remaining being Russia's undeveloped artic territories. These would take decades, if not a century, to harness. It all depends on the growth of technology and, while your scientists are among the very best in the world, they will be using sticks and stones to try to bring back the most basic computer models."

The director sat silently again for a few minutes. When the director started to talk, he said that the Professor's points were impressive, and that he would like to share the Professor's clarity with his president as soon as was possible. He would also request that the Professor and Doc continue on their schedule and keep their appearances just as if they were here for their various presentations. The Professor said that they could and would do as he requested.

The Professor deliberately did not tell the director how much he, POTUS, and his advisers knew about the possible timing of an attack. Doc and the Professor got out of their seats, and the director stood up and bowed very slightly.

He ended by saying that he would do everything he could to arrange a meeting with his president. If successful, the president would accept a meeting with the Professor and Doc to discuss options within the next day.

Prior to their departure, the director commented that they should be easier with the whiskey that they imbibed last night, but his surveillance people had nonetheless enjoyed the show. The Professor smiled and said he was most certainly going to take that advice. As they were going out the restaurant door, the security team leader stared at Doc. Doc just looked back at him and slowly nodded. It was a message to the team leader that their time for combat would come soon enough.

Since the originally scheduled luncheon had been replaced, the Professor and Doc decided to walk back to the hotel to take a break. Doc noticed instantly that the surveillance team they had earlier was now replaced with another one whose personnel did not eat breakfasts or looked bored on duty. Rather, they looked like a pack of hungry wolves waiting to pounce. This was an A-team and would now be with Doc and Professor as tight as was humanly possible. He and the Professor also observed that they could stay on the same routes and routines until the cows came home without any odds of this group being sloppy or relaxed in any way.

It would not make a difference to this team other than to increase their professional suspicions that would in turn simply cause an increase in more personnel being assigned to figure why they always took the same paths. In the blink of an eye, the Russian coverage had changed dramatically. Doc was impressed.

Once in the hotel lobby, Doc saw one of his friends, so Doc told the Professor he needed to hit the bathroom for a minute. Doc knew that the new Russian team would likely not yet have had the time to clean the hotel completely up to their new standards. Their own former surveillance team was probably still in place.

Hence, he had motioned a subtle sign to the friend to join him in the restroom. Once there, both proceeded to take different stalls without anyone in the lavatory. Doc remembered working with this specific operative several years back and that he was a New Yorker through and through—very possibly from the Bronx too. He relayed to the operative who was first pissing and then washing his hands thoroughly that the operational atmosphere had been heightened dramatically.

They had to be at their highest alert at all times for everyone's own safety, and Doc would be doing another meeting in disguise with the Linguist early this evening. He needed the hotel fire alarm system to be pulled at exactly 6 p.m., and more than just a few whiffs of smoke would be very helpful. At that time, he was going dark in disguise and on the run.

The Professor would need to have some extra coverage, which could be taken from Doc's own detail, until he was able to get back. Finally, they were to have their exfiltration plan for the Professor and Doc ironclad and ready to go at a minute's notice. Additionally, there would now be three, not two, departing once Doc or the Professor activated the signal.

The operative acted as if Doc had never said anything to him at all—not even a glance in his direction. The words were all whispered anyway; the water had been running, and only someone near him closely would understand Doc's purposeful New York slang. The entire one-sided conversation was done in less than two minutes, but Doc could tell that the streetwise New Yorker had gotten every single word.

Once in their suite, where they had a little breathing room with the TV blasting aloud, Doc explained to the Professor his upcoming run for exercise. He added that if anything came up in the hotel building while he was gone, his friends would be very close by for assistance. Doc said that if anyone approached him casually and mentioned "hyper vault," they were a friend and he should follow their instructions. The Professor slightly nodded as if he were barely listening to Doc at all.

At 5:55 p.m., Doc slipped out of his room. In the stair-well, he quickly added his disguise and adjusted his cloth-ing, adding his cap, sunglasses, and contact lenses, chang-ing the color of his eyes and his skin color just enough. He was down the stairs and on the street thirty seconds before the fire alarm sirens began. He walked with a very serious limp and looked like an old Russian war veteran. He started by riding slowly on an even older-looking bicycle for the first twenty minutes. Then he ditched the bicycle and picked up his walking pace minus the limp. He then jumped into a taxi that brought him within two blocks of the designated restaurant.

Doc got out and walked some more, surveying the area closely. When he saw the Linguist enter the restaurant, he watched to see if she had any followers as well and she did not. He then entered through a side restaurant door and instantly removed some of his major disguise pieces. He would still look very different, but not so much as to startle the Linguist. When she saw him, she maintained her slight smile and they shook hands, thereby passing a third flash drive from her to Doc.

The Linguist shared that the delegation and senior Russian officials had decided to proceed with the attack on the U.S. They would make their multiple military moves, listed and explained on the drive, in two weeks with the strong belief that the Americans would be caught totally off guard.

Doc asked when and where the very first attack would occur against the U.S. The Linguist said that it was all in the flash drive, but North Korea would begin attacking South Korea en masse and would simultaneously send nonnuclear missiles to hit Tokyo. The U.S. strikes would be from Russian submarines currently silent in the waters off its East and West Coasts. China would fly fighter aircrafts over Alaska to take out the sensors on the U.S. military bases there, and Chinese hackers would be deployed at the same time.

Doc asked if there had been any talk or decisions that involved nuclear weapons (or other WMD) being deployed in a first strike. The Linguist shook her head no and said she understood why this was the most important question. Doc was counting the minutes as he listened and she spoke to his gut. Then, she said she had one more drive.

When he asked her what it contained, she said it included the nuclear codes of all of China's nuclear weapons systems. Moreover, these codes were up to date, and they were not usually changed, but if so, would be modified only at the beginning of each Chinese New Year. Doc sensed her tension, but it was only because he was sitting so close to her. Anyone else, just a couple of feet away, would never see or feel it. Doc sat back and tried to process what he had just heard, and accepted the fourth hard drive subtly from under the table.

Doc then asked the Linguist if she had the time to answer the personal question he had given to her in their last meeting. She said that she had done so. He asked her what she had decided.

With a single tear running down her check, she said that more than anything in the world she wanted to be with her daughter. She also wanted to live in the U.S. for the rest of her life with her daughter at her side. After less than five minutes of deep thinking, Doc said that it would be an extremely dangerous and hard thing to do, but that if she was willing to, he would do all he could to make it happen and very soon. She said she was ready for whatever he decided.

Doc asked when she and the delegation were scheduled to go back to China. She said that unless changes were made by Beijing, it would be tomorrow evening. He asked if they were flying commercial or via a private jet. She indicated that it was a private government jet that was sitting at the airport now.

Doc kept running through various scenarios, and decided that the best play was to get her out now. Doc asked her how long she had before she had to return to the hotel. She said she would be missed in about an hour. Doc instructed her to call her delegation foreign minister in forty-five minutes and tell him that she had been talking with another senior Russian official over drinks and that she thought he might wish to defect to China.

Further, she was to tell her foreign minister that she was trying to turn him so he would not defect but rather become a willing agent for China. With these calls, Doc emphasized, she should be sure to use a very unusual Chinese dialect, but one the minister would understand and the local Russians officers listening would not.

He left with some money and a modest tip on the table, redid his disguise, and said for her to follow him but only from a few steps back. If anyone challenged her, she was to say that Doc stole some money from her and she wanted it back.

When Doc got outside, he did not see any cameras or tails for himself or the Linguist. This was probably because no one wanted to waste their time in that rotten restaurant, and Doc appreciated that very much.

He did see, however, two of his friends and signaled to them an immediate activation for the exfiltration plan once he got back with the Professor. One came over to his street and asked him if he had a smoke and light. Doc offered both and reconfirmed the signal. The friend nodded and walked away saying that they would both soon be jumping into one of their vehicles so be ready.

Suddenly, a van came from around the corner, and in seconds, Doc and the Linguist were inside as it moved away at a high speed. Doc asked if they had a lock on the Professor. The driver said that they did and had once again set off the fire alarms—but this time it was a real fire—and he smiled. The Professor was now in one of their rooms getting in disguise. No Russian surveillance team members had been seen yet. Doc told them to use the code word "hyper vault" with the Professor and he would know that it came from him and to follow the team's instruction. The word was a space term used as an emergency signal.

The Linguist sat back. The team had two other vehicles as blockers and in both locations—the one they were currently in and the other; the driver just radioed confirming they now had the Professor in hand too. The fire at the hotel served as an excellent barrier, and both vehicles with the three principals were en route.

The driver explained that the warning that Doc had given earlier to one of their other brothers caused the team leader to call the Colonel, who, after permission from the Chairman/JCS, arranged to have one of the JCS's best stealth birds already on the ground. It was waiting in the pre-designated rural evacuation area via the specified coordinates. The driver said that the Colonel, on the encrypted communication radio, had told his team that they had rigged an extra seat for the nice lady and it would not be too soon for them to get all of their asses on site ASAP.

The Linguist called the Chinese foreign minister and gave him the slight details. The Chinese minister offered the Linguist every good fortune and every success. He added that he had no need to know any more and his thoughts were not worthwhile anyway. The Linguist smiled and said that she could probably not get there in time for the Chinese government airplane departure. The minister mumbled to her that no one in the Chinese side of the delegation would be brave enough to ask where she had gone— they would just be waiting. The minister said he would tell the pilots to go wheels up on his orders. The Linguist said to him she understood and would return separately once she had succeeded in capturing another source for the great Chinese country.

At the same moment, Doc was listening carefully to the time line and when they would get to the F-22. The vehicle run was going to be about thirty minutes en route, and both vehicles had used up about twenty so far. The team had made one very quick stop along the way so that the three officials (the Professor, the Linguist, and Doc) were all together and put into another large delivery-marked vehicle. The other two initial vehicles were abandoned, all fingerprints were wiped away, and the stolen registrations were destroyed. The "new" cars arrived at the site promptly, and the team and the pilot had them in their seats in less than thirty seconds. The bird stayed under the radar the whole way out without detection.

# CHAPTER FOURTEEN

# THE POT IS BOILING

ONCE IN FRIENDLY AIRSPACE, DOC ordered the pilot to patch them in to the Chairman/JCS and SecDef. The pilot was to pass on that the Professor and Doc had urgent, vital, and critical intelligence for them and POTUS. While waiting for the secure link, they sent a separate message to the Guam air base commander that the secure conference room needed to be up and running as soon as they arrived. POTUS and his selected advisers needed to be online and in video as soon as the bird landed.

A couple of seconds later, SecDef and Chairman/JCS came in on a secure line and a small video screen. Doc told them that he had received reliable intelligence that there were two totally silent Russian submarines, one on America's East Coast and the one on the West Coast with weapons/missiles at the ready to be fired, awaiting orders from the Russian president within two weeks (or very possibly sooner). Doc indicated that this was the bad news but the good news was that he had acquired specific coordinates that were being transmitted as they spoke. SecDef looked directly at the Chairman/JCS, nodded his head, and Chairman/JCS immediately picked up the secure phone to the operations center and ordered that chief of naval ops and chief of naval sub ops be reached immediately.

Within one minute, both senior officers were online and Chairman/JCS urgently ordered them to validate that two silent Russian subs were on the East and West Coasts via coordinates now being provided. The validation was to be achieved without, repeat without, making any contact pending further orders. SecDef and SecNavy wanted the two hostile subs to not realize that they had been detected and identified. Doc separately told SecDef and Chairman/JCS that their bird was about to land and he and the Professor would be briefing further details once he and the Professor were in the secure conference room. SecDef said that both of them would be in it as well. Moreover, by the time they landed, SecDef would know if those Russian subs were indeed in place.

In the descent, Doc noted that the air base had been completely revamped and everything was hardened. There were personnel working around the clock with airplanes going up and down continuously. The base commander greeted the three of them and said that the video and audio–secure conference room was ready. The Professor had asked the commander to find a small room where the lady could wash up, eat, and relax.

The commander said, "Yes sir," and indicated that they had just the right place and the right officer to escort. A female captain, who spoke native-level Mandarin, would keep her company and offer protection until otherwise directed.

The Professor thanked them.

Doc asked the commander to confirm that all spec ops personnel had been successfully evacuated.

Affirmative.

Doc asked that the commander forward to them their deepest appreciation and that he and the Professor owed all of them a cold beer. The commander smiled and said it was already done.

On the large screen in the secure conference room, Doc and the Professor saw the POTUS and an enhanced number of secretaries, directors, and top advisers, all murmuring. POTUS looked around the room and ordered quiet.

He then looked at the Professor and said, "Go."

The Professor thanked POTUS and said that based on their newly acquired intelligence, the Russian and Chinese presidents had decided to go to war against the U.S. A high-level Chinese delegation had been in Russia specifically to lessen the time of the attack on the U.S. The timetable had been moved up. The attack would commence in eleven days or fewer.

POTUS, after losing some skin color, said, "Quiet," again. He asked the Professor about his level of confidence in this information and assessment, and the Professor said that he believed it to be absolutely sound.

The SecDef and D/CIA attested that much of the intelligence rendered was turning out to be accurate by analysts and factual findings.

The Professor went on, "The Russians and the Chinese have most of their military assets in place. Russians now have two of their best attack submarines silently sitting on our coasts. The Chinese are planning in the attack a hit on our cypher space grid, as well as having their planes taking out our electronic sensors with a bombing run off the coast of Alaska. The Chinese and Russians have planned with the

North Korean leader to attack South Korea first and then Japan as their opening moves."

POTUS called for a ten-minute break so that all could process the new information, the threat levels, and their present options for action. POTUS asked that the SecDef, the Chairman/JCS, Doc, and the Professor stay in the conference room and online. POTUS sat in his chair and asked that since the Russian submarine intelligence had been validated, what should the next step be?

The SecDef spoke up first and said, "We now have two of our own submarines focused on each Russian sub—silently—so that the Russian captains are unaware we are in striking range. NSA director has also tasked his people with monitoring and tracking every single bit of noise by each Russian sub. NSA is now listening closely in what they call the 'zone in' on any and all related noise that they expect to hear should the Russian captains open missile hatches in preparation to fire at our coast."

POTUS asked the Professor what he thought of the circumstances.

The Professor said that his understanding was that the subs' actual present coordinates were right on the edge of U.S. waters. "It is logical that they would also most likely breach our waters upon the go-ahead from Moscow to fire their missiles. Damage to coastal cities would be very substantial. I recommended to you, Mr. President, and the SecDef that if our waters are clearly breached, our submarine captains should have complete authorization to fire and destroy those Russian subs without delay."

POTUS looked over to the SecDef. The SecDef concurred, only adding that two surface destroyers should be authorized and approved as well—a precaution in case any subs were lost in combat.

POTUS paused for a moment. He then personally issued the order to make it so.

After the short break, POTUS said that since the Russians and the Chinese did not yet know that the U.S. was aware of the exact time of attack, the time factor could change without notice.

The SecDef recommended to POTUS that he order the DEFCON alert to DEFCON 2 but with the proviso to not announce it to the media or the public. POTUS sat back and thought about it out loud. POTUS then said that he was not ready just yet at this time to make that decision, but he would be considering it carefully for sure.

POTUS then told the Secretary of State to have his ambassadors personally and immediately warn South Korea and Japan of possible attacks on their own countries from China and/or Russia. POTUS added that Europe should also be apprised ASAP by the other local ambassadors. POTUS said that the Secretary of State would need to do his best to have each of the countries keep this intelligence to be prepared but have it remain under wraps.

POTUS then looked at the SecDef and said that with respect to any North Korean aggression, he should tell his U.S. general responsible for the region to warn the North Korean leader.

"That is to say that any attack will be the end of him, despite what China and Russia are promising. Additionally, the U.S. will do whatever is required to support our Asian allies. There is in progress as we speak a significant increase of soldiers, pilots, and weapon systems being added to the U.S. presence in South Korea.

"All of our cyberspace needs to be upgraded defensively as soon as is possible through the American tech companies and beyond. Any commercial companies that are non-cooperative will be shut down without discussion of any kind. Preemptive offensive cyberattacks by the U.S. will be unleashed as soon as it is definite, and those physical sights will be considered as high-value targets and bombed as needed from the Pentagon.

"With DEFCON still at 3, the U.S. Air Force will still be leaning forward at the ready waiting for further orders.

"The SecDef spec ops personnel will be fully distributed and deployed by the Chairman/JCS commencing now.

"Essentially a whole array of extreme military moves will still occur, both internal and external to the U.S.; the world will see it for exactly what it is: a loud, clear message. The opposition's only advantage will be when they start to unleash their standing plans of attack."

At the end of the long meeting, the Professor asked if he and Doc could speak with POTUS alone and he said yes, but along with the SecDef, D/CIA, and D/NSA and his national security advisor. POTUS said that the extremely accelerated pace of time meant that what he approved further needed to be heard by each of them in case something happened to him.

The Professor nodded and said he fully understood and agreed. The Professor said that he wanted to share some additional pieces of intelligence that the others hadn't received as part of the earlier brief.

"First: We have acquired the nuclear codes of all of the Chinese nuclear weapons and have them right now."

D/NSA said that the codes would have to be carefully validated, but based on the intelligence sources to date, he would bet that they would have full legitimacy. He asked POTUS if he could depart the meeting immediately to confirm this (one way or the other).

POTUS nodded and the director virtually ran out the door.

"Second: The Chinese individual known to all as 'Colleague,' who has been brought back with us, is an unlimited and invaluable source of intelligence, and she will need personal protection for the rest of her life and that of her daughter. It is imperative, repeat imperative, that her absence must be kept under the tightest security possible and unknown to everyone except those here in this room and to the two officers here on the air base.

"Two separate actions need to be taken—one would be to claim that the Russians have abducted her as a separate means of more control over the Chinese president. The second is to claim that she has died of a heart attack due to the stress in her job, and the Russians did not want to acknowledge it since it occurred in their country. Note that both of these are to ensure her safety and to most importantly plant immediate cracks in the trust between the two presidents."

D/CIA stated that the agency could get these two messages out worldwide within two hours.

POTUS nodded his approval.

"Third: Mr. President told me to draw up a document today indicating that as of this moment, the Colleague and her daughter are U.S. citizens and they will be given lifetime pensions. POTUS said that the Colleague has already surpassed her contribution to the U.S., but he will still request that if she is willing, she continue to provide the U.S. with her insights, thoughts, and knowledge.

"Fourth: The current Chinese president is insane and is behind this effort to destroy the U.S. He is a megalomaniac who believes he will be the savior of the world.

"Fifth: We are in the process of recruiting another exceptionally high asset who could be invaluable to our efforts. The identity cannot at this time be revealed, but myself and Doc need to have face time with D/CIA to obtain additional information about this individual and to concur and proceed."

D/CIA said that he had brought an in-depth file on the individual and could assist the Professor as soon as this meeting is completed.

POTUS said, "Get it done."

"Sixth," the Professor continued, "the Chinese president, who I believe is the architect and originator of this coming war, needs to be disposed of—and quickly. I know the right person for the job."

SecDef, after softly laying his eyes on Doc, said he had a good hunch as to who it was.

SecDef said he did endorse the operation but noted that this was certainly a real long shot and one that should be kept to only those in the room and no further. The only exception would be a Special Forces team on site.

POTUS approved the operation and said to tell the selected individual(s) that their country sincerely thanks them.

The other members in the meeting slowly looked over to Doc, but his facial expression did not change—he even looked a little bored. Most of those present knew that Doc was a serious and dangerous man.

POTUS just smiled.

"Seventh," said the Professor, "I suggest that the Russian president may still be open to betraying his relationship with the Chinese president. However, this window opens only once—according to my mental algorithms. This window will open directly after the commencement of an attack, and not before. At that time, the Russian president must see the true force and might of the United States, and, if he does, may waver.

"The Russian president's mind will teeter on whether he has made the wrong choice. If we were able to convince him in person, then I think the Russian president might jump ship. A possibility exists, but one that will not last very long. If he decides to betray the Chinese president, he will become 'loyal' for at least the rest of the war."

POTUS said that he understood the Professor's rationale and he would send the Professor to persuade the Russian president. However, POTUS said, he thought that the odds of this occurring would very much increase if the sitting Chinese president could be removed—quietly.

Immediately after this exchange, POTUS received a secure call from the D/NSA, who notified him that the Chinese codes were valid. Additionally, the D/CIA received a separate secure call advising that the agency has been successful in muddling the issue of the missing senior Chinese official.

There was already real contention between the Chinese foreign minister and the Russian foreign official, who said he was determined to learn if the Linguist was still alive. NSA also reported that the Chinese president had a call in to the Russian president stating that the woman was of the utmost importance to him. He demanded that they release her. The Russian leader denied any involvement. The Chinese president ended the call abruptly, saying that his people would get to the bottom of this.

POTUS smiled and said, "Well done."

And on that note, the Professor asked POTUS to allow him and Doc to depart so that they could get back to work. They promised that they would keep everyone in the room apprised of any new developments.

POTUS concurred, and the members in the room quickly departed as well. A few fast minutes later, when the D/CIA was in one of his own secure conference rooms in his building, he linked up with the Professor and Doc via the same audio and video conference room they had just used in Guam.

During that very short break, Doc and the Professor put through a secure call and video to the Colonel, who was the pilot that had been closely watching over the Linguist's daughter. Doc thanked the Colonel deeply and asked the Colonel if the daughter was at all available.

The Colonel confirmed the availability, and they then brought the Colleague into the room. Prior to allowing that, the Professor stressed to her that she must not divulge her present location or situation. To only tell her that she was safe and would see her soon. The Linguist's daughter came on the line.

Both started to cry and then laughed in joy to be together. The daughter said she had been praying each and every day that her mother would be OK and would come to her soon. The mother said that she missed her beyond words and was so pleased to see her well. The mother said all would be well again, but they had to be exceptionally smart and patient.

The link was then closed. The Colleague looked at the Professor and Doc and thanked them over and over again. She was beaming with joy.

The Professor told D/CIA that he was pleased to see his old friend even if it was under trying circumstances. The director returned the sentiment.

D/CIA told the Professor and Doc that keeping their operation in closed channels was both vital and prudent to successfully recruiting the individual in question. The agency had a thick file on the individual they identified, known as "Lighthouse." D/CIA said that while they did have a lot about him, they had been unable to get Lighthouse to engage with them at all.

As Lighthouse was in the Russian president's inner circle, he would be a perfect catch, however. The director said that he would be extremely valuable for one other reason: Lighthouse was in full charge of the Russian military's nuclear arsenal. He and the Russian president thereby were the only two individuals that held the codes for all of their nuclear systems. Doc looked over at the Professor, and they both nodded subtly.

The Professor asked if the director would have any objections to Doc and the Professor making a run at Lighthouse. "Moreover, would you also be willing to allow the Chief to become Lighthouse's handler if we do get some traction?"

The director thought for a long minute, said that he knew that they were seriously up to something and it would be far easier for him to acquiesce if they were to share their plan. But the director was realistic. He knew that the

Professor or Doc could easily have POTUS order him to give either of them a shot at Lighthouse. So yes, the director would approve.

# CHAPTER FIFTEEN

# UNLEASH THE DOGS OF WAR

THE DAY CALLED FOR SOME deep rest and relaxation for not only the Professor and Doc but also for the Linguist. Her world had been turned upside down. The Professor was pleased that he and Doc were able to connect the mother with her daughter, at least for a few moments. The trio had just finished their dinner and had decided to keep the Guam air base as their home away from home for the next day or so.

During that time, the Professor told the Linguist about what POTUS had said and did on his promise to Doc, the Professor, and two advisers. She and her daughter would never have to worry again about their future and lives in the U.S. They were now U.S. citizens. From this day forward, she could be of further assistance to the U.S., but that would be her choice, not a requirement.

She looked to the Professor and Doc and said she owed everything to them and wanted to continue to contribute in any way possible. She then hugged them individually.

The Professor looked at her and said that to be honest, he had been wishing to hear that she felt that way; they needed all the help they could get.

The Linguist laughed. The Professor told her that Doc was going on a mission back to China, departing the next day. The Linguist asked if she could know the purpose, and the Professor quietly told her that he was going to kill the Chinese president. She gasped, looked directly into Doc's eyes, and asked him if he absolutely had to do this. Doc nodded affirmatively and told her it was for the best of both the American and the Chinese people. He said that he was hoping that she might have some ideas on how to get him into and out of the president's personal residence or his office without being seen.

After a moment's pause, she said that she could do better than that because certain unknown tunnels led into and out of that building, and she knew them well.

The Professor knew what she was going to say next—she herself should do the mission or at least accompany Doc. The Professor interjected—impossible. Adding anyone to the mission would only slow Doc down. The Linguist reluctantly agreed, but said that she had a lifelong contact who could guide Doc into the cavern and assist in getting him out as well.

Doc asked her if she was sure of the person's fidelity, and whether she would welcome the president being moved into his next life.

The Linguist smiled and said, "Yes, very much so, on both accounts." She said that she would give him the person's name and address and a gold necklace of hers to convince her that the request came from her and her heart. Doc nodded.

He warned that he was going to be disguised as an extremely old man using some implants and a slow-walking cast on one leg. This was to deal with facial recognition technology. She said that she understood and wanted him to know that while that technology had received a lot of media attention, China's advancement was not as good as it wanted the world and its own population to believe.

Doc said that knowing that alone would be of great value to him.

He told her that his return exfiltration would be off the coast by way of direct transport.

She said that she would put a specific diagram together for his encrypted phone storage that would ensure he could make it to her special friend's house and later to the submarine.

Prior to falling asleep, Doc contacted Chairman/JCS on a secure line and briefed him on the plan. With respect to the spec ops team that was already in China, it was the same team from the last go-round. Doc said that this was great and it was more than one could hope for, and the Chairman agreed.

He also added that the team said to tell Doc that they were anxiously waiting to see his disguised face and his "limited" physicality in person. Finally, they said to tell Doc that they thought the disguise might be something he should use all the time, even inside CONUS. Doc laughed out loud.

The Chairman/JCS then smiled and said all was a go. The Chairman said that if Doc did not make it back, he would see him in hell. "However, for our collective sake," the Chairman/JCS said, "just tap the damn guy and get the hell home pronto."

Doc laughed again.

The Professor and the Linguist flew home the next day. Once they landed, the mother and daughter hugged each other over and over again. It was then that the Professor started worrying about Doc.

He would be going wheels down in another stealth bird in a cornfield. The bird departed within seconds of Doc putting his feet on the ground. One of the operatives was there in deep background, with a beat-up, extra old vehicle left for Doc. Doc ever so softly signaled him a subtle thank-you. Doc then got in the car alone and started heading toward the city. The power of the engine in the small car was surprisingly strong and impressive. Doc smiled and thought those professional Special Forces operators never missed a detail and he was sincerely more than grateful to have them.

Doc knew he did not have a minute to waste, so he mentally pulled up the Linguist's friend's address and name and recalled the map he had memorized. While doing so, Doc also mentally reviewed the Linguist's details of the president's formal office, his private bedroom, and multiple ways to get in and get out. He thought that the Linguist could have applied for the U.S. Special Forces in another lifetime. She would have been outstanding in comparison to the difficulty of finding a strong vehicle engine.

Once in the neighborhood, he took note of the surrounding area, determining what exits he could use if the situation went south. His new contact could have moved or decided she did not care for the Linguist anymore. He found a spot for the car that would offer a very quick exit. On foot, he stopped in front of the designated abode. It had a small plot of land surrounding it. He rang the bell.

A small old woman pushed the curtain of her window just enough to see him and then slowly cracked the door open about two inches. Doc stepped back and said softly that he had found this gold necklace, which had the Linguist's name carved into the back of it in ancient calligraphy, and wanted to see if the occupant might know the owner. The lady quickly snatched it and then studied it closely.

She asked where he had found it.

He said a friend had asked him to deliver it. The lady suddenly grabbed him by the cloth on his arm and pulled him into her house.

Once the door was shut tight, he could tell that she was living alone, no children or husband. Her countenance up close was vigilant, and she pressed him on how he came about the necklace. She accused him of being a spy for the Communist Party, and she said that nothing he said would change her mind.

She had, he now saw, a high-caliber pistol in her right hand, completely on mark. He told her in Mandarin that he meant no harm, and if she could point the gun slightly lower, he could explain his situation. She did not lower the gun and rather took a long step back that now substantially reduced his odds of taking it away from her. She then raised the gun higher with her two hands positioned exactly right and a fractional increase to improve her aim. Doc knew that this old woman was familiar with firearms and could put a bullet in his head competently.

Doc spoke of a mutual friend to the old lady. He told a story about the both of them, which the old lady knew well. The old lady asked whether her friend was still alive, but Doc told her that he could not say either way.

She lowered the gun about two inches, and that made his heart beat a little easier. Doc told her that he was sent on an important assignment that would ensure that their mutual friend would be safe in the future as would her daughter. The old woman lowered the pistol. She asked him how he could know about their mutual friend's daughter.

Doc said that he was instrumental in getting the daughter to a foreign country that had permitted the daughter to attend a wonderful university, where she was learning more every day. The daughter would never have to leave that country, and she would always be safe. The old woman had a tear streaming down her face and said that she and their mutual friend were the only ones who knew about the daughter. Doc nodded and said that their mutual friend wanted her to know that she missed the old woman and hoped that she was taking good care of herself.

After a minute or so, the woman asked him how she could help. Doc said that time was of crucial importance and he would greatly value her assistance if she were willing to work with him.

The old lady paused and said that they should have some tea first outside on her patio, which Doc understood was to avoid recorders or noisy neighbors. She put on a television, and then they sat down and had some tea and biscuits. He asked whether she'd ever had a husband or children. The old lady replied that her husband and three children were all murdered by the current Chinese president. Her husband had gone against the president politically. She was forced to watch their execution. She was told that she could not die. She was to show all that she had been rehabilitated so that those who went against the president would know never to test him.

For appearances, the communist politburo gave her a house and claimed that her family all died in an automobile accident.

This all occurred many years ago. It had been and would forever be in her broken heart. Perhaps in the next life she would be with her children.

Doc now understood why the Linguist had chosen this individual to be his helper. He asked her if she was familiar with the caverns and tunnels. With an open mouth for a few seconds, she again paused. She said that she knew them intimately and asked what this assignment had to do with them. Doc said that time did not offer him niceties to obfuscate so he would put his mission on the table, but she could not tell anyone.

He told her that he was going to assassinate the president.

She looked at him for a long couple of minutes and then asked him if it was possible—if he could do it.

Doc looked directly back into her sad eyes and said yes. Doc said that the more difficult part might be after the fact. Would he be able to securely get out of the country?

The old lady's face now changed. She somehow looked much younger. She smiled and said that she only had one more question: When did his assignment start?

Doc said that if he could stay with her in this house to sleep for a couple of hours, commencement would be about 2:30 a.m.—if she knew a way to get into and out of the tunnels without being caught.

The old woman said she did, and he could of course get some rest prior to his mission. Doc shared the features of the mutual friend's mental map of the presidential office and bedroom. While Doc had no intention of bringing the old woman beyond the cavern, he thought it was still good for her to know in case things went sideways. She said she was coming along, period, and there was nothing he could say or do to stop her.

The old woman directed Doc to her bedroom and told him to rest and then get ready. She said that old people did not sleep that much so she would study the tunnels to select the best routes and wake him once it was time.

Doc dozed off without missing a beat. Doc had used the old executive protection proviso for catching a few minutes of rest: eat whenever you can, go the bathroom whenever you can, and always sleep whenever you can—whether you are standing up or lying down.

At one o'clock, they were in the small vehicle on the outskirts of Beijing. The old woman directed him to one of the tunnel openings. They were walking on a field of some sort and had already covered the vehicle. On the outside, the tunnel entrance could not be seen at all. Trees and bushes covered the entrance completely, but the old woman found it effortlessly.

They went into the cave and walked on one of many paths, with the old woman leading the way. At many points, she described which was the most promising path, absolutely confident. Each time she chose a turn on a path, Doc marked it by breaking a couple of branches to remember not only for their exfiltration, but as a means that provided his friends a breadcrumb trail to track them too. After about twenty minutes, they were at one of the building's lower-access floors. Doc asked that the old woman wait. If she did not hear from him within the next two hours, she was to abandon the endeavor. If she ever got questioned on it, she should tell them that he had forced her to take her there. The woman said she understood.

Doc quietly moved into the private residence, watching the guards and their change cycles. Surprisingly, there were only a few of them, but they were numerous on the outside grounds.

Doc also observed each and every camera in sight with a small mirror assisting him around the corners. The cavern route into the floors was close to the president's suite. Doc noted that at his current specific corridor, security was not permitted. Incredibly, at the presidential suite bedroom door, no security was permitted as well. Doc smiled for a moment and quietly shook his head. People do not know that many principals will outright reject the security aspect of having officers too close to their bedrooms. The principal wants and often demands privacy because in the daytime and evenings, their personal time is nonexistent.

This applies particularly to master bedrooms. Presidents often do not bother or allow a lock on either the outside or the inside of the door. Presidents often use the ruse of asking what would happen if they need to get out of their rooms quickly and emergently. Security officers are then told to knock or call prior to entering the room.

Doc had previous intelligence that said the president never slept overnight with anyone for security reasons. He smiled and wondered if the man ever got lonely or had any affairs, but remembered that he was, at his core, a mentally ill man and a killer for sure. Any women that he had were probably quite aware of his base sickness and tried to stay as far away as possible.

At the right second, when the corridor was fully empty, Doc silently slipped into the president's room and found him in a deep sleep. Doc knew that he had to immediately pick out the electronic sensors that he could step on or activate. Doc looked around carefully and felt comfortable. He was glad to hear and see that the Chinese president snored a lot, as it meant he was in a deep sleep. Doc moved in close, carefully withdrew a clear syringe from his pocket, then plunged it downward directly into the president's heart, and then quickly removed it. He then swiftly lifted an unused pillow and placed it squarely over the president's face. This stopped all airflow to his lungs. Within a minute, the Chinese president was dead from cardiac arrest.

Doc waited, counting time on his watch for the shift changes of the guards, and then softly opened the door slightly and saw that the three closest guards, which were the ones he had to get by the most, were all having a deep rest too, with snoring to boot.

They must have been all doing a double shift. Doc quietly left the corridor, slipped down to the lowest level, and went deliberately back into the cavern. After about four minutes, he saw the old woman waiting patiently; she led him directly back the way they had originally come. They carefully uncovered the small vehicle and drove it back to her neighborhood.

The old woman looked into his face to ask whether the job was done. Doc just nodded, and she reached over and kissed him for a few seconds on the side of his face. She was starting to cry but holding it in as best as she could.

He said that not now but sometime in the not-too-distant future, a messenger would come to her house and leave with her a small suitcase. She should accept it, and the messenger would prove his bona fides by mentioning the word "Doc" and her mutual friend's daughter's first name and no more. The case would be filled with cash, and he hoped that it would be of some comfort to her.

Doc said he knew that it would never replace her loved ones, but perhaps she could move to another area in another house. She should live the rest of her life knowing that she saved the lives of thousands, and maybe even millions, of Chinese children.

The old lady stepped out of the vehicle and looked again at Doc and said she would never forget him.

Doc saw one of the vehicles behind him that was a "friendly." Doc drove off, and when he had passed a few miles, he pulled over into a dark spot. The operator got him into their car. He then wiped down his car thoroughly and took the false registrations out. After they went about three more miles, his old car caught fire and burned to a crisp. Two more vehicles besides the one he was in were used to repeatedly move him from one to the other as a security precaution. In the last one, Doc directed them based on the Linguist's specified routes.

On the small shoreline, they all got out of their clothes and into their black wetsuits, and then they all got aboard a small, motorized rubber boat and waited in darkness after sending a visual signal for the submarine.

The signal was accepted, and each dropped into the water, cut the vinyl boat so it went deep into the ocean, weighed down by the heavy motor, and were on the submarine in about two minutes. Doc told the captain that he had a secure message he had to forward to the Professor and POTUS.

The captain said he thought he might, handed him one of their secure phone lines, told all personnel to step outside and away from the communications center, and then left as well. Doc reached the Professor and said it was done.

The Professor said, "Your ride has been ordered to drop you off at the Guam air base; I'll meet you tomorrow. POTUS wants us to be in Moscow no later than that time frame for negotiations with the Russian president."

POTUS had told the Russian president that the Professor and Doc were his personal envoys. Further, any communications between the Russian president and POTUS would be through this back channel. The Professor ordered Doc to get as much rest as was possible on the air base. Doc asked that the special operations team that had been on this most recent trip be duly compensated and rewarded for their performance.

Moreover, the assistance and bravery of the old woman that the Linguist provided were invaluable. It was a success primarily because she guided him, with tremendous danger to herself, to his required destination. Upon completion of the assignment, Doc had promised her a payment of $2 million that she would receive within the coming months and well past the former Chinese president's demise. Doc requested that a capable colleague make delivery once the coast was clear. He rested some knowing that the elderly lady would be well taken care of by Uncle Sam.

# CHAPTER SIXTEEN

# DO NOT TREAD
# ON THE U.S.

ON THE SUB, A NEW secure message was coming in, one that was marked urgent. The captain read the message and handed it to Doc. It was crystal clear: two armed Russian submarines breached U.S. territorial waters and were destroyed by two American submarines on the U.S. coastline. The message went on to declare that this was not a drill and the actions were implemented based on a clear threat to the United States. From this moment of time, the U.S. DEFCON alert has been raised to DEFCON 3, and all submarines were to take aggressive positions regarding any hostile foreign seafaring ships of any kind. The captain was ordered to accelerate his delivery of Doc as much as he could.

The captain said, "Roger that, as long as we don't detect any hostiles along the way." The submarine surfaced within what seemed like a few tense hours, unloaded Doc, and then returned underwater to cover the coast of the Guam air base.

Inside five minutes, Doc was escorted by vehicle directly into the hangar and greeted by the commander once again.

The commander asked if Doc had gotten the news about the destroyed Russian submarines. Yes. Doc said that he needed to reach Washington via secure communications as soon as possible, and the commander said he figured as much and pointed to the secure conference room.

It was already linked into POTUS and the Professor, and the other major military, intelligence, state, FBI, and Homeland Security personnel were all already in place. One difference that Doc saw was that they were not in the White House Situation Report room any longer, but rather one with surrounding extra hard, solid walls. The Professor saw Doc and nodded to him. A general was walking through the taking down of the Russian submarines and probable retaliation on other U.S. assets by either the Russians or the Chinese.

POTUS asked SecDef, the Professor, and the Secretary of State what they thought the degree of retaliation would be at this time. The Professor surmised that since the massive planned attack was still scheduled for a week or so from now, the Russians and Chinese were trying to evaluate whether this hit happened because the U.S. had somehow found out about their specific time line, or because the Russian submarine captains tried to do something stupid.

POTUS took in the scenario and demanded to know if they thought the U.S. was going to get hit hard as a result or not. POTUS paused and looked at Doc on the screen and asked if he was 100 percent sure that his mission was a success.

Doc looked directly at POTUS and said yes. Doc added that his supposition would be that the lack of any public announcements was because the Chinese were trying to identify a new leader and had not yet done so. Doc said that his guess was that the Russians were totally focused now on the total loss of their two submarines. And they were completely unaware of this other major event—the demise of the Chinese leader—at this time.

Doc went on, "Respectfully, sir, if you and the SecDef want to know the degree of the hit we may soon get, it can perhaps be achieved best by having the Professor and myself travel to Moscow immediately to talk with the Russian president face-to-face. We would be acting, as you have stipulated, as your back-channel representatives to express our concerns over this terrible tragedy. The Russians may not only show their possible current reactions toward us over the submarines but also may relay their knowledge, or lack thereof, regarding the Chinese situation. Either way, we have definitely rattled their cages. And as long as this remains out of the media, we all still have some wiggle room."

The SecDef said that he did think that getting the Professor and Doc there would serve to get an accurate temperature reading.

POTUS looked at the Professor and asked what he thought. The Professor said he thought that Doc's idea could work. He would give it a 70 percent chance, and if they were able to manipulate the Russians just a little more, they might possibly be able to break the Russians' close relationship with the Chinese.

POTUS said to the Secretary of State that he wanted the U.S. ambassador to quietly approach the Russians and advised that the Professor and Doc would be arriving secretly to meet with the Russian president at his convenience, but no later than two days from now. They would be coming on behalf of POTUS with a message. There would be no media or publicity of any kind. The Professor told the SecDef that he would like to be airborne, by military aircraft if at all possible, within the next couple of hours to Guam so he could pick up Doc. POTUS looked at the SecDef and then said, "Make it happen now."

SecDef picked up the secure line and said it would be ready. Given the time factor, it would be a stealth F-22 with two other like escorts on their tail. They should have flight clearance by then to Moscow once they were ready to depart Guam Air Base. The stealth(s) would continue with the tail coverage and be ordered to protect the Professor and Doc by any means necessary. SecDef also added a special operations team to protect the Professor and Doc in Moscow.

POTUS approved it and told everyone to get rest but stay alert to any more wonderful events that were sure to come their way on this roller coaster. Everyone laughed. Humor was an excellent means to stay at the ready and to keep tension levels at a reasonable notch that ensured maximum performance.

After about twelve hours, the primary aircraft, as well as the trailing protector aircrafts, arrived on the Guam air base. The Professor and Doc spent some time catching up with each other.

Prior to their departure, the Professor reached out to the Linguist via a secure line to the New York safe haven on the Hudson. He was able to reach her on the secure line that was there. The Professor explained that he and Doc were en route overseas again. He asked her if the Russian asset who was working for Chinese intelligence had any particular vices or imperfections.

She told the Professor how the Chinese had successfully recruited him: he was a gambling addict. They waited and watched until he had an extremely high substantial loss of money on one of his trips abroad at a casino in Nevada. The

Chinese did not know what his real work involved other than that he was a high-level Russian military officer on the move. He also had a family with two young daughters, and he was very close to them.

The Chinese had blackmailed him and threatened his children's lives, but they had not pushed him all the way in the hope that his contributions could grow in the future. She added that he did send them a few sensitive documents, but they were not sure if they were legitimate or just a means of temporarily getting them off his back. The Professor thanked her and said that he had to go. She paused for a minute on the video screen and said to be very careful.

The Professor knew what she wanted to know without saying it. Had the target been neutralized? The Professor said that it was great that Doc had returned safely. Oh, and he added that Doc said to be sure to tell her that she (and her daughter) should from now on get some sound sleep. The Linguist smiled widely and said she hoped they would have a very good and safe trip.

Doc told the Professor that he now found Lighthouse to be promising in some respects. The Professor agreed and advised that a new message had just come in from the U.S. embassy. The Russian president had agreed to a meeting. It would be as mentioned, handled discreetly from beginning to end, and the Professor and Doc were both invited (but no one else was).

The note also said that the Russian president had decided to meet with them tomorrow evening at his office. He added that since Doc was going to be present, he had decided to include one of his younger and most promising generals in the meeting. Doc and the Professor smiled widely, and they could not wait to see if that was referring to Lighthouse. The message finally indicated that the director of the FSB would be picking them up at the Russian military base as a courtesy. The smile they had just enjoyed a minute ago was quickly dissolved given the very unpleasant news of the FSB director's inclusion attending to their transportation. The FSB was clearly not one of their fans!

They boarded the stealth F-22, headed to Moscow, and slept for about ten hours before waking to review their strategy. Doc said that while they were in with the Russian president, Doc would make a serious effort to create a relationship with Lighthouse. The way that the Kremlin had worded the message, it seemed to place Doc and Lighthouse in a lower but equal position. The Professor agreed but warned Doc to tread lightly.

He would play it thusly: POTUS had given the Professor a very sensitive and personal message for the Russian president, for his eyes only. The added possible lane of an exchange of some sort between Doc and Lighthouse was one they might never get again.

The bird landed and they disembarked. In less than a minute, the pilot/Colonel took off and was rejoined by the other U.S. fighter jets that had been circling above, now very happy to be heading home with an aerial refueling in friendly airspace. The director's limousine pulled up, and the Professor and Doc were escorted into the large armored vehicle. The Professor was sitting adjacent to the director, and Doc was sitting on a small bench seat that folded open. The lead and follow security Mercedes SUVs were off and running with all three vehicles riding down a lane that was reserved for official visiting heads of state—even though the mission was secret, the windows were all darkly tinted, and no media would ever intrude when it came to a motor-cade that included the Director of the FSB.

The director said to the Professor and Doc, in a low voice, that they must understand that his country's leadership was furious with the U.S. The destruction of their innocent submarines could not be forgotten or forgiven easily. Moreover, from his perspective, retaliation from the Russian motherland was likely to occur. They were certainly entering very volatile times. The Professor looked at the director and said that he agreed with his assessment that at present the future was dark. "That is precisely why we wish to talk with your president—to see if there is a way out of this very black hole."

The director mumbled that in his estimation, such a mission was damned before it even got started. It was dangerous for any American to be here at this time.

Doc stared at the director for a minute and said, "Sometimes outcomes do not end up like some people expect." The team leader up front had been listening. Doc looked at him in the mirror, and this time the TL did not try to hide his smile. The director paused, looked at Doc for a full minute, and then noted, "I think you are a bit crazy."

Doc looked first at the Professor and then the director and said, "You, sir, are not the first person to tell me that."

All was very quiet and the limousine was now pulling up to the first Kremlin gate. They went through a second inspection, which amounted to one of the soldiers looking into the limousine and matching the digital photos of Doc and the Professor. They were then asked to step out of the car. The Professor thanked the director for the generous transportation and conversation, and then got out of the limousine.

Doc leaned forward toward the security team leader and said that he hoped that they would cross paths again. Once out of the car, Doc leaned inward toward the FSB director. Doc said to him, "Take good care of yourself, for as you mentioned, we are living in very trying and dangerous times."

The director looked at Doc and then just shook his head in disbelief. The team leader, on the other hand, quietly glared at Doc and displayed his true wolf like facial features, including even some slight froth at the corners of his mouth. Doc smiled again and waved a very light kiss to him. It was Doc's longtime experience that individuals that urgently wanted to kill him (and the Professor) often suffered during any missed opportunity, and it played greatly with their minds.

Several members of the president's security detail escorted the Professor and Doc to the president's office. They sat outside the office for about ten minutes and were then invited in. Once seated, an attractive female assistant asked them if they would like any beverages. Both declined.

A very young-looking Russian general came walking in confidently. He smartly walked over to the Professor and Doc and shook their hands while welcoming them at this difficult time. The photographs matched—it was Lighthouse. He apologized for the president's late arrival but said his schedule was always full to the brim. However, it was even fuller now with the recent U.S. military actions.

A few moments later, the president came barging in and they all stood. He had an extremely unpleasant demeanor and appeared to be angry. The Russian president stared at the Professor and then at Doc and asked why they were here. He said, "Your U.S. military just destroyed two of my submarines without cause." He looked at the Professor closely and asked why he should not order an attack of similar scale on the U.S.

The Professor stared back and said, "The Russian submarines were purposely and quietly sitting off our coasts, clearly waiting further orders from Moscow.

Then, those submarines' captains moved aggressively: not only did they pass our international border lines, they pushed on directly to our coastlines. We were forced to respond."

The president paused, motioning for them all to sit down. The president lowered his voice some. He said to the Professor, "You have to understand that much of what I have just heard is different from what my naval officers told me."

The Professor paused and said that he understood that and it was why he emphasized to POTUS the value of a face-to-face visit. The matter could still be considered an accident, and the U.S. was willing to compensate the families.

The general now spoke up: the incident could be successfully handled in that manner if it was acceptable to the Russian and American presidents. Otherwise, retribution would be necessary, likely leading to full-scale actions for both sides.

The Professor knew that the U.S. would then be forced to respond in kind, making extreme escalation inevitable. The Russian president looked at the general and nodded. The Professor sensed that he seemed to be genuinely looking for an escape. The Professor took a deep breath. He might actually be able to help.

# CHAPTER SEVENTEEN

# A FRIEND IN NEED
# IS A FRIEND INDEED

THE PROFESSOR FELT IT WAS the right time to put their next ploy on the table. He asked the president whether they could have a face-to-face while the general and Doc continued to put together more options. The Professor said to the president that he did have a special message from POTUS that he was to share with him only via his eyes and ears alone. The president nodded.

Once outside the room, the general suggested to Doc that they carry on their discussions in his office. When they entered, Doc looked around and complimented the general for both his good taste and his remarkable number of medals, shining in glass cabinets. The general beamed just a bit and said, "Why don't we continue to evaluate the situation?"

Doc nodded and said that he was most impressed with the general's comments regarding the "accident" approach, and Doc asked him if he really thought they could get it by the media. The general smiled and said that it was the wisest thing to do.

Doc asked if he thought the Russians were preparing a counterstrike, and the general's eyes shifted uncomfortably. Doc felt the man out slowly; given the circumstances, a reprisal would be in line with history. The general seemed to relax a little and said that he thought their job now was to avoid such impulsive actions. Doc concurred.

Doc looked at the general and asked if it would be OK to share a few thoughts. The general nodded. Doc said he himself was a gambling man. He had even been known to hit the casinos a time or two. Gambling helped him sort out difficult dilemmas. The general smiled and said that they did seem to have some traits in common. Doc said that in their very short time together, he had felt that too. Doc said he, of course, did know that others often did not think or feel the same way. The general asked what he meant.

Doc said, "Well, look at the Chinese. They have a whole totally different culture that worries about 'face' and not being embarrassed more than almost anything else." Doc leaned forward and whispered that, to be completely honest, he tended to hate the Chinese with a passion.

The general was silent, looked closely at Doc, and then asked if Doc would be interested in getting a drink or two at a small restaurant that evening. It was one of his favorite locations that offered some privacy. Doc said he thought it was an excellent idea and nine o'clock would be good. But it was important that he not mention it to the president or the Professor. The general looked at Doc and put his index finger to his lips. They went back down the hallway to the president's office. The general leaned his ear against the closed door and said he heard some laughter, and then the door was opening. The general missed being caught by seconds.

The Russian president told the general to get a limousine for the Professor and Doc to bring them back to the U.S. embassy. The general acknowledged and pointed them to the downstairs floor, then proceeded to escort them to the waiting foyer; the vehicle pulled up almost immediately. The Professor thanked the general. Doc touched his forehead slightly to indicate that he would see the general later. It would look to anyone else like a salute.

They walked up to the building entrance and got on the elevator. The door opened and with a special turnkey, they were again in a secure conference room. The Ambassador as well as the former participants appeared present. The Professor asked if they were aware that the U.S. had one day ago taken out two Russian submarines. The military officer nodded. The Ambassador had heard a broader secure message, and it had claimed that there had been a major accident, as many foreign Russian personnel were dead. No other details.

Doc looked at the Ambassador and said that both stories were accurate to a degree. He added that it was good to hear that it was an "accident," because that was what they were trying to get the Russian president to believe. The Professor added that there was no reason to believe, at least at this point, that reprisals were coming. The president had so far agreed to going along with the accident story for media consumption.

Doc sat down with the Chief of Station and said it was good to see him again. However, Doc said he would still refer to him as simply the "Chief." He asked him if D/CIA had briefed him on his role, and the guy smiled lightly, nodded, and asked what he could do for Doc regarding Lighthouse. Doc said he was going to meet with Lighthouse at 9 p.m. at a small restaurant. The Chief said that he could get him out of the embassy and no one would see him. Doc said that he had his own disguise kit for traveling back and forth. The Chief nodded.

As they went through the preparations, the Chief asked Doc if he would mind telling him the name of the restaurant. Doc pulled the card out of his pocket. The Chief said that this was actually a very good choice by Lighthouse because it was off the beaten trail, dark and quiet, and had good points of access and egress. Doc said he planned to get there well before their set time to review, orient, and acquaint himself with the neighborhood and to determine if he or the Lighthouse brought any surveillance along and what the camera systems were like with them. The Chief said that fortunately, there was pretty much no camera system in that area at all.

The Chief got Doc all set up and got him on the street without any unwanted coverage by the Russian surveillance units. The Chief had pulled out of the embassy in a known vehicle and looked to be rushing to get somewhere. He took off like a shot out of hell to get the locals' attention. Meanwhile Doc walked slowly and casually out the main entrance. A U.S. Marine even waved his hand at Doc. Once down a couple of blocks, Doc looked in one of the nearby store windows and felt his significant disguise merited some real value.

He looked like a Russian old timer anxious to get home after a long day's work. Doc picked up his pace and then jumped in a taxi. He was at the restaurant a full half hour before Lighthouse's arrival. Doc's disguise had been removed prior to entering the establishment, and he had gotten his table toward the rear—which included very soft lights.

Doc had a bottle of vodka brought to the table and discreetly poured a third of it into a nearby plant. The restaurant was pretty empty. Lighthouse came in at exactly nine o'clock.

He found Doc waving at him in the back, greeting him by shaking hands while feeling for any wires or recorders. He did the same. Lighthouse liked the professionalism. Once both were seated, they had to lean forward to get the waiters to provide any service. Lighthouse told Doc that while the servers were less than first class, the food was excellent. Doc smiled and poured Lighthouse a shot of vodka that he swallowed right away. Doc poured another for himself and toasted to "friendship." Lighthouse seemed nervous but keenly interested in talking.

Soon after, Doc could tell that this was a man that had been carrying a heavy load. The general wanted desperately to get rid of it. Doc looked at Lighthouse and then mused that he was still a younger man who was not as experienced in the rocks and holes that life often has to offer whether one accepts it or not—and Russian and Chinese cultures were as tough as it gets. Doc lifted the vodka bottle one more time but Lighthouse put his hand over the glass so Doc placed it aside. They ordered some food, and Doc raved about it nonstop. They talked over the meal about Russian hockey and American football, and then asked for two cups of coffee to begin their real business.

# CHAPTER EIGHTEEN

# PEELING THE ONION

DOC ASKED HIM WHAT HE thought about the Russian president. Lighthouse smiled and said he was rather old and probably should have retired a few years ago. Doc was surprised by his candor. Doc asked if he thought that Russia would attack the U.S., and Lighthouse said that if it did, he did not think that the submarine incident was going to be the burning fuse or the cause. If the U.S. were attacked, it would not be a byproduct of the relatively new Russian/Chinese relationship either. Their real collective fear for their respective populations (Russian and Chinese) and their individual leaderships would be their famine, dealing with fear of the coronavirus, and lack of jobs. Lighthouse was on a roll.

Doc asked him again if he thought the U.S. would be attacked. Lighthouse looked directly at Doc and said that Doc knew he could be arrested for such talk. Doc said he did not wish to put him on the spot. Lighthouse whispered in a light voice that there was a plan in motion that called for a massive attack by the end of the next week.

Doc played it cool. "That is what some of our intelligence is saying too."

Lighthouse's eyes widened, and he said, "The U.S. is that far down the road?"

Doc said that was his opinion. He added that in his view, the Chinese were the masterminds here, and would turn on Russia as soon as they could. Lighthouse said, "We speak as one."

Lighthouse and Doc stared each other down. Doc said that he was very glad that they had met and that time was of the essence. Lighthouse then asked Doc if—were he to confide in Doc—would Doc help him?

Doc said, "Absolutely. We are kindred spirits. Together, we can save our two countries."

Lighthouse relayed that like Doc, he enjoyed a good casino gamble from time to time, that he had two wonderful daughters whom he loved greatly, and that he, too, hated China. Doc let him continue.

He went on to say that he had gotten himself into a terrible jam and needed help.

The Chinese had watched him lose a few bucks at a casino in Nevada and had since then threatened Lighthouse. They said that they would kill his daughters unless he cooperated more by feeding them higher-quality information. Lighthouse said that he had only sent the Chinese a few actual documents and that they were not sensitive. This approach had been working fine, but somehow, the director of the FSB found out about it, and he was now personally blackmailing Lighthouse too. Doc asked Lighthouse if he could be brutally honest with him and put their respective cards on the table. Lighthouse leaned forward.

Doc said that they had been watching him for many years. They had found him to be probably the most talented and promising man they had ever seen in the Russian military structure and in the Russian political structure. Moreover, the U.S. believed that he could and should be the next Russian president. Doc said that he was not exaggerating any of these points. Doc said that he believed he could take care of both of the problems for him.

Although Lighthouse's way of dealing with the Chinese, and the FSB director, had been relatively smart, he needed to remove himself and his family from both orbits immediately. Doc said, "Your daughters can be put into boarding schools abroad within a couple of days." Lighthouse asked how this could happen.

Doc said that they would be enrolled with their true identities hidden. As a general of your rank and stature, this would be very understandable and quite reasonable as a security precaution. Their tuition and all of their personal expenses would be covered because they would have entered on full scholarships. Doc said that he would personally take care of the Chinese officials that threatened him and his loved ones. They would never bother him again.

"By the way, regarding your time gambling in Nevada, we happen to have a videotape of your visit and you had not lost a dime." Doc said he could have the video authenticated so that it showed that Lighthouse had actually won, but because he had a close friend there with him, he had acted like he lost so that his friend (who is from the U.S.) was not embarrassed.

Lighthouse could then send this directly to the Chinese official. Lighthouse would then relay to the Chinese counterintelligence officer that he had enjoyed his time watching and seeing how his guys operated. But he had now simply grown tired of it. Lighthouse would say that he planned all along to use the interaction as a case study for junior cadet officers.

Doc also said that with regard to the FSB director, he would soon be no more. Lighthouse looked at Doc with his eyes wide and asked if he really meant that. Doc told Lighthouse that he had to trust in him. The FSB director would be quickly disposed of and for good. Lighthouse again leaned in forward to Doc and asked him what he would have to do in return.

Doc said being a friend of the U.S. was all. However, he would have to show it in a very clear and direct way to convince the U.S. that he was indeed a friend. Lighthouse asked what he could do. Doc said that due to the possible attack on the U.S., Lighthouse would need to pass Doc his copy of the Russian nuclear codes tonight.

Doc said he knew the general carried them with him all the time per Russian military protocol. Lighthouse sat back in his chair and looked at Doc. Doc told him that this was why he was sent on this mission.

"The Professor's meeting with the president was a means to get to you. The U.S. does hold the Chinese leadership responsible, and they are most assuredly going to be dealt with." Doc said to Lighthouse he should take the gamble. "The Chinese attempt to recruit you will collapse. With reference to the FSB director, that will be taken care of for sure in the not-too-distant future.

"Regarding your ascent to the Russian presidency, it will be accomplished but mostly by your continued growth and willpower. The U.S. will endorse you informally in the background, but that will by itself send a strong message to the world. We will always be there for you. Even if you are not elected in the future, you will still have our support as a senior general in the coming years."

Lighthouse asked how they would communicate and Doc said, "It will be done when you are abroad at any time—dropping in on your daughters at their university or attending to business anywhere in the world. We already have an individual standing by that would be your contact and conduit. For the time being, though, you will see me here, and there will be an encrypted telephone number for you if you need help."

Lighthouse gave the slightest nod, and they both got up.

Lighthouse then pulled his hand out of his front pocket and reached out to shake Doc's hand. In doing so, he deftly passed the nuclear codes to Doc.

Doc told him, "Be aware that you should not try, under any circumstances, to change them, as our people will see it happening in real time, and we will know it promptly."

Lighthouse said he understood. Doc smiled and said louder that they should have dinner again sometime when he was abroad. Lighthouse nodded and left.

Doc decided that he would leave via the backdoor. Doc swiftly put his disguise on again and quickly moved into the dark night. The Marine guard saw him coming and waved when he walked back into the compound limping. The auto cameras would record only an old man who had gone out to steal a few sips of vodka.

# CHAPTER NINETEEN

# A MAN WORTH HIS WEIGHT IN GOLD

THE PROFESSOR WAS WAITING FOR Doc in the secure conference room. He was speaking again with POTUS and the other usual characters about recent deployments and the ongoing status of U.S. military assets. At the request of the Professor, Doc gave them a full briefing from his new "source." He left out whether the source was Russian or not and just gave them the facts that the source did not think the U.S. would be attacked by Russian submarines or otherwise in the next couple of days. He could not determine if the Russians were aware or not of the demise of the Chinese president. However, the moved-up date for a broad general attack was still at the ready and likely to occur. He added that the director of the FSB, who brought them by his car from the airport to the Russian president's office, certainly seemed to be against the U.S. First off, he expressed his view that their trip was worthless, and he intimated that Russia attacking America was a certainty. He also made a direct threat to the lives of both the Professor and Doc.

The Professor then asked if POTUS would speak with them privately. The Professor added that it would also be very helpful if the SecDef, Secretary of State, D/NSA, and D/CIA (the director of national intelligence was abroad) be the only other ones in the room. Done. The Professor asked Doc to continue. Doc told the group that he was able to get from his source the Russian nuclear codes, which had to be validated as soon as possible.

Stunned, the D/NSA said to Doc, "You mean to say that you believe that you have the Russian nuclear codes?"

Doc said yes.

Doc said that he had forwarded them immediately in compartmented channels a few minutes ago to D/NSA eyes only. D/NSA got on his secure line, briefed his number two, and asked the deputy to respond as soon as they had authentication.

POTUS said, "While waiting for the NSA evaluation, we have to be pleased that there will be no strike in the next couple of days at least."

SecDef mentioned that the extra time would be "of great value as it permits us to get many more of our assets in place." SecDef also noted, "We need to consider when and how we will respond and go to DEFCON 2; when attacked, we will no longer have a choice, and it will then be a reality."

The Secretary of State agreed and said, "We may wish to take preemptive strikes against the Chinese and the Russians simultaneously with such direct precision that it sends a message."

The D/NSA was called on the secure line.

His deputy came up on screen and told them that the Russian nuclear codes had been authenticated. The Chinese codes, which had been previously validated, remained authenticated. Any changes could now be detected as well.

POTUS looked at the Professor and Doc and asked what could be done with the D/FSB and his very real threat to kill them both. POTUS said he had met this man and he was evil.

The Professor looked over to Doc. Doc spoke to the SecDef and said that with his permission, since the SOF team was already here in Russia, and by the way supporting Doc and the Professor, he wondered if he could impose on them a little more with a plan he had come up with to address this D/FSB with extreme prejudice.

SecDef looked at POTUS. POTUS just said he had no idea what Doc was talking about, but if he was a betting man and it was some strong disagreement between Doc and D/FSB, POTUS would place his quarter on Doc every day and twice on Sundays.

SecDef smiled and said that from this point forward, Doc has been approved for the additional operation. "The team on the ground is now under your command."

# CHAPTER TWENTY

# LIGHT, ACTION, AND CAMERAS

ONCE THE CONFERENCE LINE WAS off, the Professor said that they both needed to get a good night's sleep. Doc said he just needed to speak with the Chief for a couple of minutes.

Given the vital importance of this new asset to the U.S., Doc told the Chief that he would be the primary and only officer that was to meet with Lighthouse when he was abroad. Additionally, it would be wise for the Chief to return to CONUS and set up however he needed to so that he would be ready to respond to meeting Lighthouse anywhere in the world, except Russia. The Chief said he understood. He told Doc that he would give his boss a complete update and his best regards from Doc. Doc stood, shook hands with the Chief, and said that if he ever seriously needed Doc personally, he should reach out to the Professor, who always knew where he was.

Doc walked to the Ambassador's residence, found his bedroom, and collapsed on the bed. When he woke the next morning, the Professor was already having breakfast with the Ambassador. Doc took a shower, gulped a large cup of coffee, and then briefed the Professor that they were going to be in a Hollywood movie that morning—to go with the flow. The Professor nodded.

Doc then headed again to the secure conference room. He placed a video and audio communications call to the team leader's telephone, which was also encrypted. He answered on the first ring and asked the caller to stand by for one minute. He then asked for the correct signal, and Doc relayed the password and then received the leader's password in return. The TL then said his latest message conveyed that they would need to step things up a bit and the plan was going to be activated today.

Doc asked if the TL felt he and his operators had been given the time they needed to prepare. The TL said absolutely, that they were now a definite go from his end. The TL noted one more time for absolute confirmation that the main target was the powerful Russian official previously named via encrypted communications.

The SOF plan officially kicked off at 0900 hours, and it was a (false) kidnapping of the Professor and Doc by one of the Russians' largest criminal syndicates (actually some disguised SOF operatives). They were on their route to meet with the Russian president. Their embassy vehicle was forced to stop, and the driver got out and ran away. Lots of cars and vans surrounded their vehicle. Small explosives/ stun grenades and lots of gunfire were part of the theater action unfolding.

The operatives took the Professor and Doc to a secure safe house that was actually a very large but empty warehouse. Threats had already been called in to the FSB director's office. The same were sent at the same time to a couple of the top members in the Russian mob as well. The rumors got very repetitive in that it "was really a cover-up operation totally done by the FSB to irritate the U.S."

One of the threats said that the director was behind the operation and that the Russian mob had nothing to do with it. It was played as if the FSB director attempted to lay the entire setup on the mob. The Russian president called the FSB director and said he better get this under control immediately or it would end up in the media and that the president did not want that at all. An explosion (placed earlier by the SOF) of considerable magnitude was also detonated in the basement of the FSB at 1000 hours so that everyone would evacuate the building in a panic, and certain files, including the one (original hard copy only) on Lighthouse, would be left behind.

At 1100 hours, a call went through to the D/FSB on his personal cell (that NSA had provided). The caller said in a very scratchy voice that the two live victims could be picked up at a designated warehouse.

If the FSB director did not go there personally, and this matter was not resolved as an FSB matter by late afternoon, then the director of FSB would be assassinated. The voice also said that all the security details in the world would not know what hit any of them.

The FSB director decided that he did have to personally go just to make an appearance if nothing else. He certainly did not want more problems with the Russian mob.

On the rooftop of the building adjacent to the warehouse were two U.S. snipers, there to take out the D/FSB and his security team leader. It was done quickly—one shot apiece—and the heads of both the FSB director and the Russian team leader came off in a pink mist. The Russian security detail looked on in complete shock. Then several explosives outside and inside the building were detonated at the same time, as well as on two of their security vehicles. The explosives had been placed on the underside of the security motorcade, right after the basement explosions of the FSB building, while the teeming crowd was running for the doors.

The snipers purposely left their long guns on the roof. They were of the same exact make and model that was used extremely frequently by the Russian mob. Doc and the Professor had long since departed the area. They went back to the embassy entrance in a food van. The Marines had been instructed that it was not to be stopped or inspected. The vehicle was sent directly into the embassy compound parking garage. The Professor had called the Russian president's office and asked if they could push their appointment back a bit to the afternoon as he had a small cold. The president's office rescheduled for three o'clock.

In the secure conference room, it was determined that their friends were all safe. The D/FSB and his detail leader were confirmed absolutely dead. There was now a host of news and media surrounding the warehouse. The FSB headquarters remained a pile of rubble and in small fires. All supposition so far, according to the media, was that the mob had killed the D/FSB and one of his security aides.

The Professor and Doc got into the embassy vehicle en route to the newly rescheduled afternoon appointment. This time, they were immediately escorted into the president's office.

The general welcomed them both, and when he shook hands with Doc, it was a particularly strong grasp and a wide smile of appreciation. Prior to the president coming into the room, the Professor had asked if he could use the restroom. The general pointed to it right across from his office. Doc then quietly slipped to the general the original "Director of FSB—for his eyes only" file that the director had on him.

The general glanced at it and shredded it on the spot. The general looked directly at Doc and nodded with a small tear in his eyes. Doc said that he saw on the television that the news was all abuzz about some criminal activity and the killing of the FSB director by the Russian mob; what a shame. The general smiled and said, "Sometimes, these mobsters go too far. I'm sure that the perpetrators will be apprehended."

The Professor then returned to the general's office.

The president came into the room about a minute later. He went directly to the Professor and embraced him warmly. The Professor was slightly surprised, but he went with the flow of the reunion. The president said to the Professor that they had much to discuss. He went on to note to the Professor that the U.S. president had gone to DEFCON 2, and that, the Professor knew, was a very, very dangerous step. The Professor said he concurred whole-heartedly, but "to be honest, our president is at a loss to do otherwise since there are rumors now adrift that Russia and China were planning to attack the U.S. within the next two or three days."

The Russian president said that while they have been unhappy with the submarine incident, the Professor could still see, due to their great restraint, Russia was not auto-matically responding in kind. The Professor said the U.S. government had viewed this positively, as a real effort by Russia to get its country and the U.S. back on track. But this didn't allay the U.S.'s concerns.

The Russian president paused and then said that he had formally and informally withdrawn from his relationship with the Chinese president whom, by the way, he had not been able to reach in the last couple of days.

The president said he thought that perhaps the Chinese president was ignoring him so that he would not change his promise to strike the U.S. with the Chinese. The Russian president was very specific and said that the attack was indeed scheduled to be the day after tomorrow. The Professor said that if what the Russian president had just said was true, the Professor could get POTUS to again review the situation, which would definitely put Russia in a more favorable light.

The Russian president said that it was still very dangerous for all parties, particularly since the Chinese president was temporarily ignoring his calls and his messages. The Professor said he understood the problem and would need some time to address this issue. Meanwhile, he would like to go back to the embassy right away to send a message to POTUS. The Professor told the Russian president that he should not assume that the U.S. president would change DEFCON 2 status based on this alone. The Russian president asked the Professor what assurance he could give the U.S. president to show that he was telling the truth.

The Professor said that he and Doc would let him know as soon as is possible. While they were going down the stairs, Lighthouse whispered to Doc that he deeply appreciated his actions and would not forget it ever. Doc looked at him and said their friendship would always be there from now on. The general said that yes, it would. The Professor, who was a little ahead of them, paused and then said, "I do not know what you two are mumbling about."

As they pulled up to the embassy entrance, Doc noted that the Marine guards were extremely heavy with automatic weapons as well as gun turrets and machine guns surrounding the interior of the compound, with more Marines manning them.

Doc leaned over to the Professor and said, "Something has happened and it is big."

The Professor asked him how he knew, and Doc just said, "We have to get upstairs instantly."

Once in the secure conference room, the line opened and they saw POTUS and the SecDef and all of the respective JCS from the Pentagon. SecDef nodded and the Chairman/JCS began the briefing.

"North Korea has attacked South Korea, and our U.S. military is repelling them with our Republic of Korea military counterparts. A total military invasion has occurred, and all hell has broken loose.

"POTUS has directed the U.S. military to destroy all North Korean target sites, with the exception of the weapons of mass destruction (chemical, radiological, biological, and so forth)."

NSA was in the process of checking on the status of North Korean nuclear codes and whether they were included in Doc's source from China. The Professor raised his voice just a little too quickly and said that the North Korean codes were definitely included, as he clearly recalled them on one of the earlier flash drives.

POTUS said, "Excellent," and he got on the line to the D/NSA and said the same. He paused and then said to the

SecDef and the D/NSA, "If the North Koreans make so much as a futile motion of pointing to any or mobilizing any of their ballistic nuclear missiles, they are to be taken out completely prior to launch and at all costs."

The SecDef saluted the commander in chief and motioned to the air force general, who excused himself to make a few secure calls to his generals and other officers at specific locations.

POTUS looked directly at the Professor and asked what he had for him. The Professor responded accordingly.

One: The Professor commended POTUS on his order—a clear message to U.S. enemies. China and Russia would know they had better consider things carefully or risk joining North Korea as a pile of rubble and dust.

Two: The Russian president with whom Doc and the Professor met minutes ago swore that Russia was not going to hit the U.S. one day from now or in the future. He claimed to have broken his relationship with the Chinese president and was no longer interested in a confrontation with the U.S. The truth of this remained to be seen. The Russian president also had been told directly that he must immediately come up with a means of assuring POTUS that he, the Russian president, was telling the truth.

Three: The Professor also warned that if attacked, the U.S. would annihilate both Russia and China without hesitation. Testing this, he said to POTUS, would be a catastrophic mistake. The Professor added that the Russian president was unable to reach the Chinese president in the last few days and said he thought the Chinese president was blocking out the Russian president to prevent his withdrawing from or changing their agreed-upon attack strategy. The Russian president obviously was unaware that the Chinese president was dead.

Four: The Professor said that he believed that the "new" Chinese president, whoever that might be, had ordered the attack by North Korea

POTUS thought for a solid ten minutes in silence and then said to the Professor that he wanted a verbal message personally carried back to the Russian president immediately. Doc and the Professor were to relay in no uncertain terms that Russia must stage a massive attack against China (nonnuclear) to convince the U.S. of his sincerity. Moreover, Russia would end up being the savior of all, and the Russian president would be a famous peacemaker.

POTUS said that he could also report to the Russian president that the U.S. would take care of North Korea. SecDef and the other chiefs in the room were speechless. POTUS added that if the Russian president tried to fake retribution against China, he would know, and would from that point forward classify Russia as an enemy.

POTUS understood the North Korean attack as a precursor to all-out war. Hence, the window of opportunity for the Russian president was exactly twenty-four hours.

The Russian air, land, and sea soldiers, sailors, and airmen would need to mount an attack on the Chinese by that time.

The SecDef stood up and said to his chiefs, "You heard the man. His decision has been made, and we need to get off our butts and make sure we support our troops in the ROC and watch everywhere else now—particularly in the homeland."

POTUS stood up and said, "Let's get these trains moving."

The conference line was broken, and the Professor and Doc hurried to get the message to the Russian president.

Their car pulled up, and they were waved through the gates. The general bowed and asked that they follow him. While going up the stairs, the general told Doc that he and the president had heard about the North Korean attack. The general then whispered, saying that he knew for a fact that the president did not authorize it.

In the office, the president came in sat down and asked them to all do the same. He said that he had no idea that the North Korean attack would occur; the Chinese president did not seek his clearance. The Professor said that it was a true pity, as many had already died. The Professor went on to say that POTUS accepted in principle the Russian president's statements that he had broken his relationship with the Chinese president. The Russian president let out a sigh of relief and moved a little back in his seat.

Then, the Professor said that POTUS also forwarded the following:

1. Due to this North Korean massive attack, the U.S. is responding in kind and more. The U.S. will eliminate the North Korean leadership but not the North Korean people. They have starved and suffered far too long and this will be corrected—and soon.

2. The supposed timing of the massive attack on the U.S. by Russia and China remains a major concern, and he is now considering going to DEFCON 1.

3. There is only one way he can fully and completely know that your statements made to the Professor, Doc, and himself (POTUS) are true.

4. Russian air force, navy ships, submarines, and sailors along with Russia's army soldiers will all need to be focused on an immediate and massive attack against China.

5. The window for this opportunity for Russia is exactly twenty-four hours, and the clock is ticking.

6. The attack on China will have to be real and genuine. If an effort is made to fake it, POTUS said that his eyes in the sky and ears on the ground will know and they will report it immediately. The U.S. will then act accordingly.

7. If you follow these directions, POTUS will then know for sure that you are sincere. The U.S. military will, without the world knowing, assist the Russian military in their destruction of the Chinese leadership and the Chinese military. The U.S. will not permit the Russian military to fail.

8. If this attack on China does not happen prior to the timeline, then POTUS will assume the Russian president's comments were just a ruse, and Russia will be designated an enemy of the U.S.

9. It is POTUS's deepest prayer and wish that Russia and the U.S. will develop a new world for not only our two countries, but for all of the countries everywhere.

The Russian president was unable to speak as he processed the overall offer. He was clearly at a loss. The Professor said softly to the Russian president that POTUS was exact in his wording and would follow through accordingly without doubt.

The president nodded and asked the general to get him a glass of water. When the general came back, the president swallowed the entire glass. He then looked at Doc and the general. He quietly asked the general what he should do.

The general looked somewhat pale as well, but he cleared his throat, sat up straight, and then said to the president that he should order the entire Russian military to activate within the next two hours and to attack China with all that it had.

The president looked directly at the general and said he concurred. The general then told the Professor that the president had decided to follow POTUS's requirements.

The president told the general to make up the orders. Once they were signed, the general would distribute them through all secure channels to make it so as ordered by the president of Mother Russia. Within fifteen minutes, the general came back into the office and placed the numerous documents with the president's fixed stamped on each along with his signature and orders. The general then asked formally if the Russian president wanted his orders to be distributed, and the president said he did and ordered the general to do so immediately.

Within ten minutes, the distribution infiltrated throughout the relevant Russian political and military structures.

Doc and the Professor were silent en route back to the embassy. The Professor and Doc were then instantly linked in to POTUS and the rest in the secure situation room. The Professor said that the Russian president had agreed to the attack on China and to follow all of POTUS's specified requirements.

The Professor walked through each and every one of POTUS's requirements as well as the portion in which POTUS promised that the U.S. would support Russia. The Professor had told the Russian president that POTUS would neither abandon them nor permit the Russian leadership and their people to fail. However, such support would be done without the rest of the world knowing the U.S was on their side. Doc then indicated that those gathered should start hearing of the massive attack on China within the next two hours.

SecDef was asked to take a secure call. POTUS said to put it on the speaker. The Pentagon operations center advised that bombing runs by Russian air force planes in Beijing had commenced.

Submarines on the coastline of China had been detected and were firing missiles at the Chinese mainland. The Russian diesel subs, which were extremely quiet, had already destroyed three Chinese subs. POTUS and the other participants stood up and cheered.

CHAPTER TWENTY-ONE

# LOYALTY, SADLY, IS SOMETIMES FLEETING

THE PROFESSOR ADDED THAT ONCE China fully processed that the Russians had abandoned and attacked them, China had to be watched, and its actions, and potential actions, had to be evaluated moment by moment. The Professor recommended that outside study groups, comprising of scholars and elder states specialists, be appointed with backup groups every twelve-hour shift. When a country like China was attacked, the Professor stated, it would initially feel cornered without recourse, and emotions might lead it to escalate. POTUS concurred, approved the initiative, and ordered the Secretary of State and SecDef to get their respective deputies on it immediately.

Additionally, the North Korean situation remained a blood-and-guts battle; POTUS said that he had made a decision to not allow the Chinese the chance to reclaim the North Koreans in any way. He said he could no longer tolerate the Chinese using the North Koreans as a baseball bat against the U.S. every time they wanted to give Americans or American allies a migraine.

POTUS would have North Korean land and people turned over to the South Koreans once the North Korean leadership has been destroyed.

POTUS said that if the U.S. could cut off the head of the North Korean snake, it was quite possible the remaining leadership would collapse. POTUS looked directly at Doc and the Professor. They, in turn, said that the idea was sound but intelligence was needed to identify where the North Korean leader was being protected.

Was he possibly now in China, in one of the many bunkers? SecDef said that at a basic level, the U.S. military and the ROK were wrestling with this issue at that moment, and had been since the war started. D/CIA indicated that the CIA had had defectors that had provided general locations but none specific enough to pinpoint.

POTUS paused for a good three minutes, looked around the room, and stopped at the Professor and Doc. POTUS said that he had already seen enough to agree that the Russians were on the U.S.'s side. POTUS then ordered that the Professor and Doc depart Moscow immediately and fly directly to South Korea without delay. POTUS ordered that they meet with the commanding U.S. general for an in-depth, on-the-ground briefing to identify the exact possible locations of the North Korean leader. They would meet with the South Korean president on POTUS's behalf.

After all left the situation room and the audio storage was no longer active, the Professor asked the D/CIA to stand by with them. They reviewed their general success with Lighthouse. D/CIA said that he was totally briefed in now. The Chief had already been called home for the foreseeable future to handle Lighthouse whenever he stepped abroad around the world. D/CIA also noted that his two daughters were now attending one of the best universities in the U.S. on full scholarships.

He said that Lighthouse would literally change the course of history. But only they, the director, and the Chief could know of him at this time.

The Professor asked Doc to brief the director on one more piece of information. Lighthouse had been approached by recruitment from the Chinese as they had found out that he'd lost a large amount money in Las Vegas. Threats to his daughters' lives had been made. Doc had counseled Lighthouse that if he heard again from the Chinese, he should do nothing but advise his agency contact and it would be taken care of promptly. It was Doc's opinion that this would not happen again and it could be dismissed. On another front, the late director of the FSB had learned about the Chinese move recently and had also blackmailed Lighthouse. Doc added that fortunately for the U.S., the Russian mob had killed the director.

D/CIA then looked at Doc and said the timing was impressive. The director said he had read that D/FSB had died a very quick and violent death. Doc nodded and then said that apparently those Russian mobs are really tough. D/CIA smiled and said it was great that the D/FSB could no longer blackmail Lighthouse. Doc concurred and noted that the file that the D/FSB had kept on Lighthouse was amazingly recovered, as fate would have it.

Doc then provided it to Lighthouse as a goodwill gesture. Doc had also quietly sent it (this time it was a lone copy) eyes only to the D/CIA an hour ago for his own edification. The director looked at Doc and said once again that he sincerely appreciated the outstanding work.

D/CIA looked at the Professor and asked if he had anything to add. Doc spoke up and said he and the Professor wanted to ask him a small favor.

Doc said that when the Chinese president met his demise, there was an old woman that was absolutely vital to the success of that operation and who had literally saved Doc's life. The Professor said that they had promised her $2 million for assisting them and told her that she should expect a friend to one day come by and give her a satchel with the money. The director said that he understood and he would take care of it. Moreover, he would personally let them know once it was done.

The Professor and Doc reached out to their safe haven on the Hudson to speak with the Linguist via video call. The Professor asked her if everything was going well, and she said very much so. He told her that he and Doc were heading to South Korea, and she took in a breath. Doc said that they both would be fine and they looked forward to seeing her and her daughter in the not-too-distant future.

Doc said they had two quick questions. First, did she know who was or likely would be the next Chinese president? The Linguist said that she did not know for sure but her best guess would be the former Chinese president's uncle. She told them his name. He was extremely close to the late president, and they had often talked about succession in case either one of them died unexpectedly.

Doc asked if this new president would be up to the challenge of the Russian bombardment and a full-scale attack. The Linguist indicated that the uncle was definitely up to the task—he was a very serious and capable man.

Doc's second question was whether she had any contacts or could rely on anyone in North Korea, especially one that would likely know where the North Korean president was hiding and being protected. The Linguist thought for a minute and came up with another close friend that they could reach out to. Doc thanked the Linguist profusely. The Professor said he missed her and would see her soon. The Linguist smiled and said for them both to be very safe and very careful.

# CHAPTER TWENTY-TWO

# THE NORTH KOREAN VIPER

IN SOUTH KOREA, U.S. ARMY Garrison Yongsan was the center of the country and the largest U.S. military base. The commanding general greeted the Professor and Doc, and they went directly into the secure conference room. There, aside from the four-star general, there was another three-star general and two full-bird colonels—one was the formal overall briefer, and the latter was a specialist regarding the North Korean leadership. The four-star general nodded, and the briefing began. The state of affairs regarding the successes and failures of the engagement to date were reviewed. Essentially, the South Korean (ROK) and U.S. troops were taking in exceptional North Korean body counts and their side was not. That did not mean that the ROK and U.S. were not losing soldiers and navy personnel, as they clearly were, but it was on a much smaller scale. The ROK military causalities were unquestionable and more substantial. However, ROK civilians were taking casualties in the thousands due to artillery.

The general said that this number would inevitably grow. The specific areas that had been erased could be seen in both the South and the U.S. and ROK's repeated drives into the North.

The four-star general said, "We are going to succeed in the long run, but the amount in blood and loss on both sides will be horrific."

The Professor had one question—the present status of what had been the DMZ borderline. The three-star general pointed to the maps and said, "It comes down to the parts that we have successfully destroyed, and others have established large camps in preparation for our deeper ongoing invasions."

The Professor thanked the general.

The second colonel had a specific brief, which he started by showing a chart of the top present leadership composition of the North Koreans. Many were still listed as alive, and a few were listed as dead, but they had been replaced, a result of ROK and U.S. continuous air bombings. The Professor asked if there was any indication that the Chinese, who had placed about one hundred fifty thousand or more military troops on their far border with North Korea, had been engaging any of the ROK or U.S. forces.

The generals and the colonel said that they had not to date experienced any such intrusions by the Chinese. While Chinese pilots had been seen frequently flying within range of U.S. forces, they had avoided any direct challenges. The Professor thanked the general for his response.

The Professor then asked the colonel to dig down further into the N.K. leadership. The colonel said that the supreme leader had virtually disappeared a day prior to the first salvo. The best stipulations were that he was literally underground with a large and loyal security detachment that moved differently in the dark every day. Any of the

N.K. prisoners of war, or defectors for that matter, were either mum or they simply did not know. "Our most qualified interrogators' efforts have been stunted. The N.K. generals and colonels are physically dispersed to each of their commands and spread fairly wide. They report all actions of success and do not mention the losses for fear of their own execution."

The Professor asked if the remaining N.K. populace was permitted to go outdoors when there were no bombings.

"We believe they do, and very few even dangerously do so during the dark hours. The latter are shot dead if they are caught or detected."

The thinking by the U.S. and ROK generals was that the entire group of N.K. leaders were mostly puppets, but the top five or maybe even ten would have to be taken out along with the leader to effect any real change or cessation of war. The four-star general said that for this reason and to the U.S.'s benefit, they awaited the miracle one day.

"If we are then able to pinpoint the exact location of the evil supreme leader for at least a half hour, he and his closest sycophants could be erased from this earth. Such an event would bring North and South Korea again back together to become one undivided nation."

The briefing came to a close, and the Professor and Doc thanked the colonels for their hard work and insightful comments. The general then dismissed them, and the two generals sat at the conference room table with the Professor and Doc.

The four-star general said that their scheduled meeting with the South Korean president was planned for three hours from now.

The general asked what he was hoping to get from the S.K. president. The Professor indicated that he was not completely sure, but was hoping to determine the supreme leader's location. The three-star general asked if they had some information that the S.K. president was holding anything back.

The Professor smiled and said no, they did not; however, as a mathematician and one who had faced complex problems most of his life, he had to try. The four-star general looked at the Professor, paused, and said he now thought he understood what the Professor was attempting to do, but he would hold his tongue. The Professor smiled and thanked him for his understanding.

The Professor looked at both men and said that he could offer them a thought experiment. The Professor said the S.K. president was under tremendous pressure from his people, his family, and the decisions that he had made and had yet to make. If he chose wrongly, his country would not win this war. What if the U.S. decided for any reason to walk away, and N.K., with support from China (or Russia), won? The S.K. president could find himself and his family, as well as hundreds of thousands of his countrymen, dead. Well, when one looks at mathematical problems, one always has to consider what the various and endless scenarios are in terms of solutions, and it then gets weighted.

The Professor therefore had to look deeply into the S.K. president to determine whether one of those scenarios included a "fallback situation"—whether the supreme leader and the S.K. president might have made an agreement such that no matter who won the war, neither of them would permit the other to die, nor any of their respective families.

The N.K. supreme leader and the S.K. president might have had a private communication system—a "backdoor." The Professor said that this was something that could be detected if approached correctly. It was also just one very simple instance, among thousands more, that could be studied once more information was available.

Doc, who had been almost silent for the past several hours, spoke up and said that additionally, they had also come across a possible N.K. source. "This source may permit us to work with them to identify the physical location of the supreme leader."

"We know that this source is someone who has not swallowed the N.K. Kool-Aid. We have some level of confidence that this source may have exceptional access to either the leader or a close member of his family."

The Professor and Doc would forward a note from the South Korean president to the supreme leader saying that the Professor and Doc would travel to the supreme leader with an extremely important verbal message on behalf of POTUS. If this turned out to be accepted, Doc said that they would need the very best special operations team to covertly accompany them behind enemy lines.

Doc would also need specific weapons. Secure radio communications would be used for immediate delivery of ordinance bombings if they could actually get confirmation of the supreme leader's coordinates on the ground. At that time, the Professor would have come down with malaria or a lung condition and an ambulance would rush him directly to the hospital. The attending physician would say that he might be dying, so he could clearly not make the arduous trip. Doc and the source would proceed alone to other possible hidden locations, to meet personally with the supreme leader.

Doc, substituting for the Professor, would carry the message from POTUS. The message would be intimating an urgent need for a cease-fire. POTUS's message would claim that the supreme leader had won and the U.S. troops would be removed within the next month to save face. At this point, Doc would dispose of the supreme leader. The source and Doc would persevere out of the bunker, and the SOF team would escort and accompany them to the awaiting submarine on the coast for the exfiltration of all.

The four-star general said to Doc that he would have whatever he needed. The general also said he had the exact special operations team that Doc would want, need, and even enjoy. These guys had been behind enemy lines numerous times and had had substantial successes. "They will be told that you will be completely in charge."

The generals stood and saluted both of the men and said it was their distinct honor to work with them.

The meeting with the South Korean president started on time. The Professor and Doc greeted the president and relayed POTUS's best regards. The Professor and the president spoke for a long time regarding the difficulties, deaths, and damages the North Koreans had brought to the South. The Professor was sympathetic to the weight and decisions the president and his generals were making every single day. It was clear to Doc that the S.K. president was exhausted and beside himself with fatigue and pressure. Losses were mounting and expected to grow.

The Professor took note of historic models and told the president he had to understand that war was incredibly painful, but his strength and love of his people would carry them all out of this hell. The president looked at the Professor and thanked him for his genuine support and understanding of what he and his people were going through.

A small South Korean lady quietly brought in some tea. The Professor measured the South Korean president very closely and eyed his very subtle disdain for what he believed to be the arrogance of the U.S. military and POTUS.

While the president was sipping his tea, it was over the brim of the cup that he saw the president's true colors. This man did not really want them there. He seemed to also slightly blame the U.S. for the N.K. leader's attack. The numerous times that POTUS had attempted to create a relationship with the N.K. president didn't seem to factor in.

The S.K. president clearly thought that he and the N.K. leader had made real progress in finding common ground. The S.K. president thought that had the Americans not placed such pressure on the North, none of this would have happened. He personally believed that their culture was their core. He felt strongly that the Americans did not and could never understand all that.

The Professor asked the S.K. president if he considered the Chinese relationship with the N.K. supreme leader to be a factor. The S.K. president looked at the professor and said at first, they might have been involved, but the Russian traitorous attack had certainly put an end to that. Both Doc and the Professor found this answer interesting—the North Koreans and the Chinese were the "victims" of this situation and were not to be blamed.

The Professor thanked the president for his thoughts and noted that he and Doc would attempt to open the minds of both POTUS and the U.S. military. The president bowed his head to both of them and said his spirits were raised knowing they could appreciate his thinking, as it was not something that previous senior visitors could grasp at all. The Professor said that such matters took time before one could see some true progress. Confidentiality and complete trust were pivotal for the president and themselves too. The president raised his otherwise extremely low voice and smiled widely at them, knowing that they were clearly "kindred spirits."

The Professor smiled back and asked if he and Doc could impose upon him an exceptional request and a terribly important favor. It was something that had not been planned or thought of until they spent their outstanding time together.

The president said they could all talk openly now and asked what that special request was. The Professor said that before he even raised it, he wanted to stress to the president that if it were not possible, they would understand fully. The S.K. president nodded and said he would do his best. Doc purposely leaned over to the Professor and said in a loud whisper (which the president could easily hear) that it might be too much to ask. The Professor put his hand up to indicate that it would be OK. The president was by now eager to hear their request.

The Professor leaned forward and said to the S.K. president that if there was some way that they could have a similar sit-down in person with the N.K. supreme leader, it was his devout belief that he could express the S.K. president's amazing wisdom and deep understanding of the situation.

The Professor said he could convince the supreme leader that the S.K. president and he had come to a vital crossroads, and that it was now critical to their future that they together brought their respective populations back together so that Korea could once again be whole.

The Professor continued by saying that he and Doc could put together a simple verbal message, allegedly from POTUS, that would say that he was prepared for an immediate cease-fire. Moreover, they could say that POTUS was prepared to remove all of the U.S. military troops from the entire peninsula. "Thus," the Professor said, "you two can bring peace to this catastrophe and resurrect the Korea that you both love. A Nobel Peace Prize would be likely in this scenario."

The S.K. president stared at the Professor for a whole three minutes, and he then said that what he had just asked for would be most challenging and also extremely dangerous. The Professor said that in every great moment in history, a first step had to be taken by someone with a vision.

"Only you," the Professor continued, "can open some kind of a channel of communication with the supreme leader if you do not have one already. This could be arranged rapidly, and we could go to him, but only in person, to explain the purpose of our visit."

The president paused and said that while it was true that he did have a special communications channel to reach the supreme leader, it was rarely used. Even the fact that it existed must be kept in the utmost secrecy. The Professor and Doc both looked at him and solemnly assured the S.K. president that they would not mention this to anyone. It was too important a tool. The president said he valued their courage and conviction, and especially their discretion. Consequently, he would try to use the device at once.

They noted to the S.K. president that they could depart on the mission the day after tomorrow. The Professor would ensure that the U.S. military would not block or target either the plane or the specific base.

The S.K. president got up and walked over to his very old-fashioned desk, and he then proceeded to move a small latch or lock underneath the base that was almost invisible.

The president then lifted the top lid off the desk, and there, sitting in the middle, was an extremely modern computer with a very large monitor. The S.K. president carefully hooked it all up with unseen cables, and it was ready to go with the push of a button, plus very complicated passwords with multiple authentication measures. The South Koreans excelled in computer technology and were known for it around the world. They were also known as having some of the best, most secure, and fastest software and hardware devices.

The S.K. president said that he had activated and secretly provided, in the early negotiations of the North and South, one of the newest and fastest computers specifically for the supreme leader. The purpose was so the supreme leader and the S.K. president could communicate at moments just like this.

The S.K. president went on to say that since the war commenced, he and the supreme leader had spoken numerous times together, and they promised to maintain it as their own means of staying in touch regardless of emotions and distractions that occurred around themselves. The Professor and Doc maintained their steady and plain facial expressions, for appearance to avoid any disruption with the president—but internally, they were floored by this latest revelation.

Within one minute of the screen activating, the S.K. president was talking to one of the supreme leader's top aides on the screen. He told the aide that he needed to speak directly with the supreme leader. The supreme leader was soon on the screen, and he and the S.K. president first exchanged pleasantries.

The S.K. president said that he had just finished an extraordinary meeting with two senior Americans. "They were completely different and open-minded and, more importantly, had a verbal message from POTUS. They indicated that they were most interested in meeting you in person. They had to pass to you the message directly.

"The message said that it was vital to all of your, my, and U.S. interests." The S.K. president said that he was truly impressed with meeting with them and found them to know much more than the usual flunkies he had to put up with and experience.

The supreme leader paused and then said, "Why can't they just use the computer we are on now?"

The S.K. president said he had asked the same thing but was told that they could not trust any computer or the information of this message and had to share it with the supreme leader in person. They had said it was vitally important.

The supreme leader said that his security chief was not going to be happy and he was going to vet them closely when they arrived, but the supreme leader would go ahead and accept them in person. The S.K. president said, "They can arrive the day after tomorrow on an unmarked small U.N. Cessna jet to the air base that you decide."

The supreme leader then waved his hand and said his aide (who had come on screen at the beginning of the call) would take care of all that and send it to the S.K. president after the call was over.

The supreme leader asked if the S.K. president had anything else, and he responded to the supreme leader that the two individuals were truly worth listening to and their information could genuinely help the supreme leader, POTUS, and the S.K. president.

The S.K. president said, "They are the only Americans I have ever met in my lifetime that seem to really understand our culture and the current mess we are all in right now."

The supreme leader said, "Your comment means nothing; I alone will make the assessment once I have met them and heard their message."

The supreme leader paused then gave a rude "OK, stay in touch" and cut the computer link.

The Professor and Doc remained poker-faced but now understood completely that the S.K. leader was a pawn and more or less inconsequential to the supreme leader.

The screen was blank, and the aide came on again and said their plane or helicopter should land on air base number twenty-two, and they were to arrive the day after tomorrow at noon.

Doc added that they might be bringing one more person, a linguist, and the aide consented.

The S.K. president said thank you, and then the connection on the screen shut down. The S.K. president then turned off the system on the desk and pulled the desk lid back into its place with its security latch. He walked over to the Professor and Doc and said he wished them the very best and a safe return.

The motorcade proceeded away from the S.K. bunker. The Professor said to the military captain in charge of their security for the day that he would appreciate it if they could bring them to a specific address. Doc gave him a nearby address, but an inaccurate one, so that they did not expose the source from the Linguist at the safe haven in New York. Additionally, the Professor then ordered the officer to spread out the motorcade vehicles so that it looked less like one while they reached the address. The officer said that he understood and would do so.

However, the officer was compelled to inform the Professor that the area that they were going into was at best a "gray" zone; some called it the informal "border," and it therefore was quite dangerous. He said in terms of their collective safety, it was definitely not advisable. The Professor responded that he did appreciate the notification and he was now taking full responsibility for the decision.

When they were in the general neighborhood, after the driver had just made a turn, Doc ordered the driver to pull over to a side street. Doc told the officer to have each of the follow vehicles pulled into each of the three side streets as to greatly reduce their visibility. Doc said that he and the Professor would now be on their own, without escorts. The officer started to protest, but Doc said he understood and that it was totally their call.

He explained to the officer that it had to be this way as they were to meet with a very sensitive source who would not arrive at all if it appeared any other way. The officer said he understood and saluted both of them.

He added his orders were that nothing was to happen to either of them, so to please reach out if he was needed. Moreover, the officer noted that if he deemed anything a danger while they walked, then he was going to counter-mand his and the Professor's orders, and they could work it all out back at the air base bunker. Doc smiled and looked directly at the officer and said he would expect nothing less.

The Professor and Doc walked around the area until they felt that they had lost both the officer and his troops and, more importantly, any S.K. or N.K. surveillance that might have also followed them. Doc and the Professor went into the side buildings, went up to quietly cross the roofs, and then came down to the exact address that the Linguist had provided them.

They softly knocked on the door, and a middle-aged Korean woman opened it. She was very attractive and had very clear and exceptionally sharp eyes. She looked both of them over very carefully and asked them what they wanted.

The Professor said in Korean that he thought they had a mutually close friend and they were wondering if they could have a few minutes of her time. She looked him over more carefully and said she had no such friend and they were mistaken.

Doc softly said in English the contact's name, and he gave her the specific contact's phrase to pass on to her. The woman showed the slightest surprise but recovered instantly. She said that she did once know this person but it was her understanding that she had died.

Doc said to her, "That is exactly what we would like people to believe. However, she is still with us and enjoying very much every day she can with her university-aged daughter."

This time, the woman smiled widely and said that they should of course come in for some tea. She told them her name: Ha Rin Ha. The Professor smiled too and said that if he was not mistaken, her name in Chinese meant summer, great, or talented, and Rin meant female unicorn.

She smiled again and said that the Professor was indeed a learned man.

The Professor asked if this was a place that was agreeable, and when she nodded, he expressed how beautiful a home it was too. It was nice to hear her actual name, but Doc and the Professor decided to just refer to her in any future conversations as the "Unicorn" for security purposes.

# CHAPTER TWENTY-THREE

# A SPECIAL AND NEEDED ALLY

THE UNICORN PUT ON SOME classical music and a television in another room and smiled again. She looked over to Doc and looked into his eyes. She said that the Professor looked to her like a scholar and she would guess that he was quite an accomplished one at that. However, as she turned her sight to the Professor, who had smiled at her statement, she said that Doc was a much different man. He, she stated, was very amiable but also quite adroit. Doc leaned forward and said that she was generally correct on both counts.

She then looked at them both again and said that she was born with some very unusual traits that had separated her from the vast majority of normal people.

She paused and then looked at Doc directly and said that his near future was connected to the N.K. leader in a very intimate way. She said that she could not see the result of the encounter now but was quite sure it would happen. The Professor sat back and watched her. She said that their mutual friend was also a very special person and that the Professor was supposed to "be with her" as part of his fate.

She said that the Professor and their friend would live long lives but it was not so clear if the same applied to Doc.

Doc asked the woman how well she was connected to the N.K. supreme leader. She said that she was one of his favorites, fully trusted by the regime and very close to his family. She was in fact one of his favorite concubines. She had known him since she was a very little girl and grew up with him during their youth and into their adulthood. He also considered her to be one of his closest advisers and periodically talked with her on various topics.

Doc asked her what her true personal feelings about him were. She said that on the inside, she hated him because he had her mother and father, as well as her younger brother, all executed when she was a young girl. She prayed quietly every day that she could one day hear that he had been executed as well, but ideally very slowly.

The Professor asked if she would be willing to travel with Doc. She slowly nodded.

Once back on base, Doc met with the SOF commander and then with each one of his troops individually. Doc told the commander in private that he sincerely appreciated his and his teammates who were all in for this mission. He asked if he and the team had already been briefed. The commander said yes, and they were ready to go on the "fight night" at Doc's say-so.

Doc looked directly to the commander and said, "Excellent, because the mission is literally a go right now."

The commander's orders were to depart this date at dark for insertion behind the enemy's lines at a location and via an aircraft that he, the commander, saw fit. Doc regretted that this was a surprise, but it was essential that all aspects of this mission, including the actual timing, would be totally unknown to all except him, his team, Doc, and an N.K. source called "Unicorn." Additionally, Unicorn was to be kept alive at all costs and brought back. The commander nodded his head, stood up, and said he understood and would ensure the same as much as was possible. Doc then gave the TL a photo of Unicorn.

The commander smiled and said, "We specialize in surprises."

Doc asked the commander if he was informed that if Doc gave the order via coded communications to drop the bombs on a very specific location as soon as possible, regardless of Doc's location, he was to immediately order the airdrop from central command without hesitation. The commander said if he, Doc, gave the order, it would be carried out without delay. Doc nodded.

Doc indicated that barring that order, he and his team were to follow Doc's locations as much as was possible to provide a means of an instant evacuation for Doc and Unicorn, who would have the code word "clairvoyant" for identification. The commander said that he understood and hoped it would be the second order that was used.

Doc then gave him another direct order: he was to pull his team out should they be engaged in a firefight at any time. The commander looked at Doc, and he saluted him. Once near the door, the commander said that he and his team were going to enjoy working with him. Doc smiled and said he already knew the same.

Doc told the commander that he would be departing the next day, first on a South Korean military small airplane and then on an N.K. helicopter that would be monitored by central command to provide the commander geographic locations as possible. The commander left, running down the hall, while calling his sergeant out loud. Doc went to the ammunition depot approved by the general for all and any items Doc might want. Doc examined the weapons and took only the very smallest. Doc then went to his bed bunk and slept deeply throughout the entire night without delay.

Doc awoke feeling strong. Under his door, someone had slipped a large envelope marked "Very Sensitive" from POTUS to the supreme leader of N.K. The markings across the front and back made clear that this was to be hand delivered in person to the recipient only. Doc did not open the envelope, as he had no interest in it. He exercised physically throughout the morning and then went to the mess hall for a hearty meal. In the afternoon, the South Korean commercial airplane arrived exactly on time. Doc went aboard with his small and simple backpack with some extra clothes. Inside of an hour in the air, Doc was back on the ground at the DMZ.

He was then escorted to the waiting N.K. helicopter. Inside, he saw the very well-dressed and beautiful woman with jewelry whom he had met less than two days before. She was the only occupant aside from the pilots. He got on board, and the chopper lifted away swiftly and headed to Pyongyang.

In a relatively short time, while the pilots were occupied with the landing, he leaned forward as if he were sliding a bit out of his seat and almost into the woman's seat. He slid a modest ring into her hand that happened to match remarkably well with her jewelry.

Doc had noticed one of her rings she was wearing when they had spoken with her in her house. He then whispered to her that he would ask her to return it to him at some point in the meeting with the supreme leader but not before.

He returned to his seat. She glanced at his eyes and face, and then in less than a minute, she nodded perceptibly to him. She had already put the small ring on her hand, set aside from the other ring that was on her other hand.

They landed on a helicopter pad on a roof, and prior to their doing that, he quickly looked at the building and remembered everything he could see about it and its surrounding terrain. While disembarking, Doc pretended to fall down on one of the metal steps of the helicopter and rolled a bit on the roof tarmac.

An N.K. colonel, concealing his laugh a bit at seeing the dumb American stumble and fall, quickly moved to help Doc. Once Doc was upright, the colonel quickly did a very full bow in the direction of the woman who was already on the ground. It was quite clear that the colonel feared the woman so he instantly wiped any smile off his face. With the slight delay, Doc got the chance to see the surrounding city for a few more seconds.

For a nanosecond, when Doc got his last glimpse of the mountain, he was sure he saw an individual with a long-range scope eyeing him, which Doc appreciated. He knew that it was one of the SOF team members zeroing in on him to confirm his exact location. His brothers were with him on this mission.

# CHAPTER TWENTY-FOUR

# IN THE PRESENCE
# OF PURE EVIL

AT ONE OF THE ELEVATOR stops, the colonel pressed the button and motioned for Doc to get off and follow another N.K. officer that had been waiting. The elevator door closed efficiently, and the colonel and Unicorn proceeded to another floor. The officer walked him to a clear security checkpoint that had other solders at attention with weapons at the ready. Doc was ordered to place his luggage bag on the x-ray conveyor belt. He was then ordered to stand in a specific circle on the floor in this small and very narrow hallway. Doc was then fully frisked by two solders.

After they had nodded to the official that Doc was devoid of any weapons, the official then told him to disrobe completely. Doc took all of his clothes off and placed them on the side as directed. He purposely made a loud point about keeping his eyes and full overt attention on the envelope from POTUS for the supreme leader. Doc told the official that the envelope could be x-rayed but it was not to be opened. Doc then said, in a very deep voice, that he was sent here to deliver it solely in person to the supreme leader. Meanwhile, Doc received a full body scan.

It was all just a minute or less, but it allowed Doc to adroitly move and ever so slightly turn his body during the conversation so that some extremely small artificial intelligence (AI) devices he had inserted into his person were not seen or noticed by the body scan. Rather, the scan simply continued, remapping parts of his body already previously covered. The tiny devices were placed in areas that would be associated with bones and possible minor body fat, not any kinds of weapons. The AI had the unique ability to keep the microunits moving fast enough without detection from the human eye.

The officer told Doc to get dressed, and he handed Doc the special envelope that had also been x-rayed and deemed to be simply paper and ink inside and out.

The official then escorted Doc to one of the staircases; Doc had already studied each one and the exact number of floors as best as he could along with the probable basement size and configuration too.

After going down two more levels, the officer escorted him to a small room containing a bed, desk, and water. He told Doc that he would be called when it was time for him to meet with the other members that would be participating in the presentation of the letter from POTUS to the supreme leader. Doc went into the room and sat at the desk and then heard the official locking the door twice. He sat there and continued to mentally walk through all the combinations of events that could unfold in this mission.

After another hour in the room, Doc heard a knocking on his door and the separate locks being opened. At the entrance was an N.K. official that he had not seen before. Doc reviewed his mental files of the N.K. leadership and slowly recognized the visitor as one of the supreme leader's closest advisers. He studied Doc for a long moment and then asked him to follow him. Doc picked up the POTUS letter, and they walked down a long corridor to a medium-size conference room.

Upon entering, he saw three more officials in addition to his new escort—all in N.K. military uniforms; each appeared to be high-level generals. They all focused on Doc, once he sat down, and it was clear that each saw him as a simple underling. That was deliberately how he portrayed himself, selling it with anxious movements and facial expressions.

One of the men, who appeared to be the most senior, seemed to be his recent official escort, even though he wasn't wearing a uniform. He asked Doc why the Professor had not come in person, and Doc replied that he had become very ill and was rushed back to the United States. His condition was believed to be due to a strong food reaction that was affecting his ability to breathe; his respiratory tract was failing.

One of the generals asked why he was chosen, and Doc said that he was a longtime assistant to the Professor. POTUS had told the Professor that timing for the delivery was essential, it could not be delayed, and it had to be given only to the supreme leader by hand. Doc also added in a lower voice that they could be assured that he did not volunteer for this delivery mission.

The generals all laughed. One then commented that his best security division had ensured, by close x-ray, chemical analysis, and evaluation of the known type of the ink/paper, that the letter (and Doc) did not present any threat to the supreme leader. The general also added that his unit has also been meticulously careful to not read or examine any part of the actual content of the letter. The senior official said that if all in the room did not have any more comments or questions, he was authorizing this letter delivery to the supreme leader on an expedited basis.

Another general, who had not spoken so far, motioned to Doc and said that if he was nervous in this environment, to just wait until he had the distinct pleasure of meeting the security detail assigned to the supreme leader. Doc pretended to turn pale and gulp down his saliva. The generals all had another belly laugh. Doc stood up, bowed, and thanked them all for the tip. He said quietly that he planned to give the letter to the supreme leader and then ask if it was OK to leave at that point and go back home. The generals laughed even louder.

While they were walking back to his room, Doc asked the senior official whether he knew if he would get to meet the supreme leader tonight. Doc continued his poor-boy manner and asked if the meeting was within this building or someplace outside. The senior official smiled again, and he told Doc that only the supreme leader himself could answer such questions.

The officer said that when the supreme leader called for him, then two members of his security detail would escort him and take him to meet the man. Doc nodded his head and thanked the senior official. He also asked if he was permitted to have something to eat while he waited to be called. The official said that he would arrange it.

Shortly after being taken back to his room, someone knocked on the door and opened both locks. It was a kitchen boy who asked what he wanted to eat. Doc told him he would like to go to the cafeteria to see what was available. The boy said he was not sure that was possible. Doc said he needed to see the food to see what he would like to eat. The boy looked overwhelmed, then agreed.

They went down the stairs to the cafeteria. Since it was late afternoon and there was no one in the room, the boy showed him the food, and he slowly selected what he wanted.

He then sat down at one of the empty tables and waited. He looked everywhere and noted that the cafeteria was directly above the basement of the building. He was apparently in some portion of the main floor and lobby. When the boy went to the back to start cooking Doc's meal, Doc told him to heat the Kiamichi extra long with many, many hot spices.

Doc then quietly slipped back into the staircase and went down further to the basement. He managed to walk around for just a couple of minutes, but in that time, he was able to absorb the entire structure, identify each of the exits, and see the address of the building. Most importantly, as luck would have it, he looked out a small window that had what looked like a classic security detail arriving.

Unbelievably, he actually saw the supreme leader. The motorcade had continued further up to the top of the block that was about twenty-five to thirty wide strides when running. Doc saw that the leader was very slowly trying to get out of the heavily armored limousine. Due to his weight, it was a tricky process—some would have even called it an "operation" all by itself. Doc would have laughed if he had the time.

Doc judged that it would take the supreme leader about ten to fourteen minutes to get out of the car and arrive at the entrance. He was puffing and yelling at them at the same time and kept rocking back and forth but then decided to relax, catch his breath, and try again.

Doc suddenly realized that these few minutes were maybe the most important of his life and moreover, of the lives of hundreds of thousands or even millions of others. The time was now. Doc realized that the reason why there was no one in the cafeteria except the boy, or in the staircases or most likely even in the entire building, was because it had been totally vacated in preparation for the supreme leader's arrival.

Doc softly went up the stairs and quietly walked around, seeking one of the security advance officers whose sole duty now would be to ensure that no one was in the lobby while the supreme leader was entering. Doc suddenly saw the advance security site officer rounding the corner of the lobby elevator. Doc was on the other corner listening to see if there were any other security officers in this area and he heard none. Each of the other security site officers, no doubt, could be found on each floor at both ends of the building. Doc continued his light walk up to the security site officer from behind.

Doc then quickly wrapped his left hand around the officer's chin and his right around the high back of his skull on the right side and forced them in different directions. The agent's neck snapped—he was stone dead. Doc looked at the body and saw they were about the same size, so he quickly undressed and put on the man's uniform, including his weapons.

He checked to confirm the sidearm had a round already in the chamber and a complete magazine. He was also by now carrying the radio with the earpiece and wearing a hat; it was small but it would do. Amazingly, their light brown hair also matched so when the hat was on, he could look, from a short distance, like a fellow team member. Doc pulled the body beneath a dark staircase and ran back to the entrance.

After looking out of the lobby door, Doc saw that the transportation from inside the limousine was still in play. The supreme leader was stubbornly still inside and had decided to take another break or two to catch his breath.

The leader also was swearing that the back limousine seat was broken and that was "of course" part of the problem. Doc waited until the great struggle was commenced once again. Then Doc specifically jogged only on the far side of the other security armored vehicles and held his radio to his ear on the opposite side of his face so they could not get a good look at him. Several, if not most, of the other security detail members had gotten out of their vehicles, and were walking rather swiftly to the lobby entrance.

Doc continued the rushed jog with his radio until he was at the front right door of the car that was wide open. It had been since the team leader had gone over to help with moving the supreme leader out of the rear end of the car, which was the limousine's back door on the other side of the vehicle. Doc purposely dropped his radio on the front floor, leaned halfway in, raised his sidearm, and shot the supreme leader twice in the skull.

He then shot the driver in the face, reached over to the team leader, pulled him roughly by his suit jacket into the rear seat, and put two rounds directly into his head. He yelled for the one other security officer for help, and when he got close, he shot him in the eye. Doc was a second away from shooting the car's last occupant on the other side of the supreme leader's lifeless body. She was about to get her voice working enough to scream. He suddenly realized that she was the Unicorn, so he whispered his name and she abruptly realized who he really was.

From the outside of the armored vehicle, it just looked like the security officers were leaning in to continue to get the now-deceased leader out of the car somehow. Since the armored limousine had extremely dark windows, both front and back and on the sides, any splashes of blood could not be seen from the outside.

Also, due to the car's armored features, any sounds, or rounds for that matter, inside the car were entirely muffled. Doc casually walked around to the rear door, looked forward and backward, and saw no security officer paying him much mind.

He walked up to the follow vehicle that was directly behind, but it was at least a car length away, and knocked on the driver's window.

Doc saw only the driver so he slowly reached into his suit as if he was going to pulled cigarettes out, and he then quickly slit the driver's throat with his knife. Doc went back and picked up the one security officer that he had shot dead outside the leader's limousine. Doc put his arm around his shoulder and landed him into the seat adjacent to the driver he had just killed.

He then placed a prearranged "kidnapped note" in Korean that said a renegade group had taken the "supreme leader and his female companion." It further warned that the leadership should await a ransom call by late morning tomorrow. The bottom of the note said in large letters that if the supreme leader's forces tried to follow or track the limousine, the group would kill the supreme leader and his companion on the spot.

Back to the front limousine, he pushed the dead team leader into the back and on top of the leader, shoved the driver to the other seat side and reached over to pull the front door shut. Doc turned the engine on and rolled at a moderate but steady pace down the road until he saw an underground parking lot about two blocks away.

He noted that it did not have any cameras inside it or on any of the two blocks surrounding it. The woman told him the block they were on now had only very senior officials so there were no cameras. He moved the vehicle into a dark spot in a back corner of the garage and parked it. Unless one was looking for the vehicle, it would not be seen.

Doc asked the woman to carefully get out of the car, spread some of her pocketbook items around, and leave her outer jacket in the rear seat. This was so if they were captured, she could stay with the story.

He then asked her to get out carefully on her side and just wait for him. Doc also asked if she still had the ring; she nodded and he asked her for it. She then took it off her finger and returned it to him. He asked her if she happened to have an encrypted cell phone (one that could not be penetrated by N.K. techs) and she did.

He took several pictures and then forwarded them directly to the Professor's encrypted cell. He also sent fingerprints for verification. Doc said that he requested receipt of confirmation back on this number only. Doc went back over to the limousine and moved the security leader off the supreme leader's body. He then moved the dead security officer onto the ground and dragged him into another dark staircase.

Doc was about to burn the dead supreme leader to ashes, but the Unicorn asked that he not. She said that she wanted him to lose face just like he had now lost all of his power. Doc nodded and said he understood.

He then dragged the dead man out of the vehicle and left him under a staircase. Doc moved the vehicle to a far corner of the garage behind a very large dumpster and broke a few bulbs to create darkness. He took two more seconds and destroyed the faux "POTUS's letter." In all, it took less than two minutes.

Doc walked over to what looked like a brand-new Mercedes in one of the other spaces on the first level and started the engine. The owner must have been a really senior official too, as it was left unlocked. Unicorn got in and proceeded to give Doc directions on how best to clear the "hot zone." Her navigation was outstanding, up and down small streets where they would never look, and finally down a gravel road and up to the mountain evacuation point in three hours.

The commander and his team were awaiting their arrival (with word of success or failure). Doc paused and then looked the commander in the eye and said that he was not able to comment or talk about the mission either way—however, he very slightly smiled and held his thumb up to them. The men saluted him in unison. Doc introduced the Unicorn and said her assistance had been invaluable to the operation—as was their own participation. Doc added that she knew the terrain inside and out and would guide them to ensure that everyone got to the evacuation point safely.

The commander said that Doc was to make an encrypted telephone call to someone called the Professor. Doc used the commander's encrypted radio, which included both verbal and small video. Doc saw that the number patched him directly into the secure conference room. POTUS confirmed receipt of his last cell message and congratulated Doc on his extraordinary accomplishment. The Professor said that the word was already out within N.K., S.K., and Japan intelligence circles that the supreme leader was missing and being held hostage. Doc thanked POTUS and said that it would not have been possible if not for the SOF team and the source. POTUS then noted that the Chinese had moved about two hundred thousand more troops to the N.K. border. Hence, they, too, had obviously gotten the word.

The Professor suggested to POTUS and the advisers that "we may have an extremely unique window of time. While the Chinese are surely skeptical of the kidnapping scenario, they clearly do not want to make a move on recovering the supreme leader if it is real. There is an opening for us to exploit. Consequently, POTUS has ordered the South Korean military and our own U.S. military to increase their numbers on the N.K./S.K. border to exactly match the current Chinese upgrade."

Doc said that he could understand the tactics so far but not the actual move that could be put into play with the added U.S. troops.

The Professor said that the Chinese had made their dramatic troop increase on the border for a reason. The Chinese wanted to continue to control the North Korean leadership indefinitely. Moreover, China wanted dearly the N.K. nuclear weapons as a land buffer to SK—and of course to the U.S. Military.

POTUS smiled and motioned for the Professor to proceed.

The Professor said, "We have all agreed here in the situation room that the best bet at this point is for POTUS to give a speech within the next two hours.

"He will present the source as the new N.K. leader and further announce a new S.K. leader. He will say that they will march together and bring the Korean people to live as '*one*' from now on.

"It will be clear that both candidates are true visionaries and have already been in deep consultations. It has already been announced that the present S.K. president has been temporarily arrested for messaging the North Korean leader on his own.

"Meanwhile, POTUS will also announce to the remaining N.K. leadership structure that their supreme leader is dead and the N.K. people are now free. The people will be fed immediately (via U.S. air drops), the concentration camps are already being shut down at this very minute, and all will be treated as human beings from this moment forward. Mankind recalls the Nuremberg trials, and the fate of the N.K. leadership is not in doubt. To the Chinese leadership, POTUS will give a clear and absolute warning. If their troops cross the border to try to march into Pyongyang, the U.S. military and all of the Korean people (from both the former North and the former South) will fight China together until total victory is achieved."

# CHAPTER TWENTY-FIVE

# A WOMAN ON A MISSION TO CHANGE THE WORLD

THE PROFESSOR SAID THERE WAS just one issue that had to be resolved prior to commencing this strategy. Doc nodded his head very slowly and said he understood. Doc said that he would need a few minutes offline. POTUS nodded and said he and the Unicorn were in the best position to judge whether this scenario would be feasible.

Doc motioned to the Unicorn, and she came over to Doc and sat down. After a compressed explanation of the present situation, particularly with regard to her, Doc went quiet and let her absorb the data and the very real downside potential. She looked at him and then studied as much of the parameters as she could. Doc just sat back against a large rock. He observed that the woman's eyes seemed to roll back a bit in her head and for a couple of minutes, she looked like she was in a coma or a trance.

Doc had never seen anything like it before. The woman then opened her eyes and looked directly at Doc. She said that the plan was indeed feasible; the North Korean people had suffered enough, and she was willing to present herself to them. She felt their pain, but she felt their strength. She said that time was an extremely major and urgent factor in the possible success of this endeavor.

Doc thanked her and called back on the secure line and told POTUS and the Professor that she had said yes, and acting with haste would determine the fate of the world.

POTUS then said to all, "Let's make this happen within the next half hour."

Everyone left the room.

Doc told the woman to wait a minute, and 3 then went over to the commander and his team. Doc told the commander that he could commence his route to the evacuation point and get home without them. He and the woman would be returning to the capitol for an unspecified time.

The commander said he apologized in that they heard some of the conversation when Doc was on the secure line. Doc nodded and said not to worry about it as long as they pretty much kept the more important details among themselves.

The commander said that they did not hear anything telling him to accompany the woman back to Pyongyang. Doc said that he did not get any orders to that point, but given what this woman was about to do on behalf of this country, and what she had already done for the U.S., Doc felt the need to accompany her, as there would most assuredly be tangos out to kill her. The commander nodded and said that while that was for sure true, did he not think that his own back had a bull's-eye on it right now? Doc said he understood and he cared more about success than he did about his own safety.

Doc told the commander to get going. The commander said that under the circumstances, they would not be going to the exfiltration zone until Doc and the woman were also doing so. Doc paused and looked at them all and threw his hands up in the air. They all started moving, still camouflaged. No one would see them unless they were adversarial professionals or just ten feet away. Doc's mind started calculating the timing of the arrival back into Pyongyang in the Mercedes and then saw another larger and older car that the SOF team could use since it looked vaguely like a military vehicle.

While driving the Mercedes back into Pyongyang, the Unicorn guided Doc and the commander's team on very specific and small highways; she clearly was not only taking the most deserted routes, but also ones that permitted them time to avoid any military roadblocks. Doc asked her when and how she planned to introduce herself to the North Korean people without getting killed in the process.

She said she would explain it all to him, but first she needed to make a few urgent telephone calls on her encrypted cell. She asked if it would be possible to pull over the vehicles? Doc relayed to the team that they were going to stop for a short while.

The team took their positions automatically. The woman proceeded to make several telephone calls on secure lines, and after a couple of minutes, she told her contacts that she was OK and that an American SOF team had saved her life.

Furthermore, there was very soon going to be a broadcast by the American president to the world that they needed to see right away. Her contacts then said that it was just coming in now on the television and by computer video. Doc told the woman that their U.S. military central command had just put it on all channels as well. The message was indeed broadcast around the world, and the American president was sticking to his script. After about forty-five minutes, the U.S. president closed his remarks—but he had especially included the Unicorn by name and mentioned his high regard for her. He had also named the new temporary S.K. president and noted the welcomed demise of the late supreme leader.

The woman had kept the broadcast open while ensuring that her contacts had also remained on her live cell line. Once POTUS finished, she could hear and see the amazing reaction and happiness of the N.K. people; there were cameras seeing and showing N.K. soldiers and people in the street hugging each other and laying their weapons on the ground and then chanting the woman's name in unison. Several of the cameras in N.K. and in S.K. had large photographs and videos of her.

After a few more minutes, the same videos and photographs were being shown and carried throughout Asia and then in the U.S., Europe, and the rest of the globe. Doc approached the woman and smiled. The woman was then asked by her connections when she could come to them, as she needed to be seen and then to address the country as soon as is possible.

The woman said that she was in Pyongyang already, and if they could each get the media ready, she would use their outlets to address and direct the N.K. people.

She would also include the closing of the numerous concentration camps and those in prisons for clearly non-criminal acts. She told them to call her when they had it all ready but remember to ensure they were safe themselves, and the location had to be as secure as it could be under the circumstances.

The woman cut the secure line and dialed an international line to call the new S.K. temporary candidate. Surprisingly, the new S.K. candidate got on right away, and they spoke for about twenty minutes and ended with his solemn promise that he would announce immediately to the S.K. media that they would be having a meeting together within the next three days in either Pyongyang or Seoul. She thanked the candidate and said that they were going to make one Korea together.

The woman then looked at Doc, who called the commander over to his side, and she said it would be dangerous but she wanted to proceed to the capitol. Once there, she would lay low at various safe houses she knew of. She said that she well understood if Doc, the commander, or his team had to leave her at this time. They looked at her and said where she went is where they would go. The woman had a small tear running down the side of her face; she bowed deeply and then said she would never forget their incredible service to her and the Korean people. They were all real warriors.

The commander whistled and the operators all returned to the vehicles, and the cars and the truck proceeded to their first destination. After an hour, she instructed them to continue on, and they then drove into a very impressive, old Korean castle that was empty and uninhabited. It was formidable from a security perspective. It contained very modern and sophisticated weapons of all kinds.

The woman said she was going inside to shower and change into fresh clothes, and she motioned that the soldiers could do the same in several of the other facilities on the premises.

Doc and the commander looked around and also noted that the property, while not far from the city, had good cover. It had somehow melted into the nearby parkland.

At this point, they both concurred that this was a very special individual. They also concluded that they were quite glad to be on her side, no matter the odds. The woman then presented herself. She was dressed in a beautiful traditional Korean gown.

She asked Doc if they could consult on their next moves. She also said to the commander that there was plenty of food for him and his men as he thought appropriate.

There were Korean clothes of all sizes, she noted, both military and civilian, if he thought it might be of use to reduce their profiles. The commander thanked the woman and concurred.

Doc and the woman went back into one of the rooms and sat down. Doc asked her if it was OK if he knew who the owner of the place was. The woman demurred and said perhaps once they were no longer in danger. Doc said he understood and he did not mean to impose; he just found it impressive from many different angles. She said to Doc that they would have to navigate the routes they took, in daytime and nighttime, and the buildings and venues they entered extremely cautiously.

Doc said he agreed on all points and she should know that the SOF team was exceptionally perfect for these concerns. The woman said that she had already received several secure calls from her senior aides providing her an array of options for visiting various studios that could serve to authenticate her new position. She also received several other calls that were from the relatives of the dead supreme leader asking for meetings to congratulate her on her position.

Doc said that he understood and that she of course knew that none of those relatives were trustworthy. He said that she nonetheless had to create a bridge even for the untrusting and devious ones to buy some more time and then totally collapse that bridge when the moment was right. She said that it was reassuring that Doc was one of her true friends.

Doc said that from his perspective, her first task was to capture the minds and hearts of the people. Doc said this required relatively trustworthy media as soon as possible.

"Therefore," he said, "you have to pick the most reliable individual you know—with the time and place selected by you. Then we have to get in and out, ideally without being seen. Next, we have to select a different safe house, and one without the same route that we took originally to get to our destination."

Doc continued, "We also have to reach out to some N.K. military or security protective personnel that we can trust to assist us once we are inside for the video interviews. The commander and his team will operate in the 'outer circle.'" They could not be seen within the "inner circle" that he and she would create. The woman agreed. Doc said to do her very best in each of her selections.

Doc then went to check on the team and share with the commander some of her thinking as well as his own deduction of the best way to utilize the team without getting everyone killed. The commander took in Doc's perspective and agreed with the majority of it.

"In the shadows, you would have more safety and a greater ability to take out threats," Doc said.

The commander noted that he had already had his men replace their U.S. standard SOF uniforms with N.K. uniforms for working in the inner-city locales (then, under the visible clothes they were wearing, they each wore added garb that would mix in well with the N.K. populace).

The two exceptions he requested from Doc were that one of his guys remained on his six o'clock at all times but in a very discreet manner. The commander also noted that two of his men were extraordinary gifted snipers, Olympic level, and they would have to choose on their own their hiding spots, "from which they will save our sorry asses."

Doc laughed and agreed to both exceptions. Doc was called by the Unicorn to advise him and the commander that they would need to move at about 0400 hours en route to an old building (she gave them the approximate address and a map which had a specific "x") in the city.

She said that she chose to do her on-the-air broadcast that would not only be heard in both Koreas and many of the other Asian and European countries as well, but would be broadcast worldwide on the internet at 0600.

Doc and the commander said that several of their team members would do an advance at about 0300 hours and they would then stay in place. Once they radioed back that the venue was clear, they would then set up the protective zone around her and Doc.

The Unicorn said that she was going to get two hours of sleep and then write and practice her speech. Doc told the commander to contact the U.S. central command and relay to them the planned internet broadcast. It would be helpful if central command could put out some false locations as to the broadcast site.

At 0400 hours, Doc and the Unicorn were in the Mercedes, the army truck with a portion of the team already en route to the venue. Upon arrival, Doc and the Unicorn (along with Doc's "shadow"—the operator who was now attached to Doc's person at all times) discreetly entered what looked like an ancient building and then made their way into a warehouse that was buzzing with noise.

When the small group inside saw the woman, they ran up to her. The younger people hugged her and the older bowed deeply, and repeatedly did so, until the senior media adviser clapped his hands for all to get back to work.

They had an impressive amount of technical gear. The Unicorn sat down behind a large desk with two flags set up behind her, concealing the background so no one could identify it.

The media adviser turned on the monitors. He then raised his right-hand fingers and dropped each finger after the other. The woman looked straight at the screen, and she began her speech. Her countenance and her manner projected a very smooth and controlled persona. Doc and his shadow were constantly canvasing the inside of the warehouse, and the shadow communicated with his team members for periodic checks of the outside surrounding building.

The woman was on the first half of her speech, which was going well. She pointed to the two flags behind her and said that they were "what used to be the North Korean flag and the South Korean flag. Soon, we will be one Korea, and I and the new candidate have spoken and will soon meet. No longer will our people be killed, suppressed, and/or imprisoned. With the untapped tremendous natural resources of the North and the amazing technological marvels of the South, our one Korea together will become a powerhouse to all its people. The evil North Korean leadership will be gone, never ever to return."

She went on: "The United States military has been and remains our one true ally. The American president has assured us that no one will take any part of Korea, not even one inch, but the Korean people. The U.S. president has solemnly promised that he and America will stand with all of the Korean people now and in our new, bright future."

The woman said that her faith, promise, and sole belief in the unified Korean people would not waiver. She said in closing that she would be seeing the Korean people again and soon. She would relay directly to them the latest updates and wanted them to please know that she worked for all Korean people, as did the new candidate in Seoul. "We together will not sleep until this has been accomplished." She then stood up from her chair and bowed deeply.

The media adviser moved to see where the speech had been rebroadcasted or received. They were all stunned to see that the speech had been successfully broadcast around the entire world. Blogs were coming online at an incredible speed, and almost all were positive.

Doc told the media adviser that for the Unicorn's and his people's personal security, they needed to remove her and his people from the premises as soon as possible, and the adviser agreed.

The commander radioed Doc and said that they were just now observing a Chinese Special Forces team of about fifteen soldiers. They must have just zeroed in on her exact location and were surrounding the perimeter of the building. Doc acknowledged the report and asked for his opinion on their level of training. The commander said that this was undeniably an A-team.

# CHAPTER TWENTY-SIX

# TIME TO GET OUT OF DODGE CITY

DOC GRIPPED THE WOMAN BY her arm and told her that they needed to move immediately. His shadow officer was already moving ahead of Doc and the woman. He radioed to the commander that they were going to the underground basement level they had reviewed earlier. The commander said he copied that, and ordered his snipers to engage the targets immediately to buy Doc and the woman some time.

Senior officers were to be taken out first. The sound and power of the snipers' weapons were like music to Doc's ears. Within less than two minutes, the snipers had taken out five of the Chinese team leaders. An additional one which they deduced was a SOF Chinese communication specialist was also taken out along with all of his equipment.

The remaining Chinese team members were rattled and slowed down considerably in surrounding the building—particularly to the rear of it. They still did not know from where the shooting was coming—a sniper's delight.

The shadow had preselected the best door to exit. Doc nodded to him, and they were then running down the stairs. His shadow uttered to him that if they could get out of the basement door, there would be the Mercedes with its doors open for cover; it was placed there specifically for this situation.

Doc nodded and then literally picked up the woman over his shoulder and continued running; once the basement door swung open, he went directly into the vehicle. On the radio, the commander now ordered one of his two snipers to change position so that he could cover the rear of the building. The commander then told the other sniper to go fishing for one of the others in the front of the building to keep them off balance.

Doc's shadow was right behind them when a bullet fired at the right side of shadow and missed by an inch. The sniper scanned carefully for the shooter. He caught him on one of the corners of the building. He was tucked in tightly.

The commander radioed to shadow to stay glued onto and hug the building tightly until the commander gave him the green light to make it to the car. The commander told the sniper that they did not have all day.

The sniper said, "Roger that," and the Chinese guy then slowly crept his head and weapon about one inch around the concrete wall.

The sniper waited, and when the guy moved into the two-inch zone, the sniper blew the front of his head off. The rest of his body fell forward.

The second Chinese soldier, also tucked into the building, made a quick executive decision and got the hell out of the sniper's range by running to the front of the building. Many of the other Chinese operators seemed to do the same. The sniper who was waiting at the front of the building smiled and focused on getting some more fish in the barrel, catching one right after the other.

Doc had kept one door open for when the shadow would jump in and the commander told the shadow, "*Now*." The shadow took three super-large strides and flew headfirst into the back of the Mercedes. Doc floored the pedal, and the door slammed shut as the vehicle jumped forward, increasing in speed like a rocket. The snipers, who had been on the roofs of different buildings, raced downstairs as ordered, and the commander pulled the military truck up slowly enough for them to run and jump into the open back.

Their colleagues grabbed them, their gear, and their range weapons. Once they were inside the truck, their other guys asked them what took them so long and smiled. The commander smiled too and said to them all, "First-class job."

The Mercedes was running hot, and the truck was catching up to it quickly. The Unicorn gave them directions to another safe house that she knew, and it took about one hour to get there. The team jumped out of the truck and immediately set up a secure perimeter. It was another ancient house with smaller grounds and no servants or occupants, but hidden just as well.

Doc suggested that she get some rest and she agreed, so she went into one of the bedrooms. After about twenty minutes, he could hear her on the multiple encrypted cells, and he now realized that she actually had about five or more different but similar secure cell phones. Doc talked with the commander, praised him and his men, and told him to make sure they all got some food and rest if possible.

First, though, Doc asked the commander to set up a secure line for him to the White House situation room as he had no doubt that the White House wanted a "sitrep" (also known as a situation report) regarding their little trip. The commander said the call and video should be live in about ten minutes. Doc had just enough time to get cleaned up and to swallow a large bottle of water.

The secure line came on, and Doc saw POTUS, the Professor, SecDef, and all of the other advisers. POTUS looked at Doc and said that the Unicorn did a superb job. The whole world was now taken by her and listening whenever they could. Doc said that she, the woman, was the real deal and would make an outstanding president and was one who he thought could truly unite the Korean people.

The Professor asked Doc how it was going. Doc said that he would get to the point: the woman was in extreme danger of being assassinated. From his team's perspective, it would be very wise to have her visit South Korea immediately, to meet with the new South Korean candidate and the top U.S. generals there. She could still do her speeches to her people while in Seoul, and they would not know her location.

Doc then mentioned the attack on the woman and his team while they were at the recent venue that was used for her speech. Doc looked at POTUS and then at the Professor and said that the adversaries about two hours ago were a very high-quality Chinese special operations force team. "They had a squad of three or four times more A-team operators than we did. We managed to take out about ten of them prior to their running away, thinking we were a defiant N.K. trap, but make no mistake, it was an extremely close call."

POTUS leaned forward and asked if this was definitely a Chinese SOF team. Doc replied that it certainly was. "My team leader is from New York City, and he is fluent at a native level in Mandarin Chinese and has no doubt."

POTUS said, "Damn it," and that he had just gotten off the secure phone line with the *new* Chinese president, who had assured him that China did not have any military or diplomats past the far North's border.

The Professor leaned in and asked Doc if he knew who was currently in charge of the nuclear stockpile. Doc said he would get back to them, and then there was silence in the room.

POTUS asked the Professor what he was getting at. The Professor looked at POTUS directly and said that his concern was that the Chinese might be trying to get their hands on WMD. "With the pounding they have been taking from the Russians, the demise of the North Korean leader, and the now anointed woman being the next leader, the Chinese are probably extremely cornered and desperate." It was another window.

"The Chinese can be pushed back," said the Professor, "if we move all of our assets now (both U.S. military and South Korean military and any other of the former North Korean military) that will join us in this gamble of pulling the pin and moving into the Pyongyang capitol."

POTUS looked around the room. The room remained quiet. SecDef said he did understand the Professor's thinking and it was an extremely valid consideration. Doc then said that he thought it would no doubt be an enormous and daring move but he believed that the fractured Chinese leadership would ultimately fold.

However, if the Chinese did not retreat, the U.S. would have to escalate. It would likely end up with the Chinese being "all in," regardless of the price they would pay. The

Professor added that it was critical to the Korean people and the U.S. to take control of the nuclear stockpile and other WMDs.

(The Professor and Doc looked at each other after assessing POTUS's face and knew without a doubt that all hell was about to break loose. They both hoped fervently that the Chinese would come to regret their presence in the new Korea.)

POTUS said, "As of now, the Unicorn is invited and expected to meet the South Koreans for consultations right away." POTUS said to Doc that he did not care whether she agreed or disagreed; he was to get her on the bird even if he had to carry her over his shoulder.

POTUS paused, looked around the room, and stopped when he slowly laid his eyes on the SecDef. POTUS leaned into him, and then POTUS loudly announced, "From this moment forward, we are going to assist in taking over (former) North Korean land. Meanwhile, the SecDef will now commence, based on my decision at this time, to move all of our assets forward—air, sea, land, and cyber into acquiring the Pyongyang capitol. When the new united Korean country exists, all of this will be immediately turned over to the Korean people without delay."

POTUS said that this meeting was now complete, the decision had been made, and all participants were to report back to him as warranted.

The SecDef saluted POTUS and then proceeded out of the room as fast as he could, as did all of the other advisers. POTUS looked at the Professor and Doc and said, "Let's privately hope that we know what I am doing."

The Professor and Doc smiled and said that whatever happened, he could always blame them, but POTUS said he would not give it a second thought and to count on it. They all laughed for a couple of seconds, and then they, too, got up and left. The secure line was cut.

Doc called for the commander and the Unicorn and told them that some new developments had occurred and they needed to depart virtually instantly. He also said that he would brief her once they were on the road, then took her by her arm and went to the vehicles.

He asked her to again navigate them all back to their last selected exfiltration point in as fast a manner as is possible. The commander said he just two minutes ago got a secure call from central command. They instructed the new exfiltration vector points and directed that they were to arrive there for an airlift ASAP. They were all bugging out. Doc got the woman into the backseat of the Mercedes. The shadow got behind the wheel, and Doc said to hit the metal hard. Soon, they were all racing to the exfiltration point.

Two U.S. military choppers, heavily loaded, were waiting for them when they arrived. Doc and the commander's SOF team all got on board. Once the first team was in the air, the second team jumped into the second chopper and they too were airborne. Doc also noticed that two U.S. F-16s, also carrying heavy bombs and multiple machine guns, were flying on their flanks, and two more F-16s suddenly appeared on their rear and front, forming another hard circle around the two choppers.

Within less than one hour, they landed at one of the larger U.S. military bases. While being escorted to the hangar, all they could see were men and women running in every direction. It was obvious that the SecDef's order had been heard loud and clear. There were U.S., former South

Korean, and even former North Korean military going in the air constantly; aircrafts were on the move.

Troops on the ground were traveling on foot and in what seemed like an uncountable number of vehicles. Inside the hangar were an endless number of military personnel of all three brands (N.K., S.K., and U.S.) tapping away on thousands of computers. The move to Pyongyang was in motion.

Doc and the Unicorn were greeted by a four-star general and brought into one of the secure conference rooms.

"There has been some resistance by several covert Chinese SOF teams," the general said. "But fortunately, we have been able to control the situation and have taken them into custody until we can figure how far along they were able to get into the nuclear system."

Doc looked at the general and nodded. The general said that if Unicorn was up to it, she could, at this moment, be of an enormous value to the effort if she were to do a short video message to the Korean people, who were now quite scared and confused. The woman then said there was no time like the present and smiled tightly.

The general smiled and called in two video specialists, and within three minutes, they left the room and the line became active. Doc motioned to the woman, and she looked directly into the screen and spoke. The woman said that she had complete love for the Korean people, now more than ever. She said that she was with them in every way. She said that during these trying times, they had to embrace the coming future and realize that even though they were in very difficult and trying circumstances right now, it would be better—and soon.

She said that they had to remember that she was with them now and would be in the coming days and weeks ahead. She implored the people to stay at home and be safe. They must know and understand that their own former N.K. soldiers and the former South Korean soldiers were coming together to protect all of them. Along with them was the support and outstanding assistance from the U.S. military and the United States of America that only wished the two Koreas could become one and be treated properly forever.

"All three entities are now in the process of working together and quickly securing the entire Korean Peninsula to give freedom and new prosperity to the new Korean people." She said that they all had to come together at this time to prevent other countries from trying to steal their hard-earned assets and ancient and beautiful buildings and homes. The woman mentioned that one nearby country had already tried to secretly steal some of their country's assets but was stopped.

"We, both former N.K. and S.K. together, are now, with the ongoing and loving help from the U.S.A., their president, and the other countries that do not wish to steal from the new one Korea, are growing strong as *one* right now.

"The combined military forces of former N.K., S.K., and U.S. are now entering Pyongyang to make it safe." The Unicorn concluded by saying she would continue to do all that was necessary. She then stood up and bowed.

The line was cut, and she asked Doc and the general whether they thought that would be of some help, and they both smiled. The next day, each of the team members, Doc, and the woman all awoke at different times but relatively close together.

The woman asked Doc if they could talk about the next steps that she should take to continue to contribute to the

Korean people's situation. Doc said that he would recommend that she continue to go with her inner voice. He said that her speeches had fortified the Korean people. He thought it might be wise and appropriate for her to meet with the new candidate in person, and he believed that it could be arranged for later that day.

# CHAPTER TWENTY-SEVEN

# SHAPING UP THE NEW KOREAN TEAM

THE GENERAL CAME BY, NODDED to Doc, and spoke with the Unicorn. He gave her an up-to-date report on how the things were going in Pyongyang. The woman thanked him and asked if he would be willing to arrange a meeting with his former S.K. military equivalent, as well as the American ambassador, and finally with the new (S.K.) candidate, with whom she had had a couple of brief contacts.

The general said he would arrange that within the next two hours and thanked her for suggesting it. Doc then excused himself and said that he had to make a few secure-line phone calls but he would be back later. They both agreed, and Doc went to the secure conference room.

Doc called the situation room at the White House and was able to reach the Professor, who was working there alone. He smiled when he saw Doc again. The Professor gave Doc an update from their end and asked how he was doing. The Professor said they were watching the next moves of the Chinese leadership through a long looking glass, also hoping for the best.

The Professor noted that they were not out of the woods yet by anyone's measure and said they were a long way from being out of the woods. "The Chinese leadership is livid and is presently reviewing its options, and only time will tell how and if they will retaliate."

Doc asked if he had the chance to ask their Chinese female friend her opinion.

The Professor said that he had, and her honest view, as always, of the situation was somewhat limited since she knew the new Chinese leader not in depth.

Her best guess was that the new Chinese leader would at the least send his hundreds of thousands of troops past the current border just to see if the U.S. might flinch and run. Doc shook his head and said from his optic, that move had a lot to commend.

Her best estimate was that she did not believe that the new Chinese leader would "'pull the entire plug of the bathtub,' as you Westerners often say, but he will undoubtedly need to 'save face.' If we hold our ground, he will capitulate by returning his troops back to the border. However, some kind of agreement will be needed so the Chinese people can feel they have won some kind of victory. The Russians, of course, will have to stand down after that."

The Professor said he was trying to come up with an acceptable face-saving mechanism. He knew well that in Chinese culture, saving face was paramount.

# CHAPTER TWENTY-EIGHT

# THE CHINESE DECISION

IN THE WHITE HOUSE SITUATION room sat POTUS, the Professor, the SecDef, D/NSA, D/CIA, and the other advisers, and all were extremely concerned. The Chinese leadership appeared to be moving in the wrong direction. The room was quiet until POTUS looked around the room and said, "OK—lets have it all." The Professor motioned to the D/NSA, who said that they had hard coverage that the Chinese were recasting their military assets on the land, in the air, and especially on the sea.

The D/CIA and the SecDef followed up with the same conclusions but with some extra twists. Submarines had been deployed with advanced nuclear weapons. The submarine captains had their orders: run deep and out of sight. In the air, many Chinese aircraft had been rearmed with some weapons (bombs) the U.S. had not seen before. On land, the Chinese leadership had ordered their ground troops to proceed forward over the border on the Korean Peninsula and also further along on the agreed Russian Motherland border.

POTUS leaned back and said, "Well, this is certainly an unwelcome pile of crap." He looked to the Professor and asked what he thought.

The Professor said that it was his opinion that this was all a show of force to keep face. POTUS rolled his eyes and nodded. "Next."

The SecDef said that his staff had been keeping a close view of all the new activity. "Our submarines are quietly covering theirs; however, to state the obvious, if they launch a nuke, all our guys will be able to do is take out that (or those) submarines—not the missiles.

"With respect to aircraft, yes, they have some new weapons, but they're not nukes, so we are confident that our pilots will demolish them if they proceed into denied airspace.

"The land action is real, and there will soon, in the next two days, come a point where a lot of people on both sides will die. The situation is dark, and we will have to move fast to contain it. As a side note, all of the Asian countries from Japan to Indonesia have offered without reservations to fight with us against the Chinese, and the Europeans have, of course, as well."

POTUS shook his head and then held it down in his hands.

The Professor felt for the man.

POTUS asked the SecDef if the U.S. was really ready, and the SecDef said it was. POTUS asked the Professor for additional thoughts.

The Professor said that his best calculations pointed to the fact that this was a bluff; however, once all three modes of fighting (air, sea, and ground) were activated, it was a statistical certainty that orders would be misconstrued on both sides. It was dicey.

The Professor paused and then said that he would recommend that the U.S. contact every country that had expressed support and tell them all to get ready for their military units to go air, ground, and sea onto the China coastlines now. "We need to have this done immediately and let all of the press around the world know that we are doing so. We need to have Russia and all of its military stand down in hitting China until our allies have arrived.

"POTUS would then announce on television that we are again at DEFCON 2 but only with regard to the *new Korean Peninsula*. And also that the U.S. military, with their Korean military brothers, has taken full control of the nuclear stockpile that was formerly North Korea's. The United States and Russia now offer a truce: as a show of goodwill to the Chinese leadership, a delegation will meet with the Chinese, and the U.S. will remove all nuclear weapons that belonged to the former N.K."

POTUS said that if the Chinese leadership stood down, the U.S. military would do the same.

The room again remained silent, and the Professor let the idea float freely. POTUS asked what everyone thought. SecDef said he concurred completely and, in his view, it had a real fighting chance, so to speak. One or two of the advisers noted that it would require a lot of coordination with the other countries, especially Russia and Korea, but that could be accomplished. POTUS said he liked it and would proceed.

Minutes after the meeting ended, the Professor got ahold of Doc and briefed him on the situation. Doc said that he understood and asked if he could bring the Unicorn into the secure room. Once there, she said she was glad that the Professor was no longer "sick," and he smiled. The Professor briefed them both.

Afterward, she spoke to Doc in private. The woman observed that the WMD, especially with the array of potential—particularly nuclear, biological, and chemical—were capable of destroying the entire world.

Doc looked at the Unicorn and said, "You are now grasping and understanding the depth that comes with your responsibilities at the most basic and most important levels. The U.S.A. will always stand with you and your people.

"The new one Korea will now thrive."

Doc noted to the Unicorn the incredible speed and rate at which she was consuming the nuances of WMD, mixed with human political intrigue. Doc smiled and ended with saying that both domestic and foreign politics were just as critical as WMD.

That deleted portion of the proposal, in Doc's estimate, was deliberate. The Professor created it all and was responsible. Doc said that the proposal was only intended to let the Chinese leadership have some measure of "face."

Doc said that was what he had learned from this so far. Any "other" recovered WMD would be joint Korean and U.S. property. Hence, any other WMD would remain physically in Korea under the joint auspices of the future Korean president and the U.S.A. The woman nodded and thanked Doc. She said the remaining WMD, in her estimate, were vital to the Korean people. Doc said she was going to be an outstanding president.

Back in Washington, the Professor's advice, only to POTUS, was that should the Chinese inquire about the omission (biological, radiological, and chemical), the Chinese leader should be told the Chinese would not get another inch of anything. About ten minutes after POTUS's speech to the world, this was in fact exactly what happened. POTUS took the secure call, with only the Professor in the room. POTUS told the Chinese leader that if he did not concur on the nukes right away and in public, he was going to end the call immediately and move the U.S. readiness level to DEFCON 1. The Chinese leader verbally stumbled a bit and said he understood and he was only asking as a question, but not one that needed to be answered.

The leader said that his troops on the Korean Peninsula were withdrawing as they spoke. A peace pact would be made with Russia very soon. All of their air, naval, and land assets had been called back, and their military nukes were also rescinded to ensure that they and the United States would no longer have any quarrel of any kind. POTUS said he very much appreciated those gestures and once his SecDef confirmed each and every one had been effected, he would like to invite the wise Chinese leader, the Russian president, and the future (and first female) president of the new one Korea to the White House.

He also said one last thing. If the new president of Korea were to get killed or even get a bad case of the flu, POTUS would consider it an act of war. The Chinese president said he understood and looked forward to meeting in person when time permitted. The secure line then cut off.

About an hour after POTUS's speech, the Professor used the now-empty White House situation room to reach Doc via the secure line. The Professor asked that the Unicorn be contacted and be in attendance as well. The connection was made, and the Professor then conveyed the substance of POTUS's conversation with the new Chinese president. When he was finished, Doc asked the Professor whether the Chinese president's promises that China's military had been recalled were accurate.

The Professor said it was verified—a total withdrawal by the Chinese from the Peninsula and from all other ports, including air and land. "They have folded and rapidly, so if we just agree formally to the removal of the nuke stockpile, we have a deal. POTUS has also spoken with the Russians. In the next few weeks, the U.S. military and the new joint Korean military will all stand down. The war is over."

The Unicorn was speechless and simply bowed deeply to both the Professor and Doc.

Doc contacted the commander and asked him to escort the president of Korea to the Blue House for an important event. The commander saluted and rushed her and his team to get moving. Doc thanked the Professor for ensuring the welfare of so many. The Professor smiled and said that Doc had played an invaluable part as well.

Doc then asked, "If that is the case, am I now cleared to return to the U.S.?"

The Professor paused, smiled again, and said he had asked POTUS, and he had said, "Sure, why not?"

POTUS was actually not that sure what he had been doing out there, anyway. He was kidding, of course, just kidding. POTUS had in fact said that Doc was to be picked up and returned by none other than Air Force One at Doc's pleasure.

Doc smiled ear to ear and said he would need to say goodbyes for another day or so. The Professor said that would be fine and just between them, he believed the real reason POTUS was sending Doc back via Air Force One was because he wanted to be sure no errant and crazy soldier had planted explosives on the plane.

"Doc, you would be a great test case," he said.

Doc shook his head with a grin and said he would see his friend soon.

The Unicorn's inauguration took place as scheduled. The event was an unbridled success. After being sworn into office, televised live worldwide, she moved immediately into Korea's presidential offices and residence, the Blue House. First, the Korean military briefed her; then, the commerce secretary gave a brief on the Korean economy. She was engulfed and somewhat overwhelmed by numerous secretaries of state. Doc watched and concluded that the new president was, however, learning to make her moves—and yet was up to the task at hand.

# CHAPTER TWENTY-NINE

# THE NEW ONE KOREA

DOC WAS DRIVEN TO THE Blue House. He first went to the commander, who was with his team inside a room literally attached to the president's office. All of the men stood up immediately once Doc had come into the room. The commander, who had been briefing each of them on the trip that the president was making soon to Pyongyang, seemed annoyed until he turned, saw Doc, and then understood. He saluted Doc as well, and Doc did the same but then walked over to the commander and hugged him; then he did the same to each and every member of the team.

The commander smiled and said they had heard Doc was heading back to the Big House and was now on the easy road. Doc smiled and said he was guilty as charged but it was only because he needed some more experience being around the upper echelons of society. Doc said that he knew that was where they were all headed in their careers. Everyone in the room had a good laugh. Doc stepped out the door and was greeted by a Korean chief of staff who escorted him to the president's door and knocked on it softly.

Doc walked into the room and saw the president working hard at her desk. A second later, the president looked up and swiftly raised herself out of her seat and walked around the desk to bow deeply at Doc. She smiled then and embraced him. Doc returned the hug and said hello and congratulations. The president laughed quietly, and Doc laughed loudly.

The president asked him to sit down, and she did the same. A tray of tea was brought in. She looked at him for a full minute or two and then told Doc that she would miss him very much. Doc said that she was exactly where she should be and he now had to go where he had to be as well. The president looked down at the table next to her side and slowly picked up a small box that had been wrapped perfectly. She placed both of her hands, the gift clutched in them, in Doc's direction. She said that it was a very small but extremely important gift to signify to Doc their lifelong friendship. The president asked that he open and look at it when he had a moment alone in his day.

The president stood up. Doc did the same, and then he bowed deeply to her. A tear from the corner of her eye could be seen, but Doc acted as if he had not seen it. He told the president that he hoped to see her in Washington whenever her schedule permitted, since POTUS had already sent an invitation. She said she would value that very much and would welcome the opportunity to see him at that time.

Doc said that he had one last question—how did she know the various safe havens in Pyongyang? The president leaned forward and whispered into Doc's ear that they were all the former supreme leader's homes. She figured that he would not mind any longer and then smiled. Doc laughed aloud again and shook his head back and forth. Doc said that he knew the president would serve all of her people perfectly in her new position. The president proceeded to walk back to her desk. Doc bowed, smiled, and then departed.

# CHAPTER THIRTY

# A WELL-DESERVED SURPRISE

DOC RETURNED TO THE AIR base where Air Force One was waiting. He and the colonel in charge exchanged salutes. Shortly after the bird was in the air, Doc asked the colonel if there were any other officials on board. The colonel said no, as ordered by POTUS. Doc nodded and told the colonel that he was going to be one of the easiest "official" guys he ever met.

Doc said that he just wanted to be shown where he might get a long and deep sleep and asked that no one wake him for any reason unless, of course, the bird was going down. The colonel smiled and directed Doc to his cabin—fortunately, it included a luxury bathroom with a shower.

Doc went directly to the bathroom. He had carefully and totally deactivated and disassembled all of his small weapons in his temporary bunker at the base before riding and getting on to the big bird for his ride. Now, he just slowly reviewed all of the various miniature devices and pieces that were now taken apart to the most basic level, including one ring that he had used as a complete backup.

He had previously implanted each and every device into his body as covert weapons, but the ring had been kept out in the open, and it, too, had been disassembled. Sometimes, Doc had learned over the many years of his service, plain sight was the most effective hiding place. It was exceedingly fortunate that it turned out he did not need any of the devices on the Korean Peninsula trip.

Doc put on a pair of pajamas that had been placed on the bed. He gratefully closed his eyes, fell into a deep sleep, and did not open them until the aircraft speaker system announced that it was exactly one hour prior to landing. After about sixteen hours of pure sleep, Doc rose, quickly showered, and was dressed and ready within a half hour.

Doc sat down and took two items out of his bag. The first was the ring he had asked the Korean president to wear for him when they were on the helicopter and about to land on the building roof commencing the North Korea operation. That ring (now disabled) contained a miniature but extremely combustible explosive that when pressed on an exact spot, would obliterate everything within a very impressive range.

Doc had been fully prepared, if necessary, to use the ring once he (and the now-president of Korea) was in the presence of the supreme leader. Doc also saw the ring as something to be used if the whole operation failed and there were no means of escape.

The second was the gift that the new Korean president had handed to him. It had been x-rayed at the base bunker and returned to Doc as cleared. Doc opened the small box, which was wrapped with great care, and he saw that it was also another ring. It was almost identical to the one she always had on, but had a slightly more masculine character. Doc saw that it was also clearly created by a master.

This term, in Asia, described an individual who had tremendous and unquestionable skills that were rarely found. The ring had several diamonds and a very large ruby. Etched underneath the very surface of the ring was:

*This man is a hero to the new unified Korean nation. He is to always be granted all requests of any kind by any and all Korean citizens.*

A small but clear chop of the new Korean president could be seen at the very end. Doc smiled and put it in his pocket case with particular care.

Air Force One had landed, and an armored vehicle with the White House seal on the side door was waiting for him. Doc went over to the car and saw the Professor sitting in back, grinning. The Professor said that they were en route to the White House to pick something up and then they would be on their way to the Hudson Valley property. Doc looked at Professor, wondering if there was another urgent problem.

As they entered the White House situation room, POTUS and all of his most senior secretaries and advisers stood up and clapped. They shook his hand and pointed to the end of the conference table. POTUS walked over, paused, and then presented Doc with the Congressional Medal of Honor.

Doc was dumbfounded and could not initially get a word out at all; then, he thanked POTUS and all the others in the room. POTUS slapped him on his back, and everyone started clapping loudly again and smiled. Doc ended up shaking each of their hands, and they all congratulated him. POTUS said, "Now get out of here; do not forget the Medal on your way, and the Professor will get you home."

At the airport, a small commercial helicopter took him and the Professor to the Hudson Valley property. The Linguist, Zhaohui Xiaoqing, and her daughter, Mei Baozhai, both greeted them warmly. The Professor and Doc looked at them, and Doc looked especially at the daughter, smiled, and then introduced himself. He told her that he understood that her mother's name meant clear wisdom and high intelligence in Chinese and that her own name meant gorgeous, pretty, or stunning and a stockade of treasure.

They laughed. Doc said that on his honor, the Professor did not tell him this and he studied it and learned it all by himself. The Professor attested to his statement, and he said he was quite impressed. After a second or two, Doc said, "Let's go have dinner," and they all laughed again. The evening was filled with stories and laughter. After a few hours, Doc excused himself and fell, content, deeply asleep.

# CHAPTER THIRTY-ONE

# TAKING GOOD CARE OF THE LOOSE ENDS

THE NEXT AFTERNOON, DOC LEARNED that the two women had gone shopping at a popular town mall with two of Doc's security escorts. The Professor could see that Doc was still uneasy regarding everyone's personal security. Doc looked at the Professor and then explained that he still held some genuine concerns with respect to the Russian general in Moscow that had picked them up at the airport. The Professor asked what he was thinking.

Doc said that his intuition, after meeting him on the car ride, was that he might have been involved in the assassination attempt on the Professor when they were in Abu Dhabi. "Moreover, the al-Qaeda affiliate that tried to take you out here on this very property was a professional. But that foreign operator was not the brain trust that put the two pieces together in Abu Dhabi or in the U.S. Hence the contract that was put out on you, at a Russian general's initiation, and accepted by the al-Qaeda affiliate, could all still be in play."

Doc said that he wanted to speak with his team leader, who would be there the next day. Getting a more fulsome description of the event when it happened would be help-ful. "Why one of the security professionals that was dis-guised as you was killed by the sniper is not going to be unanswered. That it was done here in the U.S. opens the door to the possibility that they have a cell in the U.S.

"If we are lucky, the brain trust could also be in the U.S. right now, laying low since the incident. There are enor-mous egos with these types, and if he is here, he is now zero for two attempts on your life. In all likelihood, the master-mind was probably a psychopath as well; that alone would likely cause him to continue the job."

The Professor said that from a mathematical perspec-tive, the individual target—in order to really impress al-Qaeda—would move up in rank to a higher-stature tar-get. Doc knew the Professor was referring to POTUS. Doc asked the Professor if he thought that was even plausible.

The Professor looked at Doc and said that the mathe-matics of given situations were not possible or half right; they either were or were not. Doc looked at the Professor and asked him what he thought their next move should be.

The Professor said that he had already relayed a need for himself and Doc to have a meeting with POTUS, as well as with the director of the U.S. Secret Service, the D/CIA, D/NSA and the NDI—national director of intelligence. Two helicopters were just landing on the camouflaged concrete circle at the Ranch. Doc saw that they had USSS emblems on them. Doc was assigned to the first helicop-ter, and the Professor was placed in the second one. Within a few seconds, both were airborne and soon reached the White House internal landing zone.

They got to the door outside POTUS's office and were greeted by the four other officials. POTUS was talking on

A TRUE AMERICAN PATRIOT

the secure telephone and waved them all in. When he placed the phone back on his desk, he said, "Please begin and move slowly."

POTUS said he already knew from his long experience with the Professor and Doc that this was not going to be an invitation to one of their birthday parties. All in the room laughed, and the Professor said that he sincerely regretted having to ask for this meeting in the first place. POTUS said, "Oh boy, this one is going to be good."

The Professor let out a slight breath and said he and Doc were concerned that POTUS might be a serious target for an assassination. The Professor and Doc described the enemy group as an A-team and said that they believed the move was already in play.

D/USSS got up immediately, asked the Professor to stand by for one minute, and went directly to one of POTUS's telephones. He then got his deputy on the line and ordered him to activate "red light" now and across the board.

All protective coverage for family members under protection was to be increased instantly but without them knowing it. "POTUS's day and foreign schedules are to be hereby changed immediately via the chief of staff and under my authorization. All normal communications are being rerouted and encrypted to the highest level."

D/USSS ordered that he be advised when all was in place and for the others to please continue. The Professor asked Doc to brief the others. Once Doc finished, the Professor went on to incorporate additional factors and conclusions, drawing from mathematical calculations and unorthodox computations.

The NDI and the D/CIA both added some more factors regarding the incidents mentioned and the Middle Eastern extremist groups that seemed to be much more agitated than normal. Some of their operatives had noticed it visibly in some of their meetings. The D/NSA also said that the level of recent chatter had spiked, but the NSA was initially thinking that it was all about the Chinese and Korean War.

At that very moment, the D/USSS and Doc heard a very soft twirling sound as POTUS started to get to his feet. Both the D/USSS and Doc were very familiar with the sound and both registered it and reacted simultaneously. Doc was sitting one chair behind the D/USSS so he automatically shoved the Professor onto the floor, chair and all, with one hand. He then launched himself with the D/USSS, who had already started to move, onto POTUS. They both jumped over POTUS's desk and brought him to the floor and covered his body.

Instantly, two RPGs (rocket-propelled grenades) came through a window. They were probably mounted on a rocket (bottom) and a shoulder-mounted launcher with an RPG loaded (top). The brown part of the launcher probably rested on the shoulder of the operative firing, possibly from an open car window.

The first RPG hit the glass behind POTUS's desk, and a second exploded in the Oval Office. The sound was deafening, and the NDI was instantly killed while the D/CIA and D/NSA were both thrown across the room. Doc and the D/USSS rose unsteadily, grabbed POTUS and the Professor by their belts, and dragged them both outside the nearby door.

The D/USSS and the four agents on post outside the door immediately moved POTUS to a nearby safe room and checked POTUS's body from head to toe; he appeared to be intact. He was mildly coherent, as was the Professor, so the D/USSS yelled, "Secure."

In that moment a dozen or more agents escorted POTUS and the Professor, again holding their belts from behind to physically lift them off the floor if needed. Once POTUS was in the hard room, the White House was shut down completely and essentially frozen. A radio 'sitrep' to D/USSS indicated that no more attacks appeared likely and rings of agents with heavy weapons were now around the grounds, with local police surrounding the outer perimeter. Snipers were also deployed as were plainclothes agents on the street.

D/USSS requested an update on all transport on the grounds, both land and air, and was advised that multiple military choppers were ready to lift, as were motorcades, both with multiple decoys. The entire White House was inspected and cleared with all present occupants confirmed.

Doc looked at POTUS and the Professor and then asked how they were feeling. D/USSS was asking and answering more tactical concerns from his people, but things appeared to be calming down somewhat. D/USSS confirmed that POTUS's family was all secure and they were now in temporary safe rooms. The decision as to whether they were going to move POTUS out of the White House was being determined.

There were no more visual or audio threats; therefore, POTUS would be staying put and his family members were being transported home as a safety precaution, with larger details accompanying them as a precaution.

POTUS stepped forward and thanked everyone for their support. He said that he was fine, and other then the director and Doc knocking the wind out of his sails for a minute or two by having very professionally tackled him in a substantial manner, he was really OK. Everyone in the room laughed, and the D/USSS told everyone to get out of the room and secure the doors, as POTUS needed a little time.

The U.S. military went to a higher alert while the media was rabid with questions. POTUS looked at the Professor and Doc and said the next time he disagreed with them, they had permission to hit him in the arm. The D/USSS chuckled and said, "But only softly. Otherwise, you'll be arrested."

POTUS asked for a count, and his chief of staff said that the NDI was dead but the directors of the CIA and NSA had been moved, were now recovering, and they too seemed to be OK after the medic examination. POTUS told his chief of staff to get out the word that he was fine. Once security approved of it, he wanted to do a quick address to the nation to show that he was well and the perpetrators would be apprehended.

Reports of the individuals that carried out this attack were still inconclusive, but one report in particular did seem feasible. The USSS and local district police, in surveying the surrounding property of the outer street limits, came across what appeared to be remnants of the two RPG launchers. They immediately obtained the camera footage of the area, and a white van along with a black Mercedes were identified as possible, and even probable, vehicles used in the attack.

The plates were listed as Virginia, and they had been broadcasted for all law enforcement personnel to be on the lookout (BOLO). FBI face recognition on at least three perpetrators who were in the vehicles was being evaluated. Doc asked FBI and CIA to forward copies of the facial recognition as soon as possible. Within three minutes, copies of each individual's face were sent to Doc, and he shared them with D/USSS and POTUS's enhanced security detail.

When Doc passed the same to the Professor, he responded right away that he believed he had seen one of the three individuals when they were in Abu Dhabi. The Professor recalled glancing at the man while he was walking away quickly from the hotel, right before the explosives detonated.

Doc forwarded that specific photograph to the CIA director, and they retrieved his file instantly. He was a major player in al-Qaeda and had a particular specialty with heavy weapons of all kinds. The BOLO was reissued with an emphasis on "armed and extremely dangerous." All Customs and Immigration access and egress entries were contacted directly to see if they had any photographs in the past couple of days and weeks that might not have made it into the security net yet.

After an hour, they got a hit that showed a similar-looking individual arriving at John F. Kennedy Airport five days prior. Doc said that he would bet this al-Qaeda heavy weapons specialist was the one who fired the second RPG.

Doc looked at the D/USSS and said that unfortunately, it would be his opinion that this attack would not be the last. POTUS said, "Wait a minute. What makes you so sure of that?"

The Professor spoke up and said, "Sir, it remains that the operational mastermind does not appear to be in this group."

The thick and reinforced glass in the Oval Office would have normally withstood the blast (if there was not another RPG used). The second, following RPG hit the exact spot that the first did, and that accomplished the breach. It was very smart. Hence, that is why the Professor and Doc knew the mastermind had borrowed from al-Qaeda their best heavy weapons specialist.

Doc requested that NSA tap into their cell towers in the area—the FBI had just recovered a cell phone that had been thrown to the ground prior to the vehicles departing the scene.

He reviewed where things stood in his mind: some new FBI footage showed that the youngest individual in the group could be seen throwing the cell covertly away as they were all rushing to get out of the hot zone. NSA scrubbed the contents of the cell phone. They not only got some very interesting foreign telephone numbers, but a few stored voice conversations and unopened voicemails as well.

The NSA had just coordinated with the CIA, and they together were finding some actual safe houses that might have been used for this attack. The FBI had already dispatched surveillance teams. The couple of havens that had been compromised were being turned over inch by inch to collect intelligence. Also, an important piece had surfaced from the CIA: that al-Qaeda and ISIS were somehow joined in this frenzy. The FBI and CIA were still scratching their heads for who was the top dog in this fight, as that still remained a major concern. The NSA had also advised that the chatter was so high that there definitely appeared to be a secondary attack coming, or perhaps the first was really just a taste of what was yet to come.

CHAPTER THIRTY-TWO

# A TASTE OF THE PRESENT AND THE POSSIBLE FUTURE

LAW ENFORCEMENT AND THE INTELLIGENCE community were operating on all shifts, searching for the mastermind and trying to determine if he was acting in the U.S. or if he was out of the country. POTUS called for a situation room meeting to bring everyone up to date and to have all of his advisers providing their tactical and strategic opinions. POTUS opened it by noting that he would be giving a report to the nation in about two hours to calm citizens and assure them that their government was operating at all levels for their safety.

POTUS looked over to the SecDef and director of Homeland Security and said that he wanted to see an appearance of force both inside and outside of the country. SecDef indicated that all troops abroad had been activated to a higher level of security readiness. The Homeland Security director stated the same regarding shopping malls and schools. The Secretary of State also added that all U.S. embassies and consulates had increased their security postures. The national security advisor said that this was a real shock for the people and a brief speech would go a long way toward making them feel safer and more secure.

POTUS thanked everyone and said to continue to compliment the outstanding officers in their respective jobs. "Let them know that the speed of their reaction to this attack has been and will continue to be the key."

All in the room rose and departed. POTUS then asked that the Secretary of State, SecDef, the Director of CIA, and the Director of NSA stay behind. D/USSS and Doc were then asked to join the small group already in the room.

POTUS asked the attendees for their reactions to this close call, but first, they would have a brief moment of prayer for the deceased NDI. POTUS then looked at the Professor and said that since he was, in all fairness, the first one to determine this attack was going to occur, he could be the first one to have the floor.

POTUS looked around the room and saw some nervous faces. So he softly raised his hand and then said to the Professor (and Doc), "Could you guys the next time just please let us know a few more minutes ahead of schedule so that we can all get the hell out of the Oval Office?" Everyone in the room busted out laughing, and it went a long way toward providing some relief.

POTUS then added that from now on, the D/USSS was going to be his double, so the real POTUS could run out the nearest door when he heard any noise at all. The group all laughed again, and one or two had a tear running down their faces.

The Professor said that he thought that the mastermind was in the U.S. and his particular support structure had been good enough to keep him from being detected. He maintained his opinion on the fact that the attack, while not successful in taking out POTUS, certainly achieved one of the most desired effects—the mastermind's actions garnering worldwide attention. Next, ISIS had jumped into this situation in support of the mastermind.

"From an intelligence perspective," D/CIA said, "this tells us two things: POTUS is going to be attacked again, and that there will be a major terrorist event on our soil (which may simply serve to be a disguise or camouflage) as a way to actually 'get' to POTUS. Additionally, this may mean that this first attack by the mastermind was just a preliminary move and that the mastermind has been accepted and welcomed into the al-Qaeda family to the extent that ISIS is trying to recruit the mastermind into its own structure."

The Professor nodded his head in agreement, looked at POTUS, and said the clear acceptance of the mastermind so quickly meant that this first attack indeed was just that and the mastermind had probably already told or relayed to both al-Qaeda and ISIS that his second plan was going to be the impressive one and that it would "shake the world."

SecDef said that he would note that the U.S. population, as well as much of the world population, seemed to believe that the terrorist groups out there had broken up and were no longer a threat. "However, this is wishful thinking. They have just been dormant for a while, licking their wounds, studying their past mistakes, and accruing new and more financial means. Their attacks will, with time, become standard in their endless thirst for their own homeland in the Middle East."

D/NSA indicated that the chatter remained at a fever pitch that would definitely support all of the previous assumptions.

POTUS leaned forward and asked, "Why target me specifically?"

Doc said that in their world, POTUS was the head of the snake. He looked at the Professor, who said he would defer some of his thinking on this matter to Doc, as he was the true expert in this arena. However, he would start with a suggestion.

POTUS, to retain his personal security and safety, must successfully be seen as continuing his work for the country but needed to at the same time move himself into a fake bubble. All of his major events that he must attend could proceed; however, a couple of them should be setups so that they appeared the same as others on the surface but were handled quite differently.

The D/CIA noted that they needed to create a Hollywood version of things that actually appeared real but were just standing cardboards and fake background buildings. SecDef said this reminded him of the old World War II trick where inflated tanks and weapons passed as real from the air.

The Professor looked at POTUS and said that if he were in POTUS's shoes, he would order Doc to be his temporary "body guy" while keeping his superb USSS special agent in charge (SAIC) and his enhanced security detail with him as well. The D/USSS spoke up and relayed that he thought that was an excellent suggestion and one that he and his team would embrace given Doc's record to date.

The Professor looked at the SecDef directly and said he would also recommend and apply in deep background one or more of the Special Operations Forces (SOF) teams that so skillfully covered Doc's tail abroad.

"Lastly, at least two of the SOF operatives should be assigned to your spouse and children, again in deep background, just as a precaution." The Professor would personally work on some of the Hollywood sets. He added that he would pass them on to Doc and the USSS director so that the SAIC, who led POTUS's personal protective detail every day, could decide which would be of value to securing POTUS at any given event. POTUS looked at them all and said he was hereby ordering everyone to proceed as the Professor had said.

# CHAPTER THIRTY-THREE

# THE CHASE IS ON

THE PROFESSOR AND DOC SPOKE for a few minutes. Doc thanked the Professor so very much, and in turn, the Professor laughed. The Professor said he was going to stay at a local hotel and he would get a room for Doc just in case he ever needed it. Doc said the first thing he was going to do was have the USSS put two security escorts with the Professor 24/7. The Professor said it was not necessary, but Doc said he would not be able to sleep if he did anything otherwise and besides, he would also not be sleeping any-ways. They knew they would remain in close touch and bid each other well.

Soon after, and at Doc's invitation, D/USSS and the SAIC joined him in his office. Doc closed the door and said that first of all, he did not want to be in the way of their daily operations. He understood that he did not run the show. The director said it wasn't an issue, and that, by the way, Doc's co-tackle of POTUS in the Oval Office had been quite good. Doc laughed and said he was just trying to make sure the director was OK too since he had POTUS fully covered. The director chuckled on his way out.

Once the door was closed, SAIC was all business. He gave Doc an encrypted cell with up-to-date copies of POTUS's schedule. He said Doc would automatically be seeing them when any changes occurred—not uncommon. He also handed Doc the lapel pins, secure radio, earpiece, code words, and a firearm and badge for every day and every trip that would provide him with unlimited access inside and outside the detail at any time.

Doc looked over to the SAIC and asked if this office they were in now, which had very considerable space, was available for the both of them. The SAIC said no, that it was just selected for him alone. Doc said that it was now one third his too, and any of the remaining third was available when he thought any of the detail agents needed to catch a few minutes of sleep. The SAIC smiled and said that all of this was to be confidential; Doc smiled too and said, "Of course."

The SAIC asked Doc how he wanted to "be in play." Doc said that he would like to always be behind the agent on POTUS's six o'clock. If the SAIC was on POTUS's rear, Doc said he wanted to be on SAIC's rear or six o'clock at that time. If at any time the other agents were at POTUS's side, Doc wanted to take up the position of being on POTUS's six o'clock. When inside a vehicle with SAIC or another agent in the "hot seat," Doc wanted to be on the front right side of the vehicle immediately behind the limousine that held POTUS, not in the decoy limousine.

The SAIC said, "Is that it?"

Doc said yes, but with one other exception.

Doc said that he would need some flexibility at times. The SAIC said it would not be a problem. If Doc had to depart his position, the only stipulation the SAIC would have would be to advise him (or again the ASAIC) of the potential threat once he was making his move. The SAIC will then make the call on whether they will or will not lift POTUS off the perceived "X" to a safer location as soon as was possible. Doc said that he understood the stipulation and he would follow it to the letter.

The SAIC told Doc that it might take a day or two to get acclimated, but as there was no time like the present, they would be on a scheduled movement in three hours. Doc walked with the SAIC to the basement, and the SAIC introduced each agent on duty to him. Doc said he appreciated it. Doc was at the vehicles along with the other agents on time, and when POTUS got into the limousine, Doc was told that he would be in the real following vehicle's front seat. Doc jumped in with the other agents, and they traveled for a couple of hours to Charlottesville, Virginia, for a speech POTUS was giving at the university. When the motorcade arrived, the advance agents and the local police and state troopers were all surrounding POTUS on the outer ring. Doc got out and looked for the SAIC and joined his rear position.

POTUS went on stage to an enormous audience. They did not stop clapping for twenty minutes. POTUS looked truly touched and then began his speech. His public relations people said that it was very important for him to show himself in person for the nation, but Doc privately thought it was too early and the others won by their votes.

While POTUS was giving a rousing speech about America's resilience, Doc and the other security detail agents were scanning the crowd for abnormalities. Doc was off the stage but right on the SAIC's six o'clock. However, when he did a quick scan on their arrival, someone in the crowd caught his eye.

Once onstage, Doc saw the person again—definitely female. He kept asking himself why he had zeroed in on her in the first place. Doc then heard on his secure radio from the detail team that they had received a report from law enforcement (e.g., the FBI) that one of their subjects, a known ISIS member, was under surveillance and had successfully flown the coop.

The female was identified as being in her twenties. She might have headed south to the Charlottesville area and was the subject of a BOLO of the armed and dangerous variety. Doc then realized that the woman he had focused on, wearing a hooded robe with a hijab, was suddenly a very ripe candidate.

Doc went onto the secure single radio channel for the SAIC and said he was going to take a walk and would keep him advised. The SAIC nodded and asked Doc what had gotten his attention. Doc replied that he believed the BOLO just broadcasted was quite possibly in the building and mingling with the crowd. He was in motion now to find her, and he believed that she could be a bomber.

SAIC said, "Roger that," and he ordered the detail to contract slightly but discreetly on POTUS and his space. He then ordered to prepare, just prepare, at this time for a fast removal. The SAIC said to stand ready and go only if he gave his signal. The respective detail leaders and the agents all reported in, saying, "Copy," and, "Standing by."

Meanwhile, Doc was swiftly roaming the crowd in only the first few rows. If a true bomber, she would definitely be trying to get as close as possible to POTUS.

As he continued the search, Doc used his secure cell to contact his brother SOF snipers who were positioned at the top of the auditorium. He rapidly filled them in and said that if he found the BOLO, he was going to take her down. If they observed any other male or female bomber(s), they were hereby ordered to take them with headshots within the facial triangle. When someone was shot in the facial triangle, there was no autonomic clenching on a detonator. Doc said it officially was for the record since he made the call. The snipers knew this well but very much appreciated the verbal orders being recorded. It meant that Doc would take the heat if the shots were misplaced and the bomb successfully exploded. Doc also knew that these two particular snipers never missed anyway.

Doc thought the only other place that the potential bomber could be was in the greenroom, the room used by major guests and speakers to freshen up before and after events. When Doc reached it, he saw two law enforcement officers lying on the ground. Both had been shot in the head. Doc felt for their pulses but knew they were already dead.

Doc carefully stepped toward the greenroom door but thought it unlikely she would be inside. She was probably in a hiding spot nearby. Doc took a long step backward, very softly, and briefed the SAIC of the situation. The SAIC asked Doc what he thought he should do. Doc replied he should give the signal and then approach POTUS on the podium and whisper into his ear to wave and say he had just learned he was needed immediately back in Washington. Then, SAIC should pick him up by his armpits. Not too much but just enough so that it still appeared that he was walking on his own. SAIC was to get him to the safe haven now.

Doc took a couple of steps and saw the bomber. She was well within reach, and he saw that she was praying devoutly and was in a fugue like state. Doc saw the detonator in her right hand, her chest filled with a ton of explosives. He jumped on her and wrapped his arms and weight as tightly as he could around her body. He grabbed the detonator from her hand while continuing to keep all of her body parts frozen in place.

She resumed praying to Allah and that was fine with him. In another three minutes, a cadre of USSS agents showed up at the greenroom door, and Doc yelled at them to get the hell out of there—this woman had an ultra-bomb that could detonate at any time.

The team leader yelled at the other USSS agents and the local and state police to do as the man ordered. On the radio, he commanded the USSS bomb squad to get there pronto. The USSS team leader peeked around the corner at Doc and said he was staying regardless of orders because in the USSS, they stuck together. The bomb tech arrived, looked at the situation, and quietly cursed to himself.

Doc gave them a brief on the woman bomber and how he had snatched the detonator. The woman kept mindlessly singing her prayers. The tech got on the line and asked for the most senior and experienced bomb supervisor they had and to get there instantly.

# CHAPTER THIRTY-FOUR

# A RELATIVELY STICKY SITUATION

DOC ROLLED HIS EYES AND told the USSS team leader that he and this other guy really should get going. The tech said, "Good luck," and left, but the team leader didn't move. Doc called him a rock head, and the TL said yes, he'd been called that once or twice before. Doc asked him about the other two bombers that the tech had mentioned, and the TL said that both of them were killed by a couple of badass SOF snipers; they hit each bomber individually at exactly the same spot—a quarter of an inch up from the bridge of the nose.

Two bomb specialists showed up, looked at Doc and the girl, and said, "Ah, shit," in tandem.

Doc told them that the bomber may or may not have a firearm. Someone had killed the two policemen, and he would put her at the top of the list. The first specialist said he had a lot of experience, and the second specialist, a pretty woman, said that what she lacked in experience, she made up for in smarts. Doc said he sure felt better already, but he was not sure if he should pick one of them and tell the other to get the hell out. They said it so happened that they were professionally attached so they could learn from each other.

Doc asked who was the better of the two, and they both pointed at each other. The female bomb specialist said that she had a question for him. Doc said, "Go ahead."

She asked what Doc was doing wrapping himself around this pretty young girl in the first place. Doc said that it was a trick that the Israelis taught him a decade ago—a strong bear hug to keep the bomber from detonating. She asked him if he remembered exactly what he was supposed to do when the bomb was being deactivated.

Doc said, "Well, we never really got to that portion of the training." Both specialists kept talking back and forth to him while cutting wires and slowly moving the ones that could or should not be cut.

After an hour, the woman said, "Watch this," and with a bit of fanfare, she cut one more wire. With that, Doc had the all clear. He released his grip and immediately grabbed a handgun from the bomber's belt and moved away. The specialists slowly put a straitjacket on the young woman.

The TL asked the specialists to just cuff her ankle and stay really close to her for a minute. Doc walked over to him and said that she needed to be brought to D.C. for immediate interrogation. "There are some diamonds in that little head of hers, and it is imperative that we only use the 'soft' approach."

The specialists placed a rubber bib into the bomber's mouth to prevent her from biting her own tongue off and bleeding to death. The TL looked at Doc, smiled, and said, "You sure are demanding and even a little gruesome."

Doc smiled back and said, "You have no idea."

The TL said they should get a beer sometime—of course only when they were off duty—and Doc said he could count on it.

Doc went outside, and a USSS agent approached him and said that he was ordered to escort him to a waiting chopper to head to Camp David. On arrival, other agents greeted Doc, all with heavy weapons. Doc was told that the SAIC and POTUS, and, not surprisingly, the Professor, required his presence immediately. Doc could see POTUS's chief of staff, the D/USSS, D/CIA and acting NDI, the NSA director, and SecDef on the live feed when he entered.

After Doc gave his briefing, the D/CIA and the D/NSA revealed that the bomber was in a padded cell room at St. Elizabeth's Hospital around the clock and surrounded by USSS and the FBI. Her knowledge base and her past experiences of various attacks on entities in Syria and Iraq were high quality. She had asked for Doc and the Professor specifically and had said that she would be willing to provide them and them alone with substantial intelligence to increase her own chances of survival.

The director of NSA also noted that they'd tracked down many of her cell phone calls. She was well connected to both ISIS and al-Qaeda. She had been heard explicitly saying that her highest supervisor wanted POTUS killed and he wanted it done very soon.

She also was heard saying that the supervisor was obsessed with eliminating the American president at all costs.

POTUS leaned into to the table and said, "OK—it is true that I am not perfect and a few people really do not care for my style." There was laughter all around.

SecDef noted that if this woman could get them just a little more intelligence on the mastermind, he was confident that the DOD could eradicate him and all of his sorry friends. The SAIC and the D/USSS agreed.

Afterward, Doc went to his designated cabin to catch some rest. About five minutes later, SAIC knocked on his door. Doc said that if a beautiful woman was at the door, she could come in, but everyone else should go away. The SAIC entered the room with a grin. Doc motioned to a chair and the SAIC sat down. He started to thank Doc. Doc shook his head and waved it away. Doc said he was just glad to see that almost everything came together and that they all got their behinds out.

The SAIC started telling Doc that he had filled POTUS in on the events of the evening, but Doc just started to whistle out loud. SAIC said that if Doc was not going to listen to anything he had to say, then he should know, officially and unofficially, that the USSS now referred to him in upper-case letters as a True Hard-Ass. Doc laughed hard and threw a pillow at him. Doc then fell asleep, and the SAIC left the room after putting a blanket on him and whispering a curt *thank-you.*

# CHAPTER THIRTY-FIVE

# THE MASTERMIND MAKES A MISTAKE

DOC SLEPT THROUGH THE NIGHT and then took off early to go to the hospital. Within an hour, two USSS agents picked up the Professor at his hotel as well.

Once at the hospital, Doc found the woman's room, which had a whole group of USSS, FBI, CIA, and D.C. police around it. A nurse and doctor also sat nearby in case she tried to kill herself. Doc and the Professor went into the room and introduced themselves, and she did the same.

She seemed strong and ready to engage. The Professor spoke to her in Arabic and, surprised, she answered in the same language. She said that he was known and admired in many of her circles. The Professor asked if by that she meant ISIS and al-Qaeda, and she said yes right away.

The Professor (and Doc) looked at her directly and noted numerous scars on her body. Doc looked at her and said that life has not been kind to her. She nodded her head matter-of-factly.

The woman asked what they believed her fate was going to be. The Professor looked over to Doc and nodded.

Doc told her that she was not going to live much longer, but long enough for her to provide the information they needed—and would get either way over time. But she would have the time to decide if perhaps she had a loved one. And if so, they would and could take care of that loved one for the rest of their life. The woman looked at the Professor and asked him if he thought what Doc had just said was true. The Professor said that what his colleague just described was a mathematical certainty. The Professor told her to make her decision here and now. "There are no other paths for you."

The woman asked what they needed from her. Doc said that a start would be revealing her and her supervisor's real names, plus her husband's name and the identities of each of her brothers and sisters in ISIS or al-Qaeda. "If your supervisor is here," he went on, "then what is his address or safe haven? Is he al-Qaeda or is he ISIS, and why is he trying to kill the president?"

She leaned forward. "My name is simply the name that I gave. However, the supervisor is a man named Mohammed Ali Kamiah."

The Professor said the names meant "flawlessness and perfection," and she said, "Yes, he is a very highly educated and intellectual scholar like you. Mohammed," she said, "is also very much like you in his ways, but he is in a much, much different field."

The Professor asked what exactly that was. She said that it had to do with nuclear plants and demolitions and that he studied them both as a domestic and foreign consultant around the world. He was originally from Pakistan, had lived there most of his life, and he wanted to destroy the U.S. president on behalf of both al-Qaeda and ISIS. He was also her husband, and they were married when she was only twelve years old. She added that he had beaten her endless times and even tortured her over the years. That was why she offered to be a bomber and martyr; she just wanted to die.

Doc asked if he, Mohammed, was still in the U.S. She said yes; they had come a few weeks ago at the direction of al-Qaeda. She went on to say that previously, they had been in Abu Dhabi, and Doc and the Professor exchanged glances. Doc asked where they stayed, and she said it was an unknown family's house in Maryland.

She said that she was not afraid of dying but loved her younger sister, who was about eighteen and also a part of the mission. Her sister was also studying nuclear plants and bomb-making devices. Doc asked if she was also al-Qaeda on this mission, and the woman said yes.

Doc asked if her husband was acting on behalf of al-Qaeda on this mission, and she said yes. Doc asked where her husband and sister were now. She said they might be at a new safe haven address in Maryland; she did not know for sure, but her sister had quietly whispered to her, a week ago in confidence, about it being a very, very important place for her and her uncle. Doc said, "Exactly where in Maryland?" but the woman said she did not know specifically. However, her sister did give her an address. It was in the vicinity of Camp David.

The Professor looked at Doc with a very serious face that meant "call now."

He whispered, "Tell the advisers this is first-line stuff and not to be passed down the chain yet—but they have to be ready now."

Doc then looked at the woman and said casually that he had to use the bathroom. As he left the room, he could hear the Professor switching to Arabic to get the information they needed.

Doc used his secure cell outside of the room to reach the SAIC. He answered instantly, and Doc told him that he needed to batten down the facility to the maximum. Two or more assassins were vectoring in on their location. The SAIC said they were already set to rock and roll. Doc said he was sending him a secure email copy of the content of their interrogation so far. Doc said his air transport needed to be ready to go within a second's notice. SAIC said, "Roger that, and we are," then yelled a code word to the ASAIC, and Doc could then hear all hell breaking loose in the background as the choppers got themselves sorted.

Doc said that POTUS would need to also read the content as well, but Doc said to the SAIC that he should hand carry it to him instead of emailing, as a precaution. POTUS would, of course, have endless questions, but Doc said to tell him that the Professor was trying to confirm and nail down if a nuclear aspect was in play. The FBI and the CIA were all over these statements, and the FBI takedown teams were in action. NSA had confirmed an even higher chatter level but did not yet have any ears on the primary or the sister.

Doc elaborated. "The two main players are nuclear plant specialists. They are a Pakistani male native and his sister-in-law. They have left their last safe haven and are allegedly going to an address that somehow, and here's the kicker, matches the general vicinity of Camp David.

The SAIC said they were in full ready mode and prepared to boogie out to one of their preset caves should the need arise. Doc said, "Roger that," and added that, "By the way, if there is an attack, try to keep one of the attackers alive for me. All and any additional interrogations can be of great value." The SAIC said, "Good copy on that," and then cut the line.

The D/CIA reached out to Doc said that the CIA had confirmed Mohammed did exist and that he was apparently brilliant. The director said that based on all of their over-seas sources and their penetrations, they concurred that he was still in the U.S. The FBI called in and said that their takedown teams had successfully captured approximately thirty al-Qaeda and ISIS safe havens. However, the primary and the sister still remained unaccounted for. The Bureau's very best counterterrorist agents were interrogating those in custody and would forward any new developments in real time.

Doc looked at the Professor as he was talking to the bomber. Doc was on the other side of the glass panel, and he prayed that the Professor could somehow confirm that a nuclear piece was not part of the equation. Doc had a nag-ging feeling that something was missing; some final piece of the puzzle was not yet in place.

To Doc, it felt like there was something strange about the potential nuclear devices. The woman had said ear-lier that Mohammed knew nuclear power plants and explosives intimately. The Professor said that she had also noted to him that Mohammed always played "the role of an expert consultant." In other words, Mohammed never used the term "nuclear bomb" as it caused people in the plant building(s) to feel frightened. So he always used the term "nuclear plant"—which always seemed to keep them at ease. She also said that it always served Mohammed with getting access into any of the facilities without any difficulty. The Professor then stepped out of the room and told her to get some rest.

The Professor then asked Doc, "Remember way back when they were talking at the Hudson Valley property about who was behind the attacks? My mathematical equations and computations back then at that time showed that POTUS, and not myself, was the target."

Doc said yes, he recalled that deduction. The Professor recalled that Doc had then also said that it was most likely that the mastermind would go after a nuclear decoy of sorts—but the real target would only appear to be POTUS. The Professor paused slightly. He then told Doc that they had to now understand and realize that the bull's-eye was from the very beginning not POTUS. All of the attacks on POTUS to date were a continual *diversion*.

Doc said to the Professor that the real target was definitely the nuclear power plant. They—Mohammed and his most senior superiors—had over time used careful planning and explored every inch of that particular nuclear power plant. They ultimately had deemed it to be the perfect choice for destroying an enormous chunk of America and showing the world their true power.

The Professor said, "Yes, that is correct; we actually had the mathematical numbers in the wrong order." The Professor said again that the assassination attempts were themselves actually "decoys," and the real target was and always had been a highly defined nuclear "power" plant that could and would detonate and destroy almost the entire East Coast of America at a minimum.

The Professor said that any decoy of real value had to have believable circumstances. And if any of the attacks were successful—and all had been clearly close to the mark—than that would simply be a major bonus.

The Professor continued to mentally revise his mathematical computations. He told Doc that it had to be the case. The order, aka decoy, was actually reversed. The attempted assassinations were camouflaged every step of the way. The Russian general whom the al-Qaeda sniper had called during his interrogation was not the key. It was just the initial commencement of the attacks by Mohammed.

This meant that the al-Qaeda sniper that had mistakenly attempted to kill the Professor at the New York Hudson safe haven was a very high–level professional. He just did not know that the true Professor (and Doc) was in China— at the other end of the globe. The AQ sniper had gone to his death leaving false intelligence within the interrogation. His psychological profile—an al-Qaeda religious fanatic—showed that he followed his duties of Mohammed to the letter.

Doc and the Professor spent a minute or so consuming the facts. Both of them also realized that Mohammed was indeed a mastermind and had been treating them all as puppets. The Professor now had no doubt at all about the nuclear power plant and was going to confirm it within the next few moments. Doc mentally reviewed every possible aspect of how he was going to capture Mohammed and then kill him—before he (and his al-Qaeda and ISIS brothers and sisters) was able to activate his diabolical plan.

One thing was for sure—this mastermind had made a critical error. The Professor and Doc now knew the chessboard completely. They would hunt him down, and he would be destroyed, and his senior colleagues back home had better run for cover.

The Professor picked up the secure line and said that he needed to get in touch with the Department of Energy (DOE) secretary urgently. When the secretary picked up the secure phone, the Professor said there was no time to explain, but could he, or one of his experts, tell the Professor the location of the nearest nuclear plant? The Secretary said that would be the Calvin River Nuclear Power Plant.

The Professor thanked him and then asked him to please quietly have his people conduct an immediate inspection of that plant and get the results back to the Professor as soon as he could. The secretary said to the Professor that for anyone else, he would have reservations, but he would do it instantly because the Professor was the one requesting it; that was more than enough for him.

Doc said that he was going back into the room to find out if the female bomber knew which nuclear plant was the target. Inside the room, he looked at the woman and said that he and the Professor apologized very much for the interruption. Could she please continue with sharing her amazing knowledge and remarkable forethought?

The woman seemed pleased at the apology and nodded. Doc asked if he was correct that the address her sister had told her about confidently was unknown to her uncle. The woman nodded. Doc said that this would seem to mean that she was sure of it herself. Her sister had gotten it somehow from Mohammed, whether he knew it or not. The woman immediately said that he was correct because the only place she could have come across it was from her husband.

Doc asked why, and she responded that Mohammed was a very volatile person who demanded the tightest security. Doc thanked her for the explanation and went on to say that he had taken a short moment to look up that address in Maryland and noticed a nuclear plant nearby.

Doc said that he could not remember the name of the plant and wondered also if she knew whether her husband and sister had ever consulted there as part of their work. The woman said that if she recalled correctly, they did, because they talked about it when they were in the basement.

It was called something like Calvin. Doc nodded and said it would be helpful to know if she saw any equipment or tools or explosives when she was listening to them. She said that she did see some explosives, just like what they put on her when she was at the university. Doc asked if there was anything else she saw or could remember, and the woman said that Mohammed carried a leather tool case with a false bottom.

He also would wear a jacket that had some sort of hidden pocket but would always take it off when anyone checked him. The woman said, "He and my sister have something similar in their shoes; they even have something in their two back teeth."

# CHAPTER THIRTY-SIX

# VISIONS FROM THE PAST: THREE-MILE ISLAND

DOC STEPPED OUT OF THE room and used his secure line to reach the SAIC, who said that the USSS was reviewing Doc's latest debriefing. Doc said he understood but was calling him because the targeted plant was not that far from Camp David. POTUS needed to be moved to a more remote location.

The SAIC simply said, "Good copy." Doc heard him yelling another codeword, and then everything went on automatic. POTUS was removed from the secure room and hoisted by several agents into a tunnel that led to the helicopter pad that was in a hangar but ready to roll—the USSS also had three other identical choppers ready to depart as diversions. As all the choppers were flying their specified routes, a single missile was launched from somewhere in the woods nearby.

The pilots immediately recognized the hostile missile and took more extensive evasive actions, with one exception. One of the choppers was loaded with heavy munitions, and that chopper flew directly into the missile source area and then laid down massive amounts of firepower. A stream of USSS drones were, at the same time, fired at by about two dozen terrorists that were now running out of the woods toward the president's usual cabin. USSS tactical teams, set up in different locations, took most of the terrorists down.

A large number of highly trained attack dogs had now been released into the woods. One took down a female terrorist that had been hiding in the opening of a large tree trunk. One of the dog's handlers spotted her while the canine was busy ripping flesh out of her leg. When so ordered, the dog sat, but remained completely focused on the woman. On one command, the dog would eagerly rip her apart.

The USSS agent, the dog's handler, had her weapon zeroed in on the triangle of the terrorist's face. The agent scanned the area, saw no one else, and then shot a bullet past the terrorist's ear—a warning shot.

The agent then told her if she wished to stay alive, she would strip her clothes off now. The dog kept a nice growl going while the agent tested the terrorist via a noninvasive device that looked under the skin for any devices imbedded in her body. The agent told her to redress and then lie down on the ground and stay totally still. She suspected the woman might be the team leader of the entire attack.

Meanwhile, Doc was informed by the SAIC that POTUS was fully secure and finally relaxing after a rather bumpy ride due to an attack back home at the camp. Things were now under control. Doc said he rogered that and to please have his people reach out once they had any new information. The SAIC said that the only terrorist that was still alive was a female and she might be the leader. Doc asked if they had already removed any devices on her person, and the SAIC said they had indeed. He said, "Excellent—she needs to be flown to Saint Elizabeth's Hospital ASAP, and it is urgent." Doc then added that the protocol should be exactly, repeat exactly, the same as was implemented for the UVA female terrorist who was now in custody. The SAIC said he figured as much and the flight would be in motion shortly.

Doc gave a long exhale and said they'd just gotten lucky.

The SAIC nodded. "Well, keep that luck coming and be safe."

Doc told the Professor that POTUS had been moved from Camp David, was now secure, and might have some good news as one of the terrorists, who was the only one to have survived, might be the "sister." The Professor raised an eyebrow.

The Professor then took an urgent secure call from the secretary of DOE, who told the Professor that the nuclear plant inspection that he had requested was started but it had to stop because there was apparently a hostage situation. The Professor told the secretary to stand by as his call was being transferred to the White House situation room and POTUS would also join them from another site. Once the POTUS was online, which he and his advisers (SecDef, Homeland Security, FBI, CIA, and NSA) would soon be, the White House situation room would be ready. The DOE secretary was to give them all a briefing on the current situation. POTUS would be using the audio and video at a separate location for security purposes.

POTUS then came online. He asked the DOE secretary to give them an update on the hostage situation. Once the

DOE secretary was finished, he was also asked the size of the plant, the number of people the plant employed, the number that existed this very moment inside the plant, and if an explosion occurred, how wide a dispersal of the radiation would be to the area. All of the answers to POTUS's questions by the secretary were not good—ones either in each of the specific categories or overall terms of the situation. POTUS then turned to the Professor and Doc and asked, "Where do we stand with this new angle?"

The Professor then responded to POTUS by saying they were strongly convinced that the hostage-taker was the mastermind.

Additionally, the Professor stated that both he and Doc were now convinced that the attacks on Camp David and his helicopter transportation were meant solely as a decoy to give this mastermind and his terrorist brethren the time they needed to take over the nuclear plant—which had been their objective from the beginning. Moreover, the mastermind was, in all likelihood, going to request an exit for himself, to join his al-Qaeda and ISIS leaders, prior to exploding the nuclear plant in Maryland.

Homeland Security provided a rough figure of the number of people that would have to be evacuated and the scale of the operation if it was ordered. The FBI provided the number of agents that they could deploy but carefully qualified the time it would likely take as much longer. POTUS thanked them and said they could leave but to stand by for any new developments and above all, to keep this information to themselves only.

Doc, who was still on site in St. Elizabeth's, stepped outside and saw the USSS agent and a woman in chains. The one agent who was holding onto the woman looked over at him. He walked over and asked if she was the agent to have captured this woman, and she nodded. He asked if they still had the helicopter on the roof, and she confirmed that they did and that it was standing by. Doc introduced himself to the agents and said that they could watch through the glass.

He took hold of the woman and walked her into the room that belonged to the failed bomber. The bomber and her sister were frozen in time when they saw each other and both began to cry. Doc told them to sit down, and they moved slowly but did what he said. Doc looked at the sister and said he had to know right then if she was going to cooperate.

The bomber shook her head yes, telling her to do so. The sister wiped away the tears and said, "What do you want?"

Doc said to her, "Is your uncle at the nuclear plant now?" and she said yes.

"Is your uncle's mission to blow up the plant?"

She said yes it was and he would do so.

"How many operatives are there right now and in the surrounding area?"

Besides her uncle, there were twenty-four jihadists, and they were all planning to die.

"Does your uncle have any medical conditions?"

She said that he had a heart condition but he was not taking his medicine because he no longer felt the need for it.

"Does your uncle love you and does he love his wife?"

She said that he did not love his wife but he did love her. The bomber nodded her head too to indicate that her sister was telling the truth.

Doc asked, "Would your uncle die for you instead of for jihad?"

The sister said that yes, she believed that he would do that if she asked him to. Doc looked directly into the sister's eyes and asked her, "Would you do that to save your sister who is here now? Would you give up the jihad for your sister like your sister asked us to do for you?"

She looked at the bomber and said yes, she, too, would do that for her.

Doc said he would need her to come with him, to ask the mastermind in person, if he would give up jihad in favor for his love for her. The sister said that she would do so. Doc said OK.

He said he had two more last questions: Was the current leader of al-Qaeda the one that her uncle worked for? She said yes. Did she know of any other attacks or missions in the U.S. now or abroad? She said no, that the only real one was the nuclear power plant.

Doc said they needed to go now. The sisters hugged, and he took her back outside and asked the USSS agents to watch her. Doc walked over to the secure line where the Professor was sitting and waiting. Doc said that it was confirmed that the mastermind, Mohammed Ali Kamiah (and twenty-four Jihadists) were there now in the nuclear plant.

Doc looked over to the Professor and then to POTUS. Then he looked over to the SecDef and asked him, "Sir, with respect, how fast could you muster the SOF teams that have supported me recently?" SecDef checked with the Chairman/JCS, who reported that they could be at the venue in one hour, which would coincide with the sunset and silent requirements of the helicopter choppers. The general looked at POTUS, who said, "Make it happen under my order."

The general said to Chairman/JCS that Doc was the on-site commander and he would coordinate with the SOF team leaders once they both were on the ground. Chairman/JCS said roger that, and they would be there on time. The Professor looked at Doc and said to be exceedingly careful, as they definitely now knew whom they were up against with this guy. Doc nodded and said in this instance, he was going after this guy's heart, and he smiled.

Doc knew from the get-go that this strategy was a long shot. POTUS said that his country was counting on him and he, POTUS, was particularly counting on Doc sending this so-called "mastermind" and his colleagues all to hell.

Doc smiled again and said to POTUS, "Roger that!"

There was only room for Doc, the sister, and one other on the USSS. The female agent said she wanted to go. Doc said she could be a significant help but he had to ask if she was absolutely sure. She said it would be a walk in the park and took the final seat. The USSS pilots were briefed for the quiet arrival in the vicinity near the plant and the exact safe zone where Doc was going to meet the SOF team(s).

The USSS helicopter landed just as the evening dusk was settling into place in the woods. After two minutes, the SOF team leaders came walking out of nowhere and shook hands with Doc. The senior TL said, "You just cannot keep out of trouble, can you?"

Doc grinned and then introduced the USSS agent to him—and the sister.

The TL said he had been briefed; he and his operators were up to speed. He explained to Doc that he had five separate SOF teams in his hands and they were all operatives that Doc would have either heard or seen in the past couple of months.

Doc asked the TL if several of them were snipers, and he said, "Absolutely—Olympic level." The TL broke out a detailed map showing Doc and the USSS agent their planned approach and that each team was quietly already in motion. The TL also said that two of his Arabic-speaking SOF operatives had obtained the exact number (of the terrorists) by their count in the past fifteen minutes as twenty-four, repeat twenty-four, plus one not yet seen. As the TL was finishing the brief, he heard on his secure radio that all teams were now in place and ready; none had been detected.

The TL and the USSS agent watched him very carefully. Doc walked over to the sister, who was held by one of the USSS helicopter pilots. Doc nodded to him to back off, and the pilot left. Doc got much closer in her personal space and asked her if the twenty-four terrorists were on the perimeter inside the gates or if they were also inside the building. He told her that it was very important that she got this question right; he did not want his people surprised.

Doc also added that if she did not get this right, he would kill her slowly himself, as they stood here this very minute, until she was begging to die. A bluff, of course, but he made it sound convincing. She said, with her voice quivering, that with the exception of Mohammed, there was to be no one else in the building.

Mohammed did not want to take the chance that one or more of them would somehow screw up the plant detonation and ruin the mission. Doc looked at the TL and said, "You have a green light, right?" The senior TL got on the radio and said to all personnel that they were "good to go green, repeat, good to go green."

Within a total of five minutes, the snipers had taken out fifteen of the terrorists using silenced rounds. In another five minutes, the remaining nine terrorists were all down. Based on the added number of operatives that were available for each target—thanks to their sniper brethren having had such an admirable count—not one of the twenty-four terrorists got off a single shot. The remaining terrorists were taken down silently. The SOFs most likely killed them by knife and/or by breaking necks.

The USSS pilot had the sister in custody the whole time, and she was not informed on any of the TL's verbal reports. In fact, the pilot was also smart enough to not only keep her cuffed on both hands and feet and sitting down on the outside of the helicopter bars, but also had placed ear plugs and a large headset on her head so she actually heard nothing at all.

Doc told the TL to please deploy the teams in a silent defensive mode to see if there were any other terrorists in hiding. Doc told the snipers to stay in place. No one was found inside or outside of the perimeter.

Doc explained that the sisters' uncle, Mohamed Ali Kamiah, who was actually the mastermind, was the only one in the building and he had it fully rigged to explode. The real heavy lifting was about to begin. The senior TL and the USSS agent went a bit peaky but recovered quickly given Doc's statement, which they initially thought was a joke. Doc then decided that he was going to take his "sister" inside. He in turn would try to convince the mastermind to stand down. Doc knew that it was truly a waste of time, but it would possibly supply the sister a chance to convince him.

Doc then ordered the senior TL and all of his personnel in the five teams (with the exception of two snipers that Doc knew personally) to return to base. Furthermore, he ordered the USSS agent and the pilots return back to Camp

David ASAP. Doc said that he was officially taking over the custody of the sister.

The senior TL and the USSS agent were frozen for a minute or so and started to earnestly protest. Doc looked at both of them and said he had given them a direct order and it was not open to discussion. The last request he had was for the two SOF snipers to meet him on this hill. The USSS agents looked all shaken up, but they reluctantly moved away from the remaining mission as ordered and then went airborne.

Doc looked at the senior operational TL and said that he had not heard him tell anyone on the radio that he too was returning to base. The senior TL shrugged and said to Doc, "Where would the fun be in that?" Doc could not get him out of here with a steamroller even if he wanted to.

Besides, the senior TL said, those two SOF Olympian snipers he knew could not be left alone to their own devices. The TL smiled some more, then said he stayed so he could be sure that they were paying attention all the time while Doc was having a grand old time chasing around his mastermind in the building. Doc took a long moment looking at the TL, smiled, and then shook his head. He mumbled that the senior TL was almost as stubborn and as crazy as he was. The senior TL let out low laugh.

# CHAPTER THIRTY-SEVEN

# GETTING TO THE HEART OF THE MATTER

DOC TIED THE SISTER TO a large rock, went about three yards away, and consulted with the two snipers and the TL. They were the same guys that had worked their magic at the university attack. He had earlier briefed them both on the situation, and they volunteered but with one proviso: they would get to choose their own hiding spots.

To the remaining TL, Doc said it was imperative that he knew that the mastermind also had a very small leather case with about five glass ampules; he claimed they were for his (false) diabetes. Two tubes were actually filled with biological weapons, and the remaining three consisted of various chemicals weapons. The TL said to Doc: "Boy, you really know how to pick them."

The TL's job would be to locate and remove the biological and chemical weapons out of harm's way once the mastermind was taken out. TL said he would politely await Doc's call to enter, as he was, after all, a gentleman at heart.

Doc said, "Of course."

The snipers quietly jogged off to find direct or indirect access to get into the building. The earlier digital maps that had been provided to them, as they were flying on the choppers, were actually very helpful. Aside from gaining access, the digital maps also provided warnings; once they were inside the plant, the maps identified on each floor the explosive devices that had been inserted personally by Mohammed. What a guy!

Doc then took the sister's arm, and they walked together into the building like they were simply going to see a movie. Doc's approach was simple: Mohammed would have surely been watching the earlier shooting carnival outside, carefully looking out some of the windows alternately (as to avoid any sniper shots at himself), watching via the internal security cameras, or both. Regardless, it was certain that he was studiously watching the sister and Doc as they entered the building.

Once they were in the main lobby, the mastermind addressed them via the building's internal emergency broadcast system. They were told to go to the top floor— which was the fifth. The snipers looked at each other, both rolling their eyes as if they were laughing at their fate, and then proceeded carefully to floor number five covertly and in an ultra-quiet manner.

Doc and the sister got on the elevator and then got off on the fifth floor as directed. After another five minutes, the mastermind came out of a corridor with a sidearm and a long gun. He motioned and directed Doc to sit on the floor, and then he warmly greeted his sister. He complimented her profusely for the attack on the American Camp David. By the time the American president had run out like a little scared rabbit, the brave jihadist brothers and he were able to, almost effortlessly, take over the nuclear plant, send home all of the workers, and assume full control.

The sister looked at him and said, "Thank you for the compliment." She also added that not only did every one of the jihadists at Camp David die heroically—so had all of the brothers that had come here too. The mastermind said they were now with Allah, happy and satisfied that they had served him so well. He then said to her that they both would also see Allah together very soon.

What no one knew was that Doc had carried with him a small but extremely toxic poison device, and if he determined that this effort was hopeless, he would squeeze the poison out onto his palm and into the mastermind's skin. In that move, he would also break the woman's neck as he could not take the chance and gamble that she would change her mind. She could not be left to possibly detonate the explosives on her own after she saw Mohammed die. In a second or less they would both be dead.

The act would be highly risky for Doc, although he did have a temporary rubberized protective layer on his palm and fingers—not visible to the human eye. Once the poison was released, the toxin could potentially move into Doc's own skin; if so, he would die with the mastermind too. But Doc had already decided that he was definitely not going to let this so-called mastermind live in any case.

As for the snipers, Doc had shared this plan with them; they would serve as a backup, but if they were able to take a head shot at any time on the mastermind, they were authorized to do so as long as they did not miss the target; needless to say, it was only facial triangle head shots.

Odds of the woman being able to change the master-mind's mind were obviously extremely low, but this was to be expected. He did truly seem to love her deeply, however, and Doc was hoping it would somehow change his mindset now that he saw her again in person. The woman hugged him again and profusely cried on his shoulder. The master-mind appeared bewildered. He asked her what was wrong, as all had been exactly as planned. She looked into his eyes and said she could not do it. He looked at her and asked what she meant and told her that he would be the one to do it for both of them so she should not worry at all.

She shook her head away from him and said they needed to walk away from all this spilled blood and endless internal anger, as Allah did not really embrace it. She said that she had thought and prayed every minute since they arrived in America and she had seen that the people were kind and caring and did not deserve the avalanche of unlimited pain coming to them.

The mastermind paused, looked directly at his sister, and then shot her in the head. He looked completely pleased with himself and told Doc that they had done a good job of bending her mind in such a short time. However, he was very grateful to be able to send her to Allah so that her mind would be refreshed and his love would protect her.

Doc asked the mastermind if he could stand up. He told him that he knew his name was Mohammed and that his name was Doc. Mohammed waved his handgun at Doc, meaning that it was OK for him to stand up, as they were both men. Doc said that a good friend of his, a man known as the Professor, had asked him to send his best regards to Mohammed. The mastermind said that he was well acquainted with the man, and while he had never met him, he held him in true respect.

Doc said that from his optic, he and the Professor had a lot in common. "Although your areas of expertise are clearly in different fields, the Professor asked that you be told that he has read all of your work, and he considers it to be on a par with Albert Einstein. He said that like Einstein, yours is a true mastermind, and he wishes that he could meet with you in person one day."

Mohammed beamed and said he very much liked the title mastermind, so to please thank the Professor. Doc said to Mohammed that if he would like, Doc could put him through for a very quick telephone call, for a few short minutes, as the Professor dearly wanted to speak with him if he were agreeable. Doc said to him that he promised there would not be any tricks at all.

The mastermind said that it was truly a tempting offer and asked how he could make the call, as it would have to be a secure one for privacy.

Doc said they could use one of the lines on the counter behind him if that was satisfactory. The mastermind said that he had to be very careful since he knew that Doc must be a very senior warrior, since he had been the one chosen to bring the love of his own life here.

Doc said that he was not a senior in anything and that he had been selected simply because he had gotten the wrong side of a coin toss. The mastermind laughed out loud. Mohammed said OK, he would talk with the Professor, but he did not want to use any of the telephones in the building. Doc acted confused, and he said to Mohammed he could not think of anything else. Doc asked if he could take off his jacket because he was hot. Mohammed raised his gun and said to do so very carefully.

As Doc took off his jacket, Mohammed saw the cell phone on Doc's belt. Mohammed then said to call the Professor right now. Doc looked startled and began to ask how he could do that if he was not able to use the building phones. Mohammed smiled and said, "Look down at yourself."

Doc saw his cell phone and laughed at himself for not seeing it sooner, saying, "Of course." Doc then said he was a simple man, after all, and was quite frightened to be honest.

The mastermind then smirked at Doc and said, "Why don't you make the call on your cell phone right now?"

Doc slowly punched in the numbers, heard it ringing, and then asked for the Professor with the speakerphone on for all to hear. Doc heard the Professor say hello. Doc told the Professor that this was his lucky day as the mastermind was willing to talk with him. The Professor said he would be deeply honored. Doc said that he was going to take the phone off speaker so they could have their privacy. Mohammed kept his gun directed at Doc, and Doc moved to hand the phone over to him.

However, as Doc reached the hand with the phone in it toward Mohammed, Doc seemed to lose his grip because the phone started to look unstable. The mastermind kept his right-hand gun pointed at Doc and reached out himself to grab it. Doc then put his palm underneath Mohammed's outreached left hand and grasped his arm and wrist as if to save the phone from falling.

He then quickly withdrew and stepped sideways to the left, putting Mohammed's pointed gun away from Doc's earlier position. In less than a second, the mastermind dropped both the phone and the gun. While his legs crumpled slowly onto the floor, Mohammed loosely folded his limbs inward toward his trunk and curled into a fetal position. His heart stopped immediately and he was dead. Doc looked at his own hand, used a glove to carefully remove the fake skin, and figured that since he, too, did not collapse, he was fine. Nonetheless, Doc went immediately over to the sink and washed his hands with soap and water for about five full minutes and then exhaled deeply.

Doc curtained off the area around the body and called out to the two snipers by name, shouting, "The coast is clear." On the loudspeaker, Doc requested TL ASAP. The TL and the snipers all arrived within seconds. They made up large and multiple signs around the outside area as they waited for the hazard experts to arrive. Doc then called the Professor using one of the secure building lines on the counter. The Professor told Doc that his call was now in the situation room with all in attendance.

Doc said that he and his colleagues had just successfully dispatched the mastermind; he was dead. The facility appeared, at this time, to be intact and partially secure. He and his two U.S. military SOF colleagues, as well as the SOF senior TL, were now carefully searching for the hidden detonators/explosives throughout the building. They had already found and cordoned off dangerous amounts of biological and chemical WMD.

Doc then emphasized that the entire property—both inside the building and outside—needed to be scrubbed for explosives and anything and everything else untoward. Doc said that the very best explosive/demolitions teams should be deployed first and ASAP. Doc specifically suggested the USSS demolition team.

Doc said, "To summarize, at the most initial and superficial review, the building and grounds of the plant are safe and relatively secure. When the explosive devices are all deactivated and any chemical and biological weapons are confiscated and removed, then I'll be able to say that with a lot more certainty and complete confidence."

The situation room let out a limited sigh, and the Professor said that the needed support was on its way, ETA less than ten minutes. The Professor requested that Doc call in for one more debrief once he felt it was appropriate and safe to do so. Approximately three hours later, Doc called in to the situation room and said that the area was now totally secure—all explosives and hazmat threats (WMD) had been successfully nullified and transferred safely out of the area.

Doc announced that the USSS, the U.S. military SOF teams, the Department of Energy, and the related FBI and Homeland Security personnel were all instrumental in bringing this to a successful conclusion. POTUS looked around the room and said that he was both incredibly thankful and immensely proud of each and every one of them.

Prior to everyone's departure, the Professor requested that POTUS include an order to everyone in this room that the demise of the mastermind and the sister were not to be spoken of. The Professor said that he believed that they might be able to leverage this knowledge against the responsible terrorist leadership in the very near future.

CHAPTER THIRTY-EIGHT

# RETRIBUTION

THE PROFESSOR TOLD DOC, WHO got back to his hotel around midnight and was very gleeful that the Professor had saved him a separate sleeping room, that POTUS was going to be paying some of their adversaries a real whipping, especially the terrorist organizations that were involved in this one. Doc said it would be a smart move to remind them not to mess with the U.S. or its allies.

The Professor nodded and said that the late-morning meeting was going to be in the secure situation room, and he was expected to be there as well. Doc smiled and said for the Professor to wake him at about ten o'clock.

The Professor smiled and said to Doc, "Oh, no can do. The appointment is much earlier, so you can sleep as late as 0600 hours, but then you have to be all set."

Doc said, with a real reluctant groan, that he'd be ready in the lobby.

At exactly six o'clock, they were in the backseat of an un-marked USSS sedan, riding to the hospital again to speak with the failed woman bomber. The Professor had filled her in and had emphasized that her husband was the one who had killed her sister. She had alternated between extreme sadness for her sister and tremendous rage and revenge toward her husband. The Professor did not tell her that her husband was also dead.

Doc said that he was very sorry that she had died as they had become friends of a sort and she was very optimistic for her sister and herself until Mohammed beat her and then shot her in her forehead. The sister had tried very hard to convince Mohammed, before he beat her, and kept saying that the way was not with al-Qaeda and ISIS. "Your sister bravely rejected his thinking but to no good end."

The sister had challenged him about who else he knew in either al-Qaeda or ISIS, and he rattled off several names to convince her. However, she was still trying to get him to come to the other side, and she said those individuals were not of high rank.

The bomber asked, "What were their titles?"

Again, he repeated their names and then their titles too. Doc said that he had been made to sit down several yards from them so he only recalled a few of them.

The former bomber began to reel off every name she could think of and their exact positions in each of the two organizations. The Professor asked if they were directly involved in this specific mission, and she said they were in it from both the very beginning and right up to this day. This was expected to be one of the very best attacks that they ever carried out.

Doc asked her to provide street addresses or villages. "Your husband said that he had personally been to each of their houses and some other safe houses that they used."

She said he was talking about their homes and the places they went to travel and to train for missions. The Professor reached into his jacket pocket, took out several maps, and asked if her she could point to their locations because her husband sometimes seemed to exaggerate whom he knew and where they really lived. The woman said that was not accurate because her husband remembered everyone and he sometimes made them memorize his friends names and houses to prove they were good enough to go on missions.

She then took the maps and pointed out homes and training facilities. When Doc said to the Professor that he had also mentioned other countries, he pulled out maps and she went through those as well. She explained that once she became an authorized jihad bomber, she and her sister had free access to these places.

Doc said that they did not want to get her in trouble with her husband. She said she hoped he would very soon. She herself would slit his throat if she ever had the chance. The Professor asked her then if she knew the names of the operational commanders in al-Qaeda and/or ISIS who were actually behind this mission.

She then rattled off a number of individuals in each of the organizations by name—in all, about fifteen were identified in each organization. Doc asked her if her husband ever had the chance to meet any of the top leadership. She said he had been introduced to the most high-level leaders of al-Qaeda.

The Professor asked where her husband met them. The woman said that her husband had been blindfolded and was brought to see him via a winding motorcade from their house in Pakistan to some other site. She said that her husband had told her that when they went by vehicles it was for about two hours and it seemed to him to be by the Pakistani and Afghanistan borders. Her husband also told her and her sister that one of the men told him that he was greatly valued and his mission was a vital one. The man, after their tea, told Mohammed that if he encountered any difficulties at all along his sacred journey, he could call them directly. They had put a special encrypted telephone number in his secure cell phone. If he gave the code phrase ("Allah is always with me"), he would be answered.

Doc and the Professor said that they had to go and would return and she should get some rest.

Professor and Doc had several more meetings. One was with the SecDef, the next was with the D/CIA/NDI, and the third was with the Director of the NSA. They gave each of them the transcript as an early brief that the failed bomber had provided them and asked them to consider their next actions for POTUS's consideration. When they were with the SecDef, the Professor said that he was pretty confident that POTUS was going to respond to the terrorists.

The SecDef agreed and said that his department had already drawn up a substantial strike package(s).

Furthermore, based on the codified maps that the Professor and Doc were able to get from the failed bomber and his very best analysts, they had drawn up a set specifically for the training camps and for specific residences. Additionally, after configuring the transport routes of that al-Qaeda and ISIS meeting with the mastermind, they believed that some drones would be very effective in hitting the two leaders if they were still at that location. The Professor thanked him and his people very much for the potential preparations.

The pre-meeting with the Director of NSA was also useful. He told the Professor and Doc that the NSA was working the new information with their best analysts, tracking the cell phone that they quietly retrieved from the body of the mastermind.

The encryption that was placed in Mohammed's cell was quite sophisticated, and they were working on two aspects: one, getting the phone numbers, and two, the code relating to the phrase he was to use and in the oldest type of Arabic. He said that his people had been able to get a pretty good location of the lines indicating that it is possible that the leaders were at the least in that general location.

# CHAPTER THIRTY-NINE

# A TASTE OF HELL
# PROVIDED BY THE U.S.A.

THE WHITE HOUSE SITUATION ROOM was a virtual war room. POTUS asked the SecDef to provide options but to make no mistake; the terrorist organizations were going to be feeling some real pain in their immediate future. Five different scenarios were presented. Each was extremely precise and designed for heavy hits to produce maximum damage.

The Professor stated that he and Doc had just recently received what they would consider highly reliable, impressive, and most of all, actionable information. The Secretary of State leaned forward and said to POTUS that once they proceeded with these attacks to please remember that there were three different countries in play here: Pakistan, Afghanistan, and Syria.

The D/NSA said they were getting closer to their objective regarding the effort to obtain the encrypted cell phone numbers of the two leaders that the deceased mastermind had on his line. The Director said that they had finally found a gifted Arabic speaker, someone who was able to speak the traditional Arabic language in the oldest and most nuanced way.

POTUS asked the Director/NSA if he would know him, with all the linguists that had supported him over the years. The director smiled, and he said he believed he would remember this one very well. "We all know him as the Professor." The group laughed for a minute, and POTUS looked at the Professor and shook his head. The Professor just shrugged.

POTUS asked the SecDef if he had a high level of confidence regarding these military attacks, and he replied that he did. POTUS looked around the room, paused for a moment, and then said to the general and all of the national security directors and secretaries that he was hereby authorizing the attacks.

POTUS asked everyone in the room to depart with the exception of the D/CIA/acting NDI, the Professor, and Doc.

When everyone else had left, POTUS said to the Professor, "Do you agree with my decision?" and the Professor nodded. He asked the CIA director to proceed with his brief. The CIA/acting NDI director said that they were unanimous in their belief that they could use the female bomber as an informant if they sent her back to Pakistan. POTUS said that she could just walk away, but he saw the opportunity and approved the operation. "What a world we live in these days," he muttered primarily to himself.

POTUS looked over to the Professor and said that if he somehow, with the NSA, made it through the Arabic traditional language barrier and the coded phrase, to please tell them, "POTUS will decimate them and all that they care for and love if they try this again—period. What you are experiencing now is nothing compared to what we have in our arsenal."

In the following week, the two terrorist organizations took tremendous blows, threatening their very viability. A large number of foot soldiers were killed, as were, unfortunately, some innocents. The leaderships of both al-Qaeda and ISIS were temporarily destroyed, but there was no doubt that they would be replenished in time. It was obvious that the U.S. military had more than done its job.

The Professor was successful in using the coded phrase in traditional Arabic to reach terrorist leaders. They paused after hearing POTUS's message, and then cut the line. The Professor, after replaying the message with POTUS, said that he believed the adversaries were stunned and shocked. In his view, the message clearly indicated that they would not be bothering the U.S. for a very long time.

At the Hudson Valley property, Doc spent a month decompressing and trying to recharge his batteries. He still felt some strong need within himself that he could not seem to surface. He did not want to share this strange itch with the Professor until he had a strong grasp on it but felt at the same time he might never do so.

They both also came to know much better the two extraordinary Chinese women that were still there.

Doc and the Professor had heard, too, from the D/CIA. He had advised them that their very old but close friend in Asia (China) had received her just compensation. They both smiled, and Doc said that it most definitely made his day.

# CHAPTER FORTY

# A HISTORICAL EVENT: A DRAGON'S RESURGENCE

DOC ALWAYS KNEW INSTINCTIVELY WHEN adversaries would come knocking. They had received several threats during their "relaxing down time" that he had not yet shared with the Professor or any of their guests. However, there was one writer in particular who very much stood out when compared to the other threats. He claimed that he personally was going to send Doc and the Professor, along with the entire U.S. and, for that matter, the entire world, a substantial "gift." Doc's innate sense told him to take action. It was related somehow to Zhaohui's daughter, but he decided to not mention her until he had a more solid connection.

Doc did not walk but ran to the Professor and his now exceptionally close Chinese female friends to seek their reactions and thoughts. Doc was hoping that he was completely mistaken. The Professor and Zhaohui Xiaoqing were in one of the lodges playing Go. When Doc came into the room, both the Professor and Zhaohui Xiaoqing knew from his facial expression that something was wrong. The Professor looked at Doc and asked him to proceed as slowly as he could. Doc took a breath and slowly relayed to them his strange, persistent, and haunted feeling of the letters. He now had a new and clearer view of a major threat to the U.S.

The Professor listened very carefully, then he asked Zhaohui Xiaoqing if she knew the individual that Doc described from the numerous letters. She raised her head and softly said yes. He was young but already a full senior member of the Chinese elite and was already regarded by the Communist Party senior leadership as the best biological expert they had ever had, bar none.

The Professor then picked up the secure telephone line to the White House and asked that two helicopters be sent to their current location for transport as soon as possible. He requested that the White House chief of staff and the national security advisor be available for them upon arrival for an urgent briefing.

The Professor told Doc to get ready and then asked Zhaohui Xiaoqing if she could provide them a thorough written brief, with as much detail as is possible, on this individual prior to their departure. The Professor asked Doc to increase the security level on the property, and Doc said he had done so ten minutes ago.

A USSS agent handed the Professor a faxed document in a sealed envelope that had just arrived at the White House. It was the detailed breakdown of the young Chinese biological expert's personal and professional history that he had requested from Zhaohui. In the room, all participants were present along with POTUS, who motioned for the Professor and Doc to start the brief. The Professor relayed to the group that he and Doc had come across what they believed to be a definitive WMD threat to the country. The

Professor then put his document on screen for all in the room to read. The Professor nodded to Doc, who relayed to the group that he had been getting very specific and clear death threats by this individual within the past few weeks. At first, Doc had dismissed them.

However, as he focused and zeroed in on the individual more closely, Doc realized that he was not to be dismissed. Doc added that he had, up to this point, not understood why the individual was so eager to kill Doc. His biological expertise, as it turned out, was quite real and unquestioned, based on his acquired sensitive information. He clearly operated at a level four in any laboratory.

The Professor added that they were looking at a global threat, with an unprecedented scale, in their near future. It was biological in nature and could destroy most of not only the U.S. and their allies but the world in general. The key was the level of the threat and the biological speed and destruction in which it could spread around the planet. The Professor then also focused on POTUS and expressed his concern that this individual had gone off the rails—the Professor's personal mathematics and overall estimates showed that the scientist was likely to be mentally ill and, unfortunately, still incredibly brilliant.

POTUS held up his hand again and asked if anyone in this room had obtained, or had even ever heard of, this Chinese CCP member. The room remained silent until the D/NDI and CIA, along with the D/NSA, shook their heads no. Both said that they would need to conduct an extremely broad sweep of their digital files and those of their intelligence allies to fully identify this person. Sources in China would additionally be activated to see if they had heard of him at all or not. The SecDef said that his department would also peruse its database too to see if his physical resemblance alone might be of further assistance and would ask Homeland Security to do the same with respect to all international borders, and not just U.S. ones only, including European law enforcement (Interpol).

The Professor mentioned that this individual was a true problem in his desires for some kind of vengeance toward Doc and the United States. Moreover, his expertise in biological weapons could not be disregarded in any way, and it was imperative that the U.S., along with the Chinese leadership, determine whether he had been able to somehow secure or steal any of the various viruses from the Chinese military's secure storage facilities. Many of the more sophisticated ones would be deadly to any population of any country if they were ever to be released.

Once again, one could hear a pin drop in the room. POTUS looked at the Professor and Doc and then asked what they would recommend. Doc looked at POTUS and said that he believed they would be able to set up an operational trap in order to capture or destroy this individual and any biological weapons that he might have taken from China's own military's biological laboratories. He must be confronted and controlled swiftly. Doc looked at POTUS and said he would initially attempt to engage the individual directly through his correspondence.

The Professor added that his equations and instincts suggested that he wanted Doc and the U.S. to suffer more than anyone else. This seemed to have something to do with his dead father, as mentioned in letters to Doc.

POTUS remained quiet for a single minute and then asked if anyone in the room had anything else to say. Only silence. POTUS then said he wanted each and every cabinet member and the directors in the room to do everything possible to support this operation.

POTUS then said that he was going to make contact shortly with the Chinese president. He said that he would emphasize the clear and present danger that this threat presented, and that the possible DEFCON 2 status was on the table, as was closing America's borders if necessary.

Given China's recent history, POTUS expected that every measure would be made by the Chinese president and they would realize rapidly that this was urgent.

# CHAPTER FORTY-ONE

# THE BOY AND HIS EGO

THE CHINESE PRESIDENT CAME ON the secure line, expressing surprise and saying that he was not expecting a call from him. The Professor sat quietly in the room, out of sight. POTUS paused for a full minute then told the Chinese president that this call was most important. He added that there was a real possibility that one or more biological weapons had been stolen or removed from Chinese military laboratories by a very senior and gifted officer that was now rogue. The Chinese president's face blanched, and he looked like he had a dumpling stuck in his throat. POTUS said to the president that there was no equivocation on this matter.

POTUS stated that they were in "contact" with the rogue officer, and his intention was to destroy the United States of America and maybe the whole planet in the process using biological weapons—specifically a WMD. The Chinese president slowly drank from a glass of water with a trembling hand. POTUS said to the president that it was vital to avoid platitudes or "closed curtains."

The Chinese president then took in a considerable amount of oxygen and nodded his head toward POTUS. The president said that what POTUS said was true.

The president hoped that they could find a way to capture the deranged officer and to safely regain the biological weapon(s) he has in his possession. In the background, the Professor, still sitting quietly, was stunned at what POTUS had already identified to this point.

The Professor caught POTUS's glance and held up a pad that said, "Ask him what exactly the biological weapon(s) are," that the rogue officer now had in his possession. POTUS did so. The Chinese president then nodded and told POTUS that the rogue Chinese officer had the Ebola virus and the Chinese government was not yet sure whether he had one vial or a few.

POTUS said to the Chinese president that while they did have some contact with the rogue officer, they had not been able to pin down his exact location. The Chinese president, who now looked like he had not had a good night's sleep in months, said that to be honest, POTUS had much more clarity than they, as they had been unable to even confirm a country or city yet. This rogue officer was extraordinary in his thinking and had the ability to melt into the background.

POTUS said to the Chinese president that they needed to act in every way given the odds and circumstances, and the president concurred wholeheartedly. POTUS said that they would keep each other informed, and the Chinese president asked if they could keep this just between themselves for the time being. POTUS said they would do so for the moment. POTUS also said a full and thorough composite history of the rogue officer would be of some value to them, particularly his psychological evaluations. The president said he would send him his own personal copy within the next half hour.

The Professor sincerely complimented POTUS for using "bluffs and the inferred knowledge of our information to date" as a means of clarifying the Chinese president's thinking and present knowledge.

POTUS looked at the Professor and said he needed the Professor to somehow make this quietly go away as it might be that final straw on this camel's back. POTUS said that just between them, he honestly did not know if the American people, and their allies, could stand to bear an Ebola attack. The Professor looked back at him and said, "We will get this done, but do not be concerned when it comes to the American people. When you scratch the surface, they are fearless, faithful, and resilient, so keep the faith." POTUS then nodded toward the Professor and concurred wholeheartedly.

The Professor saw that POTUS resembled the Chinese president in one way. POTUS, too, looked like he was about to slip or step over the side of a very deep cliff with a never-ending abyss below. The Professor said that he and Doc would succeed and that he needed to try hard to get as much rest as possible. POTUS smiled, and his shoulders seemed to actually melt in place.

Back in the Hudson Valley compound, the Professor and Doc proceeded to develop their plan. Doc put on the table two copies of letters that he was going to send to the rogue officer; on one of the much older letters, the rogue Chinese officer had included a return address number mixed into one of the pages. An error, no doubt.

At the same time, the Professor's secure fax spat out a copy of the document that had just been provided to POTUS as well. Doc read through it with considerable intensity as the Professor studied the two letters that Doc had prepared.

The Professor nodded and gave Doc a quick feed on how they had come across this from the Chinese president's own desk and how he had promised it to POTUS. The brief was not only filled with extensive and useful information on the rogue officer, it included excellent photos. He had passed and exceeded all levels of studies, which included the equivalent of any U.S. universities.

At the young age of twenty-two, he had already surpassed several PhDs in micro and molecular biology and spoke and wrote in numerous foreign languages, including English. He had spent years in the Wuhan National Biosafety Laboratory as well as Wuhan Institute of Virology along with other institutes. His knowledge and experience in level-four biohazards were clearly advanced.

Despite the considerable number of Chinese MSS studiously looking and scouring many, many countries for him, in the past half year, they had not been able to locate him.

They surmised that he had also disguised himself superbly and might have had plastic surgery. Doc knew that the exact dates and times that his letters to him were marked were part of the whole, and the postal markings were generally matched to the various locales.

At times they appeared to have a slant toward Europe, and at other times within Asia—one of the letters' envelopes was boldly stamped Hong Kong and another, California. The Professor looked at it somewhat like a chessboard and matched the letter locations to various segments of the world with the correct movements of the pawns, bishops, castles, and other pieces. The Professor concluded that the rogue officer also most likely sent (false) letters to countries just so the MSS went running to them too. The letters were all handwritten in English versus computer driven, and this was peculiar as well.

The Chinese daughter of Zhaohui Xiaoqing, Mei Baozhai, entered the lodge and smiled. She was now a U.S. university senior student and asked if it was OK for her to get a soda from the refrigerator. Doc motioned that of course she could. Mei was a very pretty young woman and often spoke very softly, but she also had a very sagacious and curious mind.

Mei got each of them sodas. As they were all taking a sip, Mei looked over at the coffee table where the photos of the rogue officer had been placed. She glanced at them twice and asked if it was OK to look closely at one of them. Since Doc knew they did not have other identifying marks on the photos, he said sure. Mei blushed a bit and then said she used to know this boy quite well when she was much younger. The Professor asked what his name was, and Mei pronounced it first in Chinese and then in English.

Doc asked how long ago it was that she knew him, and Mei said about one year ago or so. They had been friends back in China for several years, and while he was not a boy-friend, they did enjoy spending time together.

The Professor asked how they first met. She said he used to walk by her school almost every day when they were just children, and he would look at her. One day, she smiled at him, and he asked if they could go for a walk together when they were finished with their academic classes.

Doc was quietly overwhelmed with this development, and it matched up exactly with the very strong connection that he felt when the rogue officer was measuring his disdain and venting about Doc through the letters. The

Professor also gave Doc an extremely light wink. They both registered the fact that the rogue officer had been and was still "in love" with Mei (who was completely unaware), and the focus of his dead father was never an issue.

The Professor and Doc then said it would be most helpful if Mei would tell them what she could remember about him. She noted that he was exceptionally smart and somewhat shy, but they still enjoyed each other's company together for many years. He once told Mei that she was very smart too. Mei said that he must be the same age, but she never knew what he did.

Doc asked if he traveled abroad at all, and if so, did he have a favorite country or city? Mei said she knew he did because he often came back with small but expensive gifts for her from time to time. Mei said she remembered that he particularly liked traveling in France, and she would ask him to tell her all about it as she hoped to go there one day. Mei said that it was very funny because instead of describing Paris, he would spend hours and hours talking about an island called Saint Helena.

He was obsessed with what was the (second) prison where the French had imprisoned Napoleon Bonaparte, but it was actually a British Island during his last years of his life.

Doc asked if he seemed to be wealthy or not and whether his parents were very smart too. Mei said she always had the impression that he was well-to-do, and in fact, it seemed to her that his parents were as well, as they wanted him to marry into a wealthy family.

However, Mei said that she knew that love was the most important. Mei smiled at Doc and asked if he would agree with that, and he said he did indeed and smiled himself.

Mei blushed again and covered her face with her hand. Doc then asked if she actually knew his father, but Mei said she did not. However, it seemed to Mei that her friend was very well situated with the Party—even though he was unknown by many people in the CCP. The Professor nodded and said the soda was great but they had to get back to work.

Doc looked at the Professor. The Professor acknowledged that the odds, while incredible, were really possible when one closely reviewed the entire collection of similarities and happenstance on top of the two children deciding to not broadcast to anyone their private times together. Doc then picked up his secure radio and ordered his director of security to discreetly double-check his personal protection coverage teams to ensure that both the mother and particularly the daughter were with the very best operatives at all times. The director said he copied and it would be done.

The Professor took the radio and asked that Zhaohui Xiaoqing, the mother, come to the lodge to have drinks. Once there, the Professor gave her a word-for-word briefing of their exchange with Mei.

She wiped a single tear that rolled down her cheek and said perhaps this would not have happened if she could have done more for her daughter. Doc said to her that she should not feel any guilt at all. She had done a wonderful job as a parent and she managed to raise a very loving and intellectually gifted young woman. The Professor concurred wholeheartedly and then gave her a review of the circumstances relating to this rogue officer. He also let her read through the eyes-only file. The Professor asked for her thoughts and whether they were missing anything that they did not mention. He added that the in-depth quick brief that she had provided them for the White House meeting was outstanding. Doc softly noted to her that in this instance of time, it was of the essence and literally millions of lives were at risk.

The Professor said that one of the blind spots they had encountered to date was with respect to the rogue officer's family—specifically, his father when he was alive. His death seemed to be a real "hot button." Zhaohui nodded her head and sat silently. She asked them if they really wanted to know. The Professor and Doc looked at her and nodded affirmatively.

She said, all the while looking only at Doc, that this rogue officer's father was the incumbent Chinese president until he had died of a massive heart attack in bed late at night. Doc winced—it was the former Chinese president he had killed. The rogue officer was a secret that was known only to a very small handful of individuals. Doc said that he was the one who sent away that Chinese president permanently and he did it without remorse or hesitation. Doc was at peace with his act; the man was a violent psychopath.

Doc looked at Zhaohui and said that he was very reluctant to ask such an important favor from her but he and the Professor had no other option. Zhaohui gazed at him for a long moment and then said she believed that she already understood his request. Zhaohui then said that he, Doc, had her permission to have her daughter speak to the rogue Chinese officer with one condition: it would be done extremely carefully and never, ever in person. Doc and the Professor both agreed to the one agreement and promised her that they would protect her daughter at all times.

Doc stood up and bowed deeply to Zhaohui. She then bowed in return and departed the lodge. As she rose up and walked out the door, Doc could see she had a tear running down the one side of her face.

# CHAPTER FORTY-TWO

# THE SINS OF THE FATHER ALSO BECOME THE SINS OF THE SON

THE PROFESSOR HAD REACHED OUT to the SecDef and requested an unmarked U.S. military aircraft at Steward Air Base that would take them to Britain to meet the British prime minister and the president of France. SecDef said it would be airborne for Doc and the Professor within the next half hour and ready to go to their respected abroad venues nonstop. All would be explained upon arrival but during the secure meetings only, and this was requested specifically by POTUS with the Professor acting on his behalf.

Additionally, he placed a request to the SecDef that the former commander and the three SOF officers (snipers) that he had the pleasure of previously working with during the nuclear power plant operation be reassigned immediately and until further notice to England forthwith. Doc contacted and provided a couple of clear digital photographs of the rogue Chinese officer for the D/CIA/NDI and D/NSA. They were requested that they provide a full and comprehensive search via satellite for facial recognition and any captured verbal communications.

There were two specific Napoleon Bonaparte sites in Europe: the first being the Mediterranean island of Elba and the second being Saint Helena—population approximately four thousand. Doc indicated that the deranged officer had a fixation with one of the two locations and might actually indeed be on one of the relatively small islands.

Doc then called the U.S. military Chairman/JCS whom he knew well on a secure line. When he gave the operator his name, he was connected. Doc was informed that SecDef had granted his SOF personnel request personally. The four specialists were already en route to England locked and loaded. The pilots were asking for the landing zone, and Doc told them to disembark the four SOF solders discreetly at the air base on Saint Helena.

Their landing approval would be granted by the time they arrived on site, as would Doc's. Doc thanked the Chairman and said he was forwarding digital photographs that showed their target, which should be passed to the SOF guys as soon as is possible. The Chairman said he was standing by for any other orders or requests and told Doc to bring him back a cold beer. Doc smiled and said he would.

About one hour later, the CIA identified a subject bearing a very close match with the rogue officer's photographs and appeared to be around twenty-two years of age, but with a facial structure that had clearly been altered. The candidate was given a facial recognition level of confidence in the high 90 percent category.

Additionally, the NSA reported that they were able to hack into the man's computer and break through the encryption. It appeared that the target was in Saint Helena.

Doc asked if the CIA could get two of their very best operatives to the island. Doc said that he needed on-the-ground exact visual pinpointed locales and the where-abouts at all times of the rogue Chinese officer. D/CIA/NDI said two of his very best would be there within the next half hour.

The Director had considered the need in advance so they were standing by with one foot off the island and as they spoke, were provided a go sign. The Director said they already had verbal and visual contact through the Chairman/JCS with the commander and Doc's three snipers. They had just landed too and were quietly hooking up with U.S. operatives now.

The commander asked, "What was taking so long for Doc to get his sorry ass in play?"

Doc laughed and said he was in descent now. The Professor had, of course, already briefed POTUS and was currently onward to brief in person the respective British prime minister and the French president. D/NSA also spoke up and told Doc that they, the NSA, were intensely looking for any possible indications of the rogue officer's hidden level-four pathogen locations or signs that he was standing by to release a trigger once found or captured.

Doc said, "Roger that."

When he disembarked, he received a secure radio call from the commander, who said his three snipers were all in place and had eyes on the target, and that he was in a town-house-type residence. They also had all access and egress points clearly identified, and there were no underground routes available for the rogue officer.

One of the snipers, positioned up high, did a visual recon of the roof; there were no escape positions there either; a helicopter extraction on that roof was not viable. The two company assets were in play. They were literally

right next door, in buildings adjacent to the target's residence. The operatives were disguised as new rental tenants.

A small and nondescript taxi with a local driver pulled
up to Doc and said he was there to transport him to a friend
of his (the commander) and the cost has already been covered. Doc got in and said it was always great to get treated
like "a somebody," and they laughed. They arrived at a
broken-down building, and Doc got out. The commander
came out and gave Doc a bear hug and then escorted him
to the top floor that was their command center.

It was filled with numerous cameras that had full sight
on the rogue officer's townhouse and the attached townhouse with the two operatives—which contained wireless
multi-cameras that were feeding back to the command center. Additional cameras had sight on each of the snipers
and their nests from very different angles, and they were
calling in whenever the target moved.

The commander handed Doc a soda and a piece of
French bread while he gave Doc a tour of the camera feeds,
the target's movements, and their own observations so far.
Doc asked if the intelligence feeds from back home in the
Pentagon and the CIA's respective operations centers were
able to confirm 100 percent if the target was their guy, and
the commander said yes, it had been confirmed—despite
the target's cosmetic face tucks.

The commander then said, "Oh yeah, by the way, our
top psychologist and psychiatrist have both agreed that
the poor rogue Chinese officer is ill in the head and not
very nice." Doc said he was glad to hear that, because up to
this point, Doc, the commander, and the snipers were the
only ones who really believed them. The covert operatives
called in on their hidden radios and quietly said they always

thought so too—but they also decided to cover their tails just in case it was not actually true.

The commander pointed to the secure line when Doc asked for it. The commander also asked if he should depart the room. Doc said, "No, please continue to monitor the target and our sites." The only proviso was that no one repeat anything they heard to anyone back home. All of the personnel were on site and in good spirits. They were also locked and loaded, awaiting Doc's provided orders.

Doc then made the secure call to the Professor. He asked if he, too, had confirmation that their rogue officer was real as he was presently in U.S. snipers' sights. The Professor confirmed it as well. The Professor said that after he dropped Doc off at the tarmac, he landed just about twenty minutes after him. He said that he had just finished briefing the British prime minister and the French president. The Professor said that the best part was when they heard it might be a possible Ebola release.

At that point, the two presidents had expressed to the Professor considerable consternation and asked that he and POTUS as well as Doc and his team were successful by all means. Doc smiled and then told the Professor he would be going to work. The Professor said, "Good hunting and work your magic."

Doc then cut the call.

# CHAPTER FORTY-THREE

# BEWARE THE MIGHTY WOLF IN SHEEP'S CLOTHING

THE PROFESSOR HAD EARLIER TOLD Doc that since they now had the rogue officer's exact location and he was contained, his mathematical computations reflected a distinct improvement in the situation with Doc's team. However, they needed the rogue Chinese officer to stay alive and remain generally coherent until they had determined exactly where the Ebola vial(s) was and whether he had triggered it already or not.

It remained possible that there was one person in the world who might get through to him. With some adroit mental reproductions of earlier "happy years together," this could actually be productive. The rogue Chinese officer also still retained a "conscience" of sorts since in fact he could have released the Ebola while in China or in any of the other countries he had been hiding in already. If the female insertion worked, he might feel compelled to not release the virus.

The Professor said that his further mathematical deductions placed the success rate of this scenario at a solid 10 percent—dependent on the level of psychosis eating at the rogue officer's brain. Doc noted to the Professor that the 10 percent and the psychosis were not exactly what one would call very encouraging. The Professor automatically dismissed Doc's concern; he was focused on what needed to be done.

The Professor said that Doc's presence with the rogue officer, combined with the female's presence on video, should cause his mental fulcrum to sway back and forth steadily and hopefully in their favor of finding and removing any Ebola vial(s).

Doc, having known the Professor a very long time, knew that what the Professor was trying to convey was that keeping the rogue Chinese officer stable in mind and emotion would increase the current 10 percent odds of success to a much more favorable level, perhaps even at the 60 or even 70 percent mark.

Doc asked the Professor to have the Linguist's daughter ready and prepared. The Professor, with a somber face, said to Doc he was to not die, but getting the Ebola vial(s) was essential to the population. Doc smiled, waved, and then cut the line.

Doc asked the two agency operatives if they could provide any additional information about the rogue Chinese officer's time in the attached apartment townhouse. They said that it was affirmative that he was definitely alone, spoke to himself almost continuously, and had slept no more than two hours. He had not spoken on any outgoing phones, and he had not received any incoming calls. They added that they had successively mirrored his phones and his laptop, and his attention to it was minimal at best. All was being provided to those back home for real-time analysis and exploitation with very low success so far. The recordings copied for examination had indicated that his continuous speaking was low, but usually still loud enough to hear him. The analysts believed that the vast majority was incoherent gibberish with some short biological constructs and formulas still in place. The specialists had ranged from basic to extremely advanced—beyond all of the experts. The target had been eating mostly salads and nuts, and he imbibed only water and hot tea.

Interestedly, he had already exhibited a need to take two showers and repetitive soaping of his hands and face; he appeared to have a germ phobia. He had a thin-to-slender physique and black hair on his head and chest. The target had older scars on his back and on his chest—probably from a whip and/or a knife. They did not appear to be self-inflicted.

Doc said he had a couple of thoughts. Since both operatives were so close to the target, he was ordering that they do all possible to not only maintain their current cover but to acquire any more breadcrumbs that came across their plates. The snipers should maintain their best and stay alert. Moreover, Doc said that it was imperative that this target not be underestimated.

The operators said they copied. The male operator added that either way, from his personal perspective, they would sooner or later have to take this guy down. Doc looked over at the commander shook his head with a significant touch of frustration.

Doc then spoke deliberately to the male operator in their audio line and got no response. Doc called for the male operator to stand down, repeat stand down. No response. After two minutes, the female operator got on the line and said that her counterpart had just knocked on the target's door. The female agent said he went against her better judgment, and she had refused to accompany him.

The target opened his door and saw the male operator walk directly into his townhouse. The operator did not reply; about a minute later, the target came out of his door and very quickly left a mid-size brown paper bag on the steps of the townhouse the female operator was in. The operator quickly opened the door to get the brown paper bag. When she opened it, she saw that it was her colleague's head, severed off from the neck up. Then she heard firing coming from the target's townhouse, directed at one of the nearby building tops.

Doc instantly looked at the commander, and he nodded his head—one of his snipers had just been shot in the head and was dead.

The two remaining snipers were asking for an immediate green light to retaliate. Doc motioned "negative" to the commander and reminded them that the Ebola had to be acquired first. The commander denied the green light twice and ordered the remaining snipers to change nest positions. The new positions had to have heavy stone cover from this point forward. The commander looked again over at Doc and said, "You do know that this guy is not leaving here alive."

Doc nodded but said, "Not before we get the Ebola."

Doc ordered the commander to have the snipers focus on the rogue officer from every angle so the female operative could safely evacuate. Doc ordered the other agency operative to retreat immediately and leave with whatever materials she could bring with her. She was being provided top cover from the snipers. He omitted the fact that the snipers were really wishing and praying right now that the rogue Chinese officer would take a shot at her and reveal himself.

The operator arrived at the Command Center without incident. She went straight to work reviewing any and all of the documents, videos, and recordings that she brought with her. She was clearly determined to learn how the target had managed to have them totally misread him. Meanwhile, the snipers were licking their teeth, waiting for an opportunity to pay back this target for their brother.

The commander came over to Doc and asked what their next move was. Doc said he personally was going to walk over to the target's townhouse to chat with the target a bit. Doc said he wanted the commander to turn on a specific, designated video/audio, to go live when he snapped his two fingers together. The commander just stared and nodded.

# CHAPTER FORTY-FOUR

# LET THE SHOW BEGIN

SHE WAS A DEVOTED UNITED States citizen but was originally from China. Doc said that this person, whose name was Mei, was a former close friend of the target. They were both now almost twenty-two years old. Mei had offered, at their specific request, to speak with the target about their earlier years together. She was also going to ask him to choose "for her" to give up the Ebola vial(s) to Doc. The commander said he understood and he would await Doc's snapping signal.

Doc then asked the commander to inform each of the snipers that he was taking his stroll and he'd appreciate it if they did not shoot him. Doc added that if the target went too far at any time or in any way, and it turned out Doc was not up to his game, the snipers were free to fire away.

Doc picked out his sunglasses, put them on his lucky neck chain from his small backpack, and proceeded to the townhouse. He rang the door button and waited until the target looked through the peephole and then opened his door. Doc nodded hello and saw the Chinese officer was carrying a Glock 17 in his right hand at his side, with one round in the chamber and the rest stored in the magazine. The officer looked both ways and told Doc to come in but to stay close. Doc asked the officer if he knew who he was, and the officer shook his head yes. They went to the sitting room and sat down. Doc took note of a big closed computer on a table. The officer asked Doc if he was armed. Doc responded no and said he had no wires either. They sat there for about ten minutes looking at each other.

The officer's voice sounded sophisticated and also as clear as a bell. He appeared comfortable and at ease with himself. He asked Doc if his trip had been very taxing, and Doc answered negatively, as he had slept through most of it.

Doc said that he imagined the officer was staying exceptionally busy, under his circumstances, as the Chinese leadership was still looking everywhere for him. The officer smiled and asked Doc how he managed to catch up with him. Doc said that as he aged, he found Sherlock Holmes and his books became wiser, so he put two and two together and ended up with this small island and the outstanding full history of Bonaparte.

Doc said he would, as a small show of good faith, let him know that his former Chinese brethren still did not know his geographic whereabouts even to this day. The officer said he was grateful for the tip. Doc asked if he would kindly explain why he chose to decapitate one of their people and then shoot a long gun at one of their officers lying on the hill. The officer let out a sigh and said to be completely honest, he was getting bored and he felt the need to let them know that he could not wait forever. Doc lowered his head and said, "Next time, just drop me a call or visit," as it would be much more efficient.

The officer let out a laugh and then said, "What makes you think there will even be a next time?"

With this, Doc had a good long laugh but even louder.

The officer asked Doc why he had killed his father. Doc waited a minute, moved much closer, and he responded, "Your father, while almost as smart as you are, was a sociopath. He murdered an incredible number of the Chinese populace primarily because they did not have the same religion and were mostly poor. Your father also planned to go to war with the U.S., and become king of the world. I know your father would show his love for you by whipping and cutting you and then he would laugh at your pain."

The officer waved his hand and said, "Enough." Doc could see tears running down his cheeks. The officer raised his head and looked at Doc closely. He then drew his gun and pointed it directly at Doc, who had moved in even closer to the rogue Chinese officer. The gun was wavering in the officer's hand but his index finger was still on the side of the gun and not yet in the trigger housing. The officer looked at Doc and again said, "Enough."

Doc could see that he had hit the right buttons. The officer was now in a physical head-and-body slump. He also had put his gun down by his side.

They sat like that for about five minutes and made no sounds at all. When Doc looked over at the officer and he determined he was recovering and it was time to strike again, Doc said he had brought a real surprise.

Doc snapped his two fingers. At the same time, he opened the large computer screen on the table. For a second, he saw a piece of the Professor, and then suddenly Mei came on the screen. The officer looked at the screen, turned away, and then back. On the third go-round and after hearing Mei's voice, the officer zeroed in on her face and let out a child's sound. He then smiled widely from ear to ear. He asked if she was real, and Mei stepped back and said yes, it was her. The officer asked her if she was all right and whether they had punished her in any way because of him. Mei smiled again and said no, that it was the opposite. She said that when she heard his name, she asked if she could see him again, and they said OK. The rogue officer was still trying to process this, so he kept staring at Mei and listening to her every word. Mei asked him how he was doing, and he said he was not doing that well. Mei asked him what was wrong, and the officer put his head down and then said that he was in big trouble.

Mei told him that they were still too young to get into any real, serious trouble. In fact, Mei said she still had many pictures in their younger years. She then opened a book and started to show them next. The officer looked at each one and kept shaking his head, as if it was simply a vision or trick. Gradually he seemed to realize that it was all very real. The officer said he would give her a test of sorts to see if it was really the Mei he remembered even today. She smiled again and said OK "fire away"—this could be fun. Every time he asked her a question, she would complete part of the question and then give him the whole answer. They both looked at more pictures and even cried a little together.

# CHAPTER FORTY-FIVE

# MEI: THE APPEARANCE OF A NATURAL OPERATOR

THE OFFICER WAS CONVINCED, AND he could only keep looking at how pretty she had become, and she in turn told him that he sure had matured as he looked almost like a Hollywood star. He blushed and told her that he had missed his special friend more than she could possibly realize.

Mei asked him what he was so upset about and how he got into so much trouble—maybe she could help him. The officer cried again and said that it was a very long story. The officer told her about his time working in the biosafety laboratories and his repeated upgrades, achievements, and promotions in his field. He then said he became bored and angry with the Chinese leadership. He said that its corruption was endless and he decided to make them pay for it. He stole some vials of the coronavirus and released it in the country. At first, he did not think that it was too bad because he figured they would just contain it quickly and they would have learned an important lesson.

Unfortunately, all did not go well, and it essentially exploded around the world. When he saw the result, he said he was at first beside himself with regret, but he could not believe that the leadership was so inept and incompetent as to let it even happen. He was interrogated and beaten, so he decided to leave, and he knew he could because he had a good mind.

Mei said, "Go ahead and tell me the rest of the story." She said that she knew he had a great mind and was very strong but she needed to know what else had been done. Maybe together, they could find a way out of this terrible situation because if the leadership had been trustworthy, this would never have occurred in the first place. The officer said to Mei that was exactly right. Nonetheless, this time, he left the country and with a matter of personal insurance because he knew that the MSS was searching for him everywhere, he took a strong vial of Ebola. Mei said that at this point his action had an explanation in that he took it for self-survival reasons and not to harm anyone else.

The officer said she understood him better than anyone else on earth. Mei said she thought this situation could be resolved. The officer said he hoped so and then he could go back to living in a normal way.

Mei then asked him if he thought he could trust her completely, as she thought that maybe they could get back to each other in person in the future. The officer then said that he did trust her completely.

Mei said, "OK, then." Could she ask an extremely important and personal question? The officer motioned to go ahead. Mei asked him if he currently had the Ebola vial(s) on his person. Doc now focused on the officer's every move and his microscopic facial features. The officer told Mei that he did have it on his body and it was only a single vial for his own protection. He asked what he should do now. Mei said that it was very good that it was only one vial as it showed he was sincerely only trying to survive.

She then asked whether the single vial of Ebola was "inside" his body, and he replied "yes." It was inserted into his left side into a soft spot. The officer said the surgeon was unaware of the content. The officer then asked Mei if she trusted Doc 100 percent. Mei answered his question by saying, "There is no one, and that means no one, that is more trustworthy than Doc."

The rogue Chinese officer then said that he thanked Mei from the bottom of his heart and wished her every success in the future. Mei then wiped a tear and pushed the button to cut the line off.

The officer motioned for Doc to follow him, and they went into a small cabinet area with a large tabletop. He used a scalpel to cut the area right below his rib cage, but still above his hip, to free the vial. It had a slight but very strong rubber case. Doc helped clean the outside and then took the vial. The officer told Doc that he regretted having threatened him with the letters. He added that Mei was the kindest and most sincere person he had ever met in his "very tortured life," which he knew full well was about to end. The officer looked at Doc. He understood that Doc could have handled this in a much different manner.

The officer then asked Doc if he could please have one last request fulfilled. Doc raised his head an inch and asked what the request was.

The officer asked that the story of his being mentally ill be kept alive. It would really be best for everyone. He then paused and said, with tears rolling down both sides of his face, that he intended it particularly for his mother, who had also lived a very distraught and exceedingly painful life. Doc focused in on the officer, saw he was sincere, and said it would be done. The officer then walked back slowly to the main sitting room. Doc knew his next move and simply watched to be sure. The officer picked up his Glock 17, put it close to his temple, and blew his brains out.

Doc carefully placed the Ebola vial into a larger and thicker cushion casing. He walked back carefully to the command center and set it into a sealed hazardous materials container. The Professor was on a secure screen. He looked directly at Doc and nodded, meaning "well done."

Doc had already showered as a usual precaution. The team then arrived in their hazmat suits and cleared the center for all except Doc. They then conducted a small test and deemed the Ebola vial to be fully authentic. The commander and the agency operative as well as a large burst of many people in the Pentagon and the agency ops centers exploded with joy.

Doc walked over to the female operative and told her that she needed to know something and they stepped aside. Doc said to her that the scars she (and her deceased colleague) had collected and described regarding the rogue Chinese officer's back and chest were absolutely critical to the mission's success. The operative started to wave off his kindness, but Doc shook his head and went on, talking in a very serious tone. He said that her and her partner's work had been extremely valuable to the effort. He would never have been able to concoct lines about the scars and torture otherwise—and those lines had ended up breaking the Chinese rogue officer's will and psyche in half to their collective benefit.

The commander came over to Doc and said to not forget that beer he promised to the Chairman/JCS, and Doc smiled and thanked him for the reminder. Doc thanked the commander and his team and said that none of this could have worked without the commander's and their superlative support. Doc asked the commander to please let him know when the burial service for their brother would be performed, as he and the Professor would like to attend. Warriors like this fallen brother deserved the highest and very best final salute.

The commander then asked Doc if he could ask him a question. He asked Doc why he had worn sunglasses and the gold chain with the dangling amulet to the rogue officer's townhouse; he had never seen Doc wear anything like that before. Doc smiled and then said that both of the items had special aspects to them. The sunglasses gave him the ability to actually see through the Chinese officer's body like an x-ray so he knew exactly where the Ebola vial was on his person as soon as he had fully opened the front door. The gold chain and the amulet allowed Doc to use them as an instant paralytic—all he had to do was pull either the chain or squeeze the amulet a certain way when he was about two feet or closer to the officer. Once they were past the door and inside together, he was always within two feet of the rogue officer at all times.

Doc said he was either practically behind or in front or at his side always. Moreover, their sitting on the sofa closely, facing apart from one another, was ideal. Doc knew that he could spray the officer faster than that officer could raise and shoot him because the officer had kept his finger off the trigger and always had his finger on the side of the Glock 17. Doc said he also was gambling that although the officer did definitely have a bullet in the chamber, that side finger meant that the officer was not intending to shoot him either consciously or unconsciously. Doc added that when they were interfacing with Mei on the computer screen, he was actually sitting only one foot from the rogue officer at all times. Once Mei had determined and visually confirmed that the officer had only one Ebola vial and not any others, then the team's odds improved substantially.

The commander took it all in and said he now understood. However, if things did not work out for Doc, what would he have done?

Doc said the spray would have instantaneously immobilized the target and he would have then removed the Ebola vial from the officer's side with a scalpel. But if he sprayed the target prematurely, the number of Ebola vials and their potential locations in the U.S., and other countries, would remain in question. The only other recourse would have been to interrogate the rogue officer, but one had to consider that if this rogue officer was already acquainted with torture, what that would accomplish. The commander thanked Doc for sharing, paused, thought it all over, and expressed out loud that he was very glad that Doc was on their side. Doc smiled lightly and noted that "fate" was fortunately on their side.

Doc took a moment to let some thoughts run through his head. All that happened. The resulting loss of two exceptionally fine U.S. government employees—both lost their lives for the love of their country. The rogue officer died via his own bullet due to his demented mind. The rogue Chinese officer did live a relatively short existence with a father who tortured him regularly: the deceased president of China.

The rogue officer did at least take his own life in repentance. He also, in doing so, saved the millions of lives around the world that would have unquestionably died from Ebola. And the officer's last simple request was to let his mother live without the pain and suffering from her past too. Doc welcomed putting down the late Chinese president. Doc was prepared for killing the rogue officer—had he not done it himself.

Doc then gratefully ran hard to catch his seat in the military airplane because it was about to return him home to the great U.S. of A.

# CHAPTER FORTY-SIX

# PEACE AND CALM: RESPECT FOR THE DEAD AND HOPE FOR THE FUTURE

THE PROFESSOR HAD HIS U.S. military plane head home but not before they did a quick layover to pick up Doc and the SOF and agency teams.

Another U.S. plane had already arrived and transported back the two fallen officers to Andrews Air Force Base, the American flag draped over their caskets. Their loved ones, POTUS, and the SecDef met them on the ground.

POTUS and his advisers, directors, and secretaries were all in the situation room the whole time the situation had been progressing, getting updates, and they suddenly came on a screen via video and audio on the aircraft that carried Doc and the Professor. They all stood up and clapped their hands for the Professor, Doc, Mei, and the entire group.

Doc and the Professor could see the relief on POTUS's face; he proceeded to say how proud and grateful he was for each and every one of them, particularly the two fallen officers who gave the ultimate sacrifice. POTUS noted that both the British prime minister and the French president forwarded their deepest gratitude as well. And, for what it was worth, the Chinese president could not be happier. POTUS ordered all of them to go home and get plenty of rest for as long as they wished. When they were ready, they would be having a quiet get-together at the Oval Office for a more formal show of appreciation.

Once home, Doc and the Professor softly collapsed for several days. With the approval of her mother, they had the opportunity to express the incredible way Mei had performed, under great pressure, an outstanding performance.

Mei thanked her mother for even allowing her to participate, and she was most happy to have contributed in some small way to resolving a terrible situation. Doc then asked if anyone was as hungry as he was; they all smiled together and headed to the dining room. A few weeks later, the White House invited all who had been on the quiet mission to come visit POTUS and other official invitees.

POTUS provided military and agency medals to all of the team members, along with the two wives who were there to represent their husbands, who had given all for their country. Toward the end, as the other attendees started to depart, POTUS discreetly asked the Professor to have his smaller group of Doc, Mei, and her mother join him for a few minutes in the Oval Office.

POTUS expressed his profound gratitude to each of them for their incredible contributions. The SecDef, the D/CIA/NDI, and the D/NSA were also present in the Oval Office, and they all nodded their heads in respect to the Professor, Doc, the Linguist, and Mei. POTUS went on to say that after previously having had the honor to meet with her mother, he was so very pleased she was able to come here again.

POTUS then asked Mei to stand up and step forward. POTUS pinned on her a Medal of Freedom, the highest medal that could be granted to a U.S. citizen, reserved for those who had been of heroic service to the United States of America. POTUS then looked at the Professor and Doc. He said that there were, at this point, no words or comments for them from him. The sacrifices, courage, and strength that they had had and given over the years were beyond description. There were no longer any medals or commendations that could be provided. POTUS looked for a few seconds at each person present in the Office and said the best possible compliment was this: "We have standing here before us two American patriots."

As they traveled back to the Hudson Valley, the Linguist and the Professor were sound asleep in the backseat. Doc and Mei were in the front. Doc found himself thinking about the rogue Chinese officer. As the brilliant and very young twenty-two-year-old, who decided to kill himself with his gun on the British Island, was about to pull the trigger, Doc knew that he could have probably intervened and stopped the kid. Doc thought more about it, and he figured in those few seconds, he could have likely consciously reached him too. Mei asked Doc what was on his mind.

Doc hesitated and then shared his thoughts with her.

Mei softly said that she did think he did the right thing and it was the only real recourse that the officer had.

Mei added that she had cried once they were cutting the secure screen because she knew that he was going to die. Doc asked how she was so sure, and Mei just shrugged and said she could feel it in her heart. Doc asked Mei if she knew it from her exchange of memories with the officer and seeing each other again after so many years. Mei said no, she knew it once she saw the photos in the lodge.

Doc said, "You knew that the Chinese officer was going to kill himself back then?"

Mei said yes. Doc did a small double take on Mei after she had closed her eyes to rest like the others, and wondered whether this was one of the gifts that her mother had alluded to. Doc decided that he was best off just remaining silent on the issue.

# CHAPTER FORTY-SEVEN

# RECUPERATION

THE PROFESSOR APPROACHED DOC AND said they needed to recover from the intensity and pressure they had both have been under for the past few years. The Professor had already requested that the White House refrain from any new deployments. Doc looked at the Professor, nodded his head, and said that he agreed. Moreover, he had given the director notice that he and the Professor were going to travel a bit, along with their current guests, Mei and Zhaohui. The Professor said he was impressed—he assumed Doc would resist any thought of a vacation.

Instead, Doc smiled and said it was an urgent requirement. However, he hadn't yet come up with an idea as to where they should spend their time. The Professor laughed heartily—Zhaohui and Mei, he said, had already covered that piece of the operation. They had recently informed him that they were all departing early the next morning by helicopter for an undisclosed location. At that time, the two ladies appeared and told Doc that his suitcase already contained all of his necessary luggage and suggested he just bring a summer hat and sunblock. They all laughed together, and Doc said he would not miss this for anything.

The Professor pulled Doc aside and said he planned to ask Zhaohui to marry him. He would like Doc to be his best man. Doc looked at the Professor and said, "Well, it's about time," and then grinned widely and told the Professor that he would be honored.

The Professor said that it was still a secret but her daughter also knew and had agreed to be her mother's maid of honor.

Doc laughed and said, "It will be interesting when you pop the question to Zhaohui," and the Professor said to just please keep it quiet until he managed to build up enough courage.

Doc said the Professor could not have made a better decision.

## The End

# ACKNOWLEDGMENTS

I WOULD LIKE TO ACKNOWLEDGE my book agent, Lacy Lynch of Dupree Miller & Associates, who deftly guided me throughout this entire project from rough conception to bound book. A special highlight of the project for me was working with editor, Will Murphy, whose expertise helped give focus and structure to the story of *A True American Patriot*.

My thanks as well go to Heather King, managing editor, and public relation specialist, Melissa Smith, of Permuted Press. I especially appreciate the important contribution of copyeditor, Kate Post, of Post Hill Press who polished the final version.

I also want to express my heartfelt gratitude to my wife and three children who selflessly provided encouragement, advice, and support at every juncture. I have truly been graced with an amazing team who can all take credit for their essential contributions.

# ABOUT THE AUTHOR

DANIEL J. O'CONNOR HAS SPENT twenty-six years in the CIA as an Executive Senior Intelligence Service (SIS) Officer and was the Chief of Security for Five Different CIA Directors of Intelligence (DCI) and their Deputy Directors (DDCI). He served both at home and overseas ensuring that the Directors were protected while they were in office. He had the distinct honor of working with outstanding DCI/DDCI team members and was responsible for their safety and security as well. Separately, he also served abroad for many years in multiple U.S. Embassies in Asia, Europe, Africa, and South America and received two medals with distinction from the CIA upon his federal retirement.

Following his Agency career, he ran a small private security firm working with high level corporate executives and ultra high net worth individuals and their families. This work included extensive domestic and international travel. Close collaboration with former U.S. Special Operation Forces (SOF) personnel was essential to success, whose skill and experience are unmatched in their field. Over the last several years, he has focused his time and efforts on creating an exciting action thriller with a fictional premise.